BROTHERS

IN

ARMS

(MATT DRAKE #5)

BY

DAVID LEADBEATER

ACKNOWLEDGEMENTS

This book is for all the readers who send the emails and connect on social media. The ones past, present and future. The ones who stay in touch and make my day with their kind words and enthusiasm.

You know who you are. . .

Other books by David Leadbeater:

The Bones of Odin (Matt Drake #1)
The Blood King Conspiracy (Matt Drake #2)
The Gates of Hell (Matt Drake 3)
The Tomb of the Gods (Matt Drake #4)

Chosen (The Chosen Few trilogy #1)

Walking with Ghosts (A short story)

Connect with David on Twitter - dleadbeater2011
Visit David's NEW website – *davidleadbeater.com*
Follow David's Blog - *http://davidleadbeaternovels.blogspot.co.uk/*

All helpful, genuine comments are welcome. I would love to hear from you.
davidleadbeater2011@hotmail.co.uk

CHAPTER ONE

The old man stared hard through the grimy window, liver spotted hands gripping the neck of the half-empty wine bottle with a shaky chokehold. His eyes were wide, the fingers of his left hand trailing slowly down the pane as if following a mysterious pattern.

Outside, demons stalked the night.

He knew these demons. He'd seen them before, many times. He was safe. They wouldn't come for the likes of him. Like the hounds of hell, they rampaged through his unstable home, singling out fitter, younger specimens, always the sort who wouldn't be missed and could be put to some future, diabolical use.

From his lofty and secluded vantage point, he watched, his fear and disgust jaded from untold years of existing on the streets. A tall demon, dagger in one hand, pistol in the other, strode carelessly among the fragile dwellings of the street people, smashing and crashing and hurling their precious belongings out of his path. His minions followed him with glee, cackling and capering, their tiny eyes alight with the reflected flame of the growing fire.

The homeless—the vulnerable and the lost—cowered in their wake, hoping the storm would pass them by. The old man brought the lip of the bottle to his mouth and drained the last dregs, making a deep sucking sound as he coaxed every last drop of liquid from the liter bottle. His gaze strayed momentarily across the rooftops, only a few hundred yards to where the Spanish beaches lay glittering under the moonlight, awash with surf. Soon they would be carefully groomed and raked, piled high with deck chairs and parasols, resources reserved for shameless tourists but never for downtrodden- locals.

Back in hell, the prey were scattering. The old man watched as the tall demon examined man after man, casting most aside like the rag dolls they were, not caring where they landed. The old man counted himself lucky that on this night, of all nights, he had chosen a different place to sleep and drink his wine, a place where no one might disturb or rob him in his sleep. The bad men down there didn't care what damage they did. Hurt and pain and even death meant little to them. If ordered and paid handsomely enough, they would do the same in broad daylight at a popular beach.

The old man crossed himself, at the same time wishing his bottle hadn't run dry. He might be lucky this time, but it hadn't always been so—and it wouldn't be in the future. The demons visited infrequently, but at least twice a year, seeking their candidates before moving on, taking the fittest kicking and screaming along with them. Where they went on other nights, he didn't know. Did they visit other such places? He suspected they did, but it was not his job to speculate. Life had shredded his hopes and dreams long ago and he had no wish to jeopardize his long-accepted position by challenging what most considered the norm.

Once, months ago, he remembered being caught in the purge. He still recalled the feeling of bone-shaking fear and the metallic taste of dread that had filled his mouth. The tall demon had taken hold of him and shook him hard, making all his limbs dance like a possessed marionette. The stink of evil had clung strong to this man. Close up, he was Satan—the Devil incarnate.

The old man had been thrown to the ground, discarded for being all used up. Luckily, his limbs had only been bruised, not broken, or he might've died from his injuries. The demon had passed by, boot heels dragging through grit and dirt, scraping across the ground with a metallic rasp. And then, they had stopped. A menacing exclamation had scraped through the air.

"This one will do." A thick, guttural accent. Others spoke Spanish, but this demon sounded Russian. Or one of those new breakaway states. The old man had no real grasp of facts anymore. It didn't matter anyway for the demon's next words froze both the blood and the marrow in his old bones.

"Do not fret, little rabbit. You have a little time left, yet. There is more than one country you must pass through before you end as — a lab experiment." Harsh laughter tore at the very fabric of the air, echoing around the makeshift campsite long after the minions of hell had gone, leaving nothing but mayhem and despair in their wake.

And now, the old man watched soundlessly as history repeated. His eyes would not see; his mouth would not speak. His heart would break.

These days, the world was an uncaring, selfish place, not for the needy and dependent. Who out there would stoop down to help them?

CHAPTER TWO

Homeland Security HQ is located in the Nebraska Avenue complex in Washington DC. Though not thought of as a primary port of call for intelligence alerts, it is nevertheless heavily concerned with terrorist threats, both domestic and abroad. On January 14th, 2013, it received a message that, whilst surprising and urgent, had no one screaming or reaching for the panic button.

Not like they would be in a little over a week.

The message originated out of Asia, somewhere off the coast of Korea. Speculation was that it came from one of the deserted islands out there. The body of the message, though short, was ultimately stunning.

"Our warship returned to the curious island I previously spoke of today. This time, I was allowed to disembark and go ashore. Saw everything unexpected. A vast, well equipped lab. Bodies of European descent. And worse— experimentation. Many weapons—American made, state of the art. Some futuristic. And one other thing—the briefest mention of a possible target. US Senator James Turner."

It came from a Japanese agent named Dai Hibiki, a man who had been deep undercover with the Koreans for many years. This man was buried so deep that it had been rumored several times that he'd been turned. Or murdered. His messages were few and far between, so any contact from him was given the highest priority.

It was routed through a Japanese intelligence agency to Homeland and then immediately to a small, covert agency because of a recent agreement between the Japanese and American governments.

The small, covert agency was brand new, and had a big new name. Special Response and Recon. Some of its members had taken to calling it SPEAR for short.

The new agency was in its infancy, still seeking agreements with some governments—the Swedes were playing major league hardball, and even the British were proving surprisingly prickly. Something to do with an unresolved matter concerning an SAS base that didn't exist on European soil. Other agencies, like the Japanese, who were quick to sign an agreement, were more than likely playing for an angle. Offices had been rented, cleaned and furnished on tree-lined Nebraska Avenue, Washington DC, with park views on one side and a University campus on the other to help promote a relaxed ambience. The space was large, and roomy, but would take a long time to feel comfortable. Computers were up and running, a new mainframe buzzed with activity, and the telephone system was online. Other than that, operational systems and physical hardware was still being installed. Several much anticipated "toys" had not yet appeared. Offices were cluttered with discarded boxes and reams of flayed wire. An interrogation room was being built along with a secure parking garage and a state-of-the-art warning and ventilation system.

But the transition was always going to be hard. The sheer diversity of the team members was a recipe for disorder. In Mai Kitano and Alicia Myles, there was both brilliance and instability. In Hayden Jaye and Mano Kinimaka, there was discipline and restraint, which, of course, led to limitation. In Ben and Karin Blake, there was both genius and a kind of broken insecurity. In Torsten Dahl, there was the superman you could always count on. Komodo was a soldier and a strong friend.

And then there was Matt Drake. Destroyed by the death of his wife, rebuilt by the love of Kennedy Moore and then ripped apart again when the Blood King arranged her murder, he was a man struggling to cling on to the blasted pieces of his life. Constant action and mayhem had helped him cope, but the last two sluggish weeks had him asking some major questions.

By day, the team was organizing their new HQ and starting to monitor handpicked communications, by night they tried adjusting to a brand new situation, a fresh life in an unfamiliar city. They were still living out of hotel rooms, the powers-that-be never quick to assign housing.

Now, Mai cut across the main communications room of their new HQ, nodding to Drake and tucking her hair behind both ears. "Bored?"

"Aye." Drake had stopped trying to lighten up his broad Yorkshire accent around her. They were becoming closer by the day. He wasn't trying to hide anything anymore. He pointed to the banks of TV screens. "A hundred channels and nowt to bloody watch."

Alicia chuckled. "You that desperate to dive straight back in, Drakey? The battle in the Czech Republic not big enough for you?"

"It had its moments." Drake acknowledged. "But inactivity kills nearly as fast as a bullet. You know that."

"I'd hardly call this 'inactivity.'" Mai gestured around her. Engineers were installing the special insulation and ventilation system. There was currently a lot of head scratching going on. Some of the specs didn't measure up.

"He means action." Alicia narrowed her eyes. "I'll take one of 'em out if you like."

"When you say it like that"—Drake sighed—"I don't know if you mean you want to shoot him or shag him."

Alicia nodded in agreement. "Either's possible."

Drake watched as Hayden drifted over to listen to the conversation, the ever-watchful Mano Kinimaka at her side. The last fortnight had seen both of them pussyfooting around some serious issues. Neither one, it seemed, was willing to make the first move. For Mano, it was because the whole thing was so important to him. For Hayden, it was something else all together. Something that combined the melancholy around her breakup with Ben, the pressures of her job—she had been appointed team leader of SPEAR—and the demands she levied against herself because of her father's great name. It didn't matter that she had probably already surpassed the greatest deed he ever did. He made her believe she would never live up to his legend—no matter what she achieved.

Drake stepped out of the room and wandered into the small canteen. Komodo, in addition to being a remarkable warrior and Karin's sensitive boyfriend, had also proven to be a kick-ass cook and coffee connoisseur. He'd already saved them from starvation more times than Drake could remember with his quick culinary genius.

Komodo squeezed the garlic press as Drake entered. The Englishman took a whiff. "Smells lovely."

Komodo blinked. "It's just spag bol, man."

"To you maybe." Alicia had walked in behind him. "But after weeks of field rations that taste like Odin's arse, I'll tell you, *Trevor,* your sweet fare tastes divine."

Komodo shook his head at her. "My girlfriend has a lot to answer for, telling you—of all people—about that."

Alicia emptied the coffee pot. "We're all friends here, mate. No hidden agendas. I'm sure you'll find a way to make her pay, eh?"

Drake concentrated on the bubbling contents of the pan. The fact that Alicia raised the question of hidden agendas only brought attention to her own. If indeed she had one. . . But Drake had known her a long time. He could not pinpoint a time when she hadn't been secretly working for herself.

He squeezed past her, leaving Komodo to fend for himself. Across the narrow corridor, the conference room stood empty, deemed the least important area to make ready. Farther down the hallway, he knew workmen and technicians were working on secure offices, an interrogation room, and a basement bunker for the arms cache. Maybe even more clandestine things he wasn't party too. Who knew what top-secret, hush-hush ideas Jonathan Gates really had for this place?

Not even Hayden Jaye, Drake was sure.

He paused for a moment, alone in the empty conference room. His life was in tatters, his past naught but ashes. But dreams could arise from ashes as easily as they could be born in glory. His future was a blank slate, purposely so. Mai Kitano remained an enigma, but a desirable one.

He ran his knuckles across the rough walls, the texture like sandpaper, harsh to the touch. The room's single window looked out on to a busy street. Cars flashed past and pulled into the strip mall opposite, odd to someone who'd lived in the UK his entire life. The White House stood resolutely to the south east, an awe-inspiring sight he'd never even seen, Langley and the CIA to the west.

His future was a blank slate.

But the past had to be dealt with. Many layers of profound regrets and deep-rooted guilt had to be raked through, evaluated, and faced. The saner part of his mind asked, *what can you do now? What good will dwelling do?* But the darker side wanted more. It craved action.

And so did his body to help dissuade and deflect the dark side. It offered a promise that said the harder he threw himself into the present, the farther his guilty nightmares would recede. Someone once said *time heals all wounds.* What a load of crap. Time would only cover it with scar tissue. The heart and mind would actually deepen the loss.

A hubbub erupted across the hall. Hayden's voice and then Gates's and then Torsten Dahl's. The big Swede didn't sound happy. Someone—it sounded like Karin—was trying to shush him. *Good luck with that one.*

Drake sighed. The so-called experts had probably installed the wrong ventilation system. A little depressed, he drifted back into the operations room and was surprised to see Mai, usually the picture of reserve, arguing animatedly with their boss—Jonathan Gates.

His radar perked up.

On one of the big screens a message was repeating:

"Our warship returned to the curious island I previously spoke of today. This time I was allowed to disembark and go ashore. Saw everything unexpected. A vast, well equipped lab. Bodies of European descent. And worse—experimentation. Many weapons—American made, state of the art. Some futuristic. And one other thing—the briefest mention of a possible target. US Senator, James Turner."

A blue flag attached to the message symbol on the screen indicated that it had come direct from Homeland. When Karin used her keyboard to open the internal message, Drake saw it had been forwarded from the Japanese Defense Intelligence Headquarters in Shinjuku, Tokyo.

Mai touched Gates on the shoulder. "I know this man. I know Dai Hibiki very well. Years of his life have been devoted to this mission. You can't—"

"You got it, Mai. My point exactly. *Years of his life.* Even the Japanese aren't entirely sure Hibiki hasn't been turned."

"I just told you, Gates. I know him."

A silence descended, frosted around the edges. Dahl was shaking his head at the both of them. "It really is a no-brainer," he said. "It's information about a threat to a US official. It has to be investigated."

"Agreed," Hayden, perhaps seeing the need to exert some authority and remind everyone of who was in charge, tapped the side of her coffee mug sharply against a screen. "The question is—should *we* take it or pass it on?"

"There's not only the senator to consider," Mai said patiently. "It is also the island that should be investigated. What is going on there?"

Drake read it through again. The words *European, experimentation,* and *weapons* stood out like warning signs. "Special Response and Recon. Sounds right up our street." And anything that added distraction to his days was worth pursuing.

"But don't trust Hibiki," Gates insisted. "Not until you get him alone."

Mai stayed tight-lipped.

Hayden allowed a half-smile to form on her lips. "New team. New mission. New rules. We respond. We don't initiate. We're recon. Not assault. And we're official now. So keep it above the law."

"And if you can't," Alicia piped up, "make sure no one ever finds the bastards."

"There *are* people who want this team to fail," Gates told them seriously. "Rivals on the Hill. I could name two without thinking. I'm just not sure yet how far they're willing to go."

Drake understood but it was combat, not politics, that concerned him. "You take care of them. We"—he indicated the big screen—"will take care of this."

Hayden stepped in quickly. "Mai. Drake. You get the flight. The rest of us will start looking into Senator Turner."

Alicia blinked in surprise. "What about—?"

Mano turned to her. "I think you're classed with the rest of us.'"

Alicia turned on him. "Really, Mano? *Really?* You're taking the piss after all I learned about you in that bar?"

The Hawaiian grunted and held his hands up. Truth be told, he couldn't remember telling her anything the night they, along with Belmonte, spent drinking and spinning yarns as the Austrian night gave way to the red dawn of what might be their deaths. For one of them it had been, but Belmonte had gone down fighting.

Kinimaka stayed cautious. "Well we won't exactly be baking cakes here in DC."

Alicia shot a glance at Komodo. "Don't count on it."

Drake checked his watch and walked over to Mai. "It's a good plan. We'll take a small team. No incursion, just surveillance. Maybe Mai will be able to contact Hibiki. He knows her. He would make allowances for her." He headed for the door, shouting over his shoulder. "Send me the details in flight. About time we got some more bloody action!"

CHAPTER THREE

The Lockheed C-130 undertook many varied missions for the United States Air Force, but tonight, it transported Matt Drake, Mai Kitano and a small, four-strong team of Marine Force Recon soldiers over the North Pacific Ocean toward their destination—a small, nameless island off the coast of Korea.

The atmosphere in the four-engine military transport possessed an air of subdued excitement. Drake and Mai spent some time in the communications area, but learned nothing new during the flight. The team back home had begun investigations, but with necessary discretion—a directive from Gates.

And not Drake's way. Nor was it anyone else's way, but they were legal now and their benefactor, Gates, was being observed from all angles.

Back in the main seating area, the four marines sat around, idly chatting. These men were at ease, but still nothing escaped them. When Drake and Mai returned their leader, a man called Romero, sat up.

"All well?"

"Could be better." Drake grumbled.

"Problems back home?"

Drake blinked and stared. At first, he'd assumed the soldier meant *back home in York*, and was about to tell the grunt to mind his own friggin' business, but then realized the reference was to the HQ. *Christ,* he thought, *gotta stop mixing business with pleasure.*

And then Mai touched his arm, her presence and her contact immediately shattering even that small resolution.

"Yeah," he said. "Senators get death threats every day. It's gonna take a miracle to convince him to lay low even for a couple of days."

"Maybe it's just that. A threat." Romero shoved his square-jawed face forward, testing the room.

Mai strode toward him. "You think a Japanese agent who managed to dig himself in so deep with the Koreans would surface for no good reason, Romero?"

"I guess not." The American backed down. "But we'll be sure to find out. We're all on the same team here, miss."

"Call me Mai." The wiry-framed operative passed so close she touched the Marine as she continued to the bar. "Drink?"

The marine frowned. Drake looked momentarily hopeful, then forced himself to pretend he was joking. He wouldn't drink again. Those nights spent in Hawaii in a drunken stupor, hunting down the Blood King's men, still sat with him as a low point of his life. No way he wanted to go back to that.

He watched Mai pour herself a straight whisky and knock it back. The marines regarded her warily. No doubt they knew something of her past and prowess, but they could never guess even half her story. Drake knew it all. They had been lovers once, inseparable, all their secrets laid bare.

It would only take some chance lighting of the touchpaper to kindle the spark and make it all happen again. But was it too soon? Recent events were still raw. New revelations were cruel and new enough to cause constrictions in his chest.

A shout rang out through the cabin. "Thirty minutes to target."

Drake collected himself. The plan was to fly over southern Japan and get as close to the unidentified island as they could without arousing any Korean suspicions. Then, the team would deploy amphibious craft and the airplane would head back to Japan. The return journey was, as ever, somewhat ambiguous.

Wouldn't have it any other way, Romero had said, grinning, when he heard.

Drake had smiled. Romero had passed the first test.

The other three members of Romero's crew, Smyth, Wardell and Matthews now stood up and began final checks. Drake strapped weapons and gear around his body, hefting the parachute and making sure the Gore-tex jump suit was secure. After a few minutes, everyone turned and checked their partners. Drake knelt on a seat and pressed his face to a window, trying to peer through the midnight murk that blanked out most of the East China Sea.

Heavy, dark swells undulated below him like the monstrous body of some mythic sea serpent.

Romero was at their back. "Don't worry." He grinned "We've done this before."

At that moment there was a flash and an ear-splitting roar the like of which even Drake had never heard. The aircraft lurched. Time stood still for a second and then, as they turned, the entire far wall of the plane seemed to disintegrate.

A fireball rolled through the sky outside, keeping pace. Chunks and shards of metal fizzed and zipped through it all. Romero cried, "Someone. . .someone shot us down!"

Mai grabbed him and pulled him down. "Not yet."

Drake knew that, with plane crashes, Hollywood took a lot of artistic license. In real life a bullet-hole or a small hole wouldn't suck you out to your doom, but a hole as big as this? They were going down. Fast. He took hold of a seat, wrapping his arm entirely around the armrest and clasping it tightly with his other. The pilot was shouting, screaming as he struggled to slow the descent.

Even his most valiant effort raised the nose only a little. The C-130 hurtled inexorably toward the sea.

"We need to get out of this fucker," Drake said. "Prime altitude. Give the chutes time to work."

Mai nodded. They glanced around at the others. It was then they realized both Wardell and Matthews had been caught in the initial explosion. Both men lay prone and torn apart on the cabin floor, and were now being pulled toward the big jagged hole.

Drake felt the tug on his body. The wind whipped and whistled around the cabin. The noise was tremendous, like a freight train roaring in his face. It would be easy to let themselves be dragged out, but their escape had to be controlled like any normal jump. He spotted the other marine, Smyth, clinging to a fixed table in the middle of the cabin, eyes steady and locked on to his bosses, awaiting orders.

Good, Drake thought. These men were among the elite of the US forces. The amphibious craft could be released too. They had three CRRC's, Combat Rubber Raiding Craft, or Zodiacs to use the more popular term. It would take a huge effort. . .but sure as hell wasn't beyond them.

The pilot was the problem. They needed—

—a second explosion shook the beleaguered plane to its metal core. A great shrieking, grinding sound spoke of unbearable stress. It rocked and shuddered through every joint. A fireball hit the cockpit, exploding through into the main cabin and taking out the pilot in the blink of an eye.

"Move!" Drake reacted instantly. As the fire died away, he pushed Romero toward the yawning hole. Mai scrambled over to Smyth, using the chair backs as stepping stones, cat-quick and assured.

The Zodiacs were stacked at the rear of the plane, big black inflatables with 55hp, two-stroke outboard engines. Drake knew from experience that a special fuel bladder and storage bag full of equipment would be housed at the front of the boats. He also knew that chasing after a Zodiac through thousands of feet of turbulent air into a raging sea wasn't exactly the best way to go, but some evil bastard had taken that decision clean out of his hands.

Drake grabbed something solid and made his way slowly toward the inflatables. It would be easy to just leap out of the plane, but that was a big-ass sea down there, and they would need shelter and even the meager security the Zodiacs offered. His head whipped back as a mighty gust of wind slapped him full in the face. A splinter of metal, flapping frantically in the gale, finally tore off and fizzed through the cabin, embedding itself deep into the far wall. Seat moorings began to groan as the pressure grew. It only took seconds, but Drake fought a lifetime to get within reach of the carefully stacked Zodiacs.

Mai was waiting. "Ready?"

"If I'm ever ready to do this shit, that's when I'll quit," Drake yelled back at her.

Then Mai unsnapped the security cables and the Zodiacs shifted. Mai and Smyth manhandled the first to the gap. Drake and Romero struggled with a second. The downward angle of the plane helped them heave the heavy boats into place. Only minutes had passed since the first explosion. Parts of the fuselage were on fire, streaking flames and fuel into the pitch-black night. Drake wondered what the pilot's last communication had been. Did anyone know they were about to ditch? He double-checked his parachute.

"Any last words?" Romero was breathing heavily at his side, eyes fully focused on the serrated gap that had been blown in the plane.

"Just one." Drake heaved his Zodiac off the plane. "Bollocks!" And jumped out into the furious, violent night.

The rampant seas swelled, as if reaching up to claim their latest sacrifice.

CHAPTER FOUR

The University of Baltimore had been chosen by Senator James Turner as the ideal place to host one of the most significant speeches of his whirlwind east-coast tour.

By the time Alicia arrived, the crowds were gathering and the stage was in the last phase of preparation. The atmosphere was happy, expectant, the noise a slowly mounting swell. Alicia made her way to the outskirts, a little unsure of how to proceed. The team had still not confirmed any major threat to the senator. She had volunteered to take a quick inspection as much to get her out of the office and into the field as anything. Like Drake and Mai, she was a soldier. Inactivity did more than make her stale; it blunted her predator's edge.

She made her way to the top of a grassy knoll. The winter sun beat down, making her shield her eyes. A sea of people chattered and bobbed around before her, waving pamphlets and campaign flyers, texting friends and flicking at their iPads. The small stage in front of them was no more than a raised dais, backed by a curtain and fronted by a microphone and a couple of chairs. Senator James Turner required no luxuries. He was famous for his outspoken stance on gun control, his ties to the community and the consistency of his promises. A clever senator, and well-funded.

Alicia could see movement on and around the stage, the senator's many aides prepping for the speech. She glanced at her watch. About twenty minutes to showtime. Not much time to get up close.

She skirted the crowd as best she could, bought a coffee from an enterprising vendor, and moved in. Any minute she expected a call from Hayden, telling her that they had verified the threat. Her faith in the team was high, and with Karin's off-the-charts IQ, she fully expected someone to find something.

So, with only three minutes to go, Alicia dropped the half-empty coffee cup and sent a worried gaze across the crowd. Perhaps this threat wasn't any more substantial than a thousand others Turner had no doubt received. Maybe this wasn't the time or the place. But the security here was shambolic. Any fruitcake could take a pot shot.

She pulled out her cell and rang Hayden. "Any luck?"

"We've got squat at this end. How's it lookin' over there?"

"Busy." Alicia said. "Dangerous."

"Keep at it. We're still digging."

Despite their differences, Alicia trusted Mai's instinct. If the Japanese woman said her old friend Dai Hibiki hadn't been turned and was even now still providing dependable information, then Alicia believed her. She studied the stage, wondering if she should just mosey on up there and introduce herself to the guards. But that wouldn't work. They hadn't even been issued badges yet.

Not that Alicia wanted one. In her time she'd worked for all sides—the good, the bad, and the motherfucking ugly. This field, this situation, was a little out of her comfort zone. Her usual tactics—intimidation, assault, and taunting wouldn't work here. She had accepted the job out of curiosity. She didn't expect to stay long with Drake and his team. Other than Drake himself, the only other person she could identify with was Kinimaka, and he was still in recovery mode, not to mention fawning helplessly over his bloody boss. At last, she reached the barrier that separated the stage from the crowd. Little more than a row of old sawhorses, painted and hung with leaflets and bunting. Not even a low fence. Apparently, the senator was a quick, lively showman. He'd take the stage, warm the crowd up, deliver his message, and be out of there before the dust settled.

Much like most of her ex-boyfriends, she mused.

Then a cheer went up. Men in black suits took to the stage and fanned out to both sides. A couple of aides ran out, smiling and waving. The curtain twitched. People around Alicia started to shout the senator's name. A tumult of noise greeted the man as he stepped from behind the curtain and took center stage. His aides melted away into the background, still smiling.

The senator basked for a moment before speaking. He was a tall, aging man with grey hair and a wiry frame. Dimples pitted the sides of his cheeks, giving him a cheery demeanor. He raised a hand.

"My friends, my friends, thank you. What a turnout. Even the sunshine has greeted us today!"

Alicia scrutinized the packed bodies as best she could. The sway of the crowd and the excitement of those in the front few rows made it next to impossible to make any kind of judgment. Maybe today wouldn't be the day. . .

But the timing of Hibiki's message was disquieting. Why would the Koreans target such a low-key figure anyway? She shrugged it off, briefly wondering how Drake and the sprite were faring. Lucky bastards.

The senator droned on to continued applause. If this was the kind of fieldwork the new team was all about, she couldn't see herself lasting long. Her feet itched to chase someone. Her fingers kept reaching for a gun that wasn't there. It had been said before, but the problem with a "secret" agency was that no one knew it existed.

Ironic, eh? She smiled to herself. But when the first shot was fired, she glanced instinctively to her right. The crowd quieted and ducked their heads. The second shot galvanized them to either hit the deck or bolt. On stage the security detail stormed forward, trying to cover the senator. The man himself stood in shock, mouth agape, as if trying to stare his would-be assassin into submission.

Another shot. Another miss, but this time, one of the aides went down, clutching her neck as blood sprayed. All around Alicia there was suddenly a terrible uproar and she was jostled and knocked and almost tripped to the ground.

But she had seen the shooter. In those frozen seconds, she had studied his face and stance and manner.

It just didn't make sense.

By now, the senator had been wrestled to the floor and the security detail was leaping from the stage and rushing toward the shooter. Alicia maintained her ground, watching it unfold. The man with the gun was the most normal, all-American looking guy she'd ever seen. He was clean, well-dressed and well-groomed. The way he held the gun spoke of training, but the way he conducted himself spoke of something else all together.

His eyes were blank. His movements slow as if he struggled through thick molasses. His mouth hung slackly. Even from where she stood, Alicia could see a string of drool hanging from his lips. The guy looked like a zombie. A real-life, bona-fide member of the living dead.

And as the bodyguards closed in, the shooter slowly turned the gun around, aiming it at his own heart. Without a second's hesitation, he pulled the trigger and fell to the ground.

Alicia raced toward him, wrestling her cellphone out and appraising the situation on the stage as she ran. Two guards down. The aide down, not moving. And a shaken senator, happy to be alive and nestled underneath his security detail.

Hayden answered immediately. "What happened?"

"I've been doin' this a long time," Alicia shouted as she ran. "But I just saw some of the craziest shit ever go down. You'd best prepare for a storm."

CHAPTER FIVE

Hell and high water besieged their every horizon.

First panic and then rage consumed Drake as he struggled to make any progress. Darkness pounded at him, rolled at him, and assaulted his consciousness with waves of disbelief and amazement. Every inch of his body cried out with pain. Water splashed and dragged at him until he learned to see through the salty sting. A continual swell sent him up and down like a nightmare elevator that never stops. His gaze swept the menacing seas.

Where were the others? Where are the Zodiacs?

Dark clouds obscured any faint light that might have shone down from the skies above. Lightning flickered in the distance, marching across the waves like old gods. Thunder rumbled threateningly. His heart sank as he studied the blackness, seeing nothing to raise his spirits.

Kept buoyant by his life jacket, Drake attempted to move. The Zodiacs wouldn't come to him. He remembered to switch on the shoulder light, but it was like a pinprick trying to illuminate the solar system. With a huge effort, he surged forward, plowing through the gloomy waters. At first, he made progress, but each successive, mountainous wave dumped him back where he started. It was all he could do to keep his head above water.

Then, a shout came, *"Move!"* desperate and plaintive, barely heard above the sea's menacing roar. Drake paddled around to see his salvation. A Zodiac, manned by Romero and Smyth, aiming straight for him. The Recon guys had come through. They reached him in seconds, skillfully guiding the light-framed boat through chop and wave crests and a hard, driving rain. The terrible sea clung to him as hard as it could, but Romero and Smyth, anchored by their guide ropes, hauled him out of the water.

Drake collapsed, breathing heavily, feeling utmost relief for about half a second. Then he sat up.

"Have you seen Mai?"

Romero shook his head. "Shit, man, do you know how lucky we were to find you?"

"We can't leave her." Drake secured himself through a set of guide ropes and rested his back against the side of the craft.

"We ain't going anyplace, bro," Romero told him. "That these goddamn waters don't want us to. Since you don't seem to get it, let me explain—this ain't no rescue mission."

Drake nodded. Spray showered over the sides of the boat, then a torrent of water poured over him. They crested another wave and plummeted off its back side into an abyss. Drake gripped the ropes until blood began to seep through his fingers, but he couldn't relax his hold. A cold rain struck at their exposed faces so hard it constantly made them flinch.

Lightning struck the seas a hundred feet from their position, boiling along the waves, drenching the whole scene with an eerie glow. The roar of thunder and water made it impossible to even think clearly.

More peaks and more troughs as the waves rose even higher, five and then six meter summits. And even the wind lent the weight of its fury against them, caterwauling among the peaks and troughs, gusting hard when the boat dropped to its lowest, whipping at them when they topped out.

The Zodiac struggled resolutely onward. Its occupants never stopped twisting and turning in their harnesses, always vigilant, always searching for their lost companion. The minutes passed like hours, and the hours like days.

"Stupid question!" Drake yelled once. "Anyone still got comms? Did you manage to get a message out to Hayden?"

"Shit, just a snatch." Romero shouted back. "After impact. Smyth?"

"Yeah. Just *we're ok* and then the lights went out. Not sure it even transmitted."

"Sounds about right," Drake muttered in broad Yorkshire. "If summat can go wrong, summat will."

As if to emphasize his point, a torrent of water deluged the boat. Drake stopped breathing as the inundation crashed into his face. A few seconds passed and then he lay there panting, exhausted.

It was good they were strapped in. As the onslaught continued, their muscles grew weary and their brains foggy. There were other dangers here, including hypothermia. When a surge of water flooded the boat, the colliding forces came together in a white fizzing froth, relentless and merciless. They braced themselves against each other, against the boat, and closed their eyes as the sky became the mountainous sea and the sea suddenly crashed away to reveal the turbulent sky.

Drake wished he knew what had happened to Mai. If this hell was to be his final resting place, he wanted to go down knowing the truth. But he had no intention of going down at all. He was stronger than that. With Mai fixed firmly at the forefront of his mind, he found the strength to ignore the peril by peering inward. Whilst not avoiding the Japanese agent recently, he had ensured that their relationship didn't develop.

Might have been a mistake. The thought came a little grudgingly, but it came straight from his soul. If a man gave up the chances that came his way, he would regret it for the rest of his life.

Drake opened his eyes and watched the other two men in the boat. Romero sat easily, a reserved calm smoothing out his features. It took moments like this to find a man you could truly rely on in any given moment of danger, and the Force Recon team leader was one of them. Smyth looked a little scared, a little green, but gazed hard into the tumult as if trying to find the paths of his future.

They were good men. Hard men. And if they survived this battle, brothers for life.

At last the skies began to lighten to the east, easing their torment if only a little. The great seas quieted, the enormous waves gradually flattening out. An hour passed and the sun began to rise, an orange ball of fire that burned off any last vestiges of the storm. Overcome with exhaustion, the trio fell into a deep sleep, waking later as the sun blasted down from high overhead.

Without a word, Drake unhooked himself from the ropes, every muscle burning, and tried to crawl across the bottom of the boat. His tongue was glued to the roof of his mouth, his skin burning from exposure to the sun. Every nerve and every sinew screamed in protest, but he forced his body to inch its way to the sealed storage bag that nestled in the front of the boat. It would hold tools, an inflator and patches, and also water.

He lifted his head. Sunlight blasted off the sea, dazzling his eyes and setting off a pounding pain. The marines would have reflectors in their packs.

Later. For now, he unbuckled the storage bag and opened it. Then he took three bottles of water out and passed them around. Never had water tasted so good.

Romero fished out the anti-glare glasses, groaning as he moved. "Damnit, man, feel like I went nine rounds with the Hulk."

He carefully fixed the glasses around his eyes and gazed out to sea for a while. Judging from the expression on his face, Drake guessed he didn't see a whole lot.

"We don't know where we landed, where we drifted, or where we are." Smyth was also surveying the area.

"No, but we do know east and west," Drake pointed out. "Maybe we didn't drift so far. And, if we head due north we should hit land." He didn't add the requisite *eventually.*

"That's the plan." Romero said, staying upbeat. Drake thought that being stranded with the marine wasn't half as stressful as it might have been with Alicia. He sat up, trying to avoid the raging sun and the glaring sea. Salt granules stuck to his skin. Scrapes and bruises stood out harshly on his arms.

"We need to cover up too," Drake said. "You guys have anything we can use?" The question was rhetorical as Drake searched the storage bag and came up empty. "Guess it'll have to be our vests."

Slowly, Drake stripped out of his Kevlar jacket and shirt. He wrapped the vest tightly around his head and tied an end. Makeshift, but effective for now. "So," he said, "we gonna start paddling?"

Romero sighed. "Fuck."

The trio of battered men unstrapped the paddles and started to dig at the sea. As one they groaned. Due north looked no different than due south, but once they had it pinpointed, they kept the horizon in their sights and put their backs into it.

After a half hour, Romero spoke up. "You guys think we'll be rescued?"

"Bugger all chance of that." Drake snorted. "Hayden thinks we're *ok*. No one else knows we're here."

"Rations are exactly that. Rations." Smyth shook his webbing, letting the few packets of food rattle. "A day or two tops."

The sun beat down. The men grew tired, and rested as the heat passed its midday peak and waned into late afternoon. They drank water and laid back to conserve energy. A couple of rogue waves sent them scaling liquid cliffs again only to plummet once more to impossible depths. Sea creatures bumped the boat, investigating, some just curious, others questing for food. When the dirty white fin of a shark broke the surface, Romero sat up angrily. "Now that's an ice cold mother of a threat."

Smyth stared at the fin as it cut its way back and forth. "We used to take bets back in training as to how we might die. Could've got a cool hundred to one on becoming shark food."

"But who would've collected the winnings?" Drake smirked.

Smyth shrugged. "Didn't think that far."

They waited until the fin vanished and then started paddling again, but there wasn't a single pair of eyes that didn't constantly keep a lookout for that chilling, telltale sign.

But as night began to encroach, the men became quiet. The ocean grew still. A thin sliver of moon rose steadily, casting its stark glow across the undulating, mirror-like surface of the sea. Drake found himself dwelling on Mai, and the ordeals she might be enduring. He couldn't bring himself to think she might already have died. Couldn't even imagine it.

His heart froze when a shadow loomed ahead, gliding silently toward them across the gentle swells of the sea.

CHAPTER SIX

"The gunman missed Senator Turner," Hayden said aloud. "But killed his aide—a Miss Audrey Smalls—and two bodyguards." She hung her head. "Senseless slaughter."

Ben tapped his monitor. "That woman from the Washington Post has vanished," he said with some relief. "Finally."

A reporter from DCs biggest newspaper had been hanging around the new facility for days now, sensing a meaty story, haranguing them every time they stepped out.

"Sarah Moxley?" Hayden said. "Oh, she'll be back."

Alicia paced the room. "What do we know? That some all-American kid tried to assassinate a US Senator. That the kid's being dissected to give us a clue as to why the hell he did it. The video feed—" She paused, glancing again at the TV screen they'd all been watching. "Showed his face. Did he look sane to you?"

In a corner of the room, Gates was attempting to find out what had happened to Drake and Mai. The secretary's voice rose. Whoever was on the other end of the line wasn't doing himself any favors. "Then *fetch him."* Gates almost yelled. "I'll wait."

"We're contacting all the agencies," Karin spoke up. "Trying to find a connection between Senator Turner and the Koreans. Failing that. . .it could be anything." The blond girl shot a quick glance at Komodo. The big soldier nodded back at her without smiling. Karin knew him well enough by now to see the distress in his eyes. The wait for news was as traumatic as an operation in the Middle East.

Kinimaka moved to Hayden's side. The big Hawaiian was moving much easier now, the deep bruising caused by gunshot subsiding. "This proves that Mai's agency friend was on the level, boss."

"Sure." Hayden was distracted, studying the video of yesterday's event yet again. "Look at his eyes, Mano. His eyes."

Kinimaka looked. He'd already looked a hundred times, but he looked again because Hayden asked him too. The shooter, now identified as Michael Markel, from the DC area, had been a thirty-five-year-old teacher. He was a loner, but nothing about him stood out as wrong. His house had already been turned inside out—but whatever Markel's reasons were for his act, they still remained a mystery. So far, the man stood out as the perfect citizen.

"Look deeper," Hayden told both Ben and Karin. "This man has a skeleton hidden away somewhere."

Hayden felt her thoughts being knocked awry. The new job came with some already deep-rooted problems—one namely Ben Blake. The pair had treated each other cordially so far, but there was no getting away from the coolness that existed. Hayden found herself not wanting to ask too much of her ex-boyfriend, whilst he clearly found it hard acknowledging the new arrangement.

And something had changed Ben back at that third tomb of the gods. When the soldier died in his arms, when Ben's hands dripped with the man's blood, a revolution had begun in his brain. Maybe its purpose was to bring out the man and discard the boy forever. Or perhaps it was just another ordeal, a trauma that would twist his psyche.

Hayden knew his pain. She almost wished he had endured an ordeal of that kind before she'd made her decision. The boy needed help, but it wasn't right for her to step up.

The man at her side was the biggest reason—in more ways than one. She was finding it increasingly hard to maintain a strictly professional relationship with him, especially since their relentless days and months of crazy exploits had ended. What she needed was a distraction. Something that would focus her mind on work.

Of course it didn't help with Karin and Komodo making constant lame excuses to disappear together. Or with Torsten Dahl's brooding. The Swede was already having second thoughts about switching jobs, but kept them mostly to himself.

Gates put the phone down at last. Every eye in the room turned to him.

"Drake's plane was shot down by the Koreans. Not officially, of course. But the bastards claim they were protecting their territory from an unidentified attack. There's a lot of tiptoeing around to be done before we decide what to do."

Dahl slammed a desk with his fist. Hayden butted in quickly before the Swede could say anything stupid. "The Koreans aren't supposed to have anything that would detect that plane flying at that height, Mr. Secretary."

Gates shrugged. "Dai Hibiki's message warned of 'futuristic arms,' I believe."

"What can we do?" Ben spoke up, fingers hovering over his keyboard.

"Nothing with that thing." Dahl growled. "We need to send a team in. Now. Our brothers are in danger."

"Politically—" Gates emphasized the word. "We must wait. Besides, Drake and Mai are pretty capable. And we didn't send 'em along with a bunch of cheerleaders. Those were Force Recon marines."

Alicia had listened to it all perched on the end of a desk. Now she pushed off. "Drake would lead a team," she said. "He'd do it for you. For any of us."

Gates's eyes were hollow. "The old Drake might have. The new Drake seems a little different. I may not be a soldier, but I do share some experience with him. I think he'd never again make that promise to save anyone."

Alicia paused. She didn't remind anyone that she'd also lost someone recently. It wouldn't help anything. Besides, the American had a point. Drake was a changed man.

"So let's help him another way," Hayden said whilst the argument paused. "How does a squeaky-clean American man with no previous convictions end up attempting to assassinate a senator? Riddle me that."

"And how does it all link to the North Koreans and Dai Hibiki's transmission?" Kinimaka added.

Hayden started the video of the shooting yet again. "Let's get to work."

"I think we need take-out." Karin looked around innocently at Komodo. "Wanna drive me round the corner?"

The Delta man had the grace to look slightly embarrassed as he whispered, "I'll do my best."

CHAPTER SEVEN

Drake shouted a warning. Romero and Smyth shot up, staring wildly around. The bulk drifted closer, on a collision course, and now Drake recognized it as a piece of smashed wing.

"Paddle!" Drake cried

The marines suddenly remembered their oars and dug them hard into the calm waters. The light craft responded immediately, shifting its course sharply, but the wing loomed over them, a dark, dead force that could capsize them without malice or concern.

Drake ducked. Part of the wing, angled out of the water, grazed the top of his head. The Zodiac skimmed out of its shadow a second before the two masses collided.

The three soldiers sat in silence, watching the remains of their plane float away. Romero finally took a swig of water, chewed on some remaining rations and motioned at Smyth.

"Keep paddling. No one else is gonna save our asses."

Drake forced himself to stay alert. It was too easy to let the unending vastness lull him and drain him of all hope and motivation. If they kept busy, they had a better chance at survival. Lethargy, after all, helps kill the brain. He occupied himself studying the constellations, inventorying their meager possessions, and checking the Zodiac for bumps and scrapes. When full light came, he would dive overboard to check the bottom. Silently, he knew they all hoped and prayed there wouldn't be another storm. This part of the world was renowned for its cyclones, a weather anomaly that would truly wipe them off the face of the earth.

Daylight came quickly. The soldiers and Drake did their best to keep the craft heading north where, they'd reasoned, lay the nearest body of land and their only chance of ever stepping foot on terra firma again. More visitors began to glide around them, visitors from the pitiless deep. Long white shapes cruised underneath the boat, triangular fins occasionally cleaving at the surface.

Drake was the first to overcome his fear and wonder aloud, "Anyone know how to fish?"

Romero shrugged. "I fished a little. You would need a lure, a line and a hook. You got a hook?"

"We sure have line," Drake told him, indicating the guide ropes. "And we could use your blood as a lure."

"*My* blood?"

"Why not? My Yorkshire blood's tainted, y' know. Too many fish and chips. The scent would put 'em off."

Smyth shook his head, offering a tight smile. "Couldn't we just shoot one of the mothers?"

Drake thought of the single handgun secreted in the storage bag. "That might be needed to fend off larger predators yet. That's our last resort."

Smyth eyed the waters speculatively. "Larger predators? What the hell are you expecting? The Kraken?"

"Of the non-gilled variety." Drake smiled without humor. He took his turn at the paddles whilst Romero rested, donning the anti-glare specs and trying to ignore the smell of sweat that clung around his body. Didn't matter how many salt-baths you took, there was no replacing good old-fashioned soap.

The sun beat down, a harsh non-stop glare. Drake kept an eye to the skies, hoping for a brief shower, anything to top up their dwindling supplies, but there was no respite from the endless pounding of the sun's rays. By mid-afternoon a fair bluster had whipped up, thrashing at the seas and sending several unpredictable waves their way. Drake and the two marines quit talking. There seemed no end to the monotony, no release from the torture.

And always they tracked north, sometimes sent astray by the currents or the prevailing winds, but incessantly north. Drake realized after a while that the lack of chatter was more than worrying, it was bordering on deadly.

"Hey!" He pushed himself to his knees and shook the other two. "Hey. Who the hell do ya think shot us down, anyway?"

Romero snapped out of his somnolence straight away. "They told us the plane couldn't be detected. Bullshit."

Drake shook Smyth again. "You alright, mate?"

"Yeah, yeah," Smyth said irritably, coming around. "You pulled me out of a damn fine dream, man."

"You're welcome," Drake said pointedly. "Now. The North Koreans, right? Goes without saying—but what on earth do they have to hide?"

"Are you kidding?" Smyth snorted. "They carry out nuclear tests more often than Tribune reruns *Friends*. Course they got something to hide."

Drake nodded. "Yes. But this is a secret island with links to the U.S. And they shoot us out of the sky without even gloating about it first?"

Romero cast his gaze around. "Well once we get our asses back on land where they belong, we can all go back to being soldiers again."

Drake watched as the day began to diminish. A blackness began to seep down the western horizon. The north, for now, remained vivid—brilliant light shimmering around scudding clouds. The low mass out there, at first, went unnoticed, and even when Drake's eyes focused on it, they didn't quite comprehend what they were seeing.

Then the message reached his brain.

"Paddle!" he shouted, almost screamed, his throat husky and raw. "Look!"

Romero and Smyth sprang into action, marines again, recognizing a last chance when they saw one. Drake glued his eyes firmly to the prize, spirits rising at every stroke with which they swept themselves nearer. The land mass formed into rock and a sweep of sandy beach and stands of dense trees. It felt like he held his breath the entire hour it took them to paddle there.

By then visibility was low. But there was no mistaking the presence of hills and high rocks—the promise of safety.

There were no expletives passionate enough for the trio as they let the boat drift finally into the shallows. Rarely had Drake felt such a sense of utter relief wash over him.

Then he saw the black shape waiting for them, moored on the beach.

"Oh my. . ."

The second Zodiac. And Mai sitting cross-legged in the sand beside it, a bewildered expression on her fair face. "Drake? Where the fuck have you *been?*"

CHAPTER EIGHT

Mai helped them secure their Zodiac and then led them farther up the beach without a word. For Drake, just the simple act of stepping out of the boat onto solid ground was an indescribable heaven. He stood there a moment, watching Mai stalk away, and just reveled in the luxury.

Romero and Smyth marched past him, shaking their heads and unable to stop smiling. Didn't matter where they'd ended up so long as they were out of the treacherous seas.

Drake started to walk. Something bothered him. A feeling that had leapt into his heart on seeing Mai. A feeling he shouldn't have, something so genuine and warm it scared him.

It took a while for Mai to reach her destination, and by then the sunlight had faded and the stars were twinkling on high. A cool breeze swept the beach and whispered through the bordering trees. Mai cut inland a little, leading them to a sheltered glade. Silvery moonlight illuminated the shelter she had crafted from tree branches, leafy plants and her Zodiac boat cover.

"It's not much," Mai muttered. "But a girl can only do so much in three hours."

Drake walked right up to her and held her close. "Thank God," he whispered, then, "You've been sitting there for three hours?"

"Of course not. I came back down to the Zodiac for supplies, saw yours coming in and thought I'd wait and surprise you."

"Thank God." Drake said again.

"Like He had anything to do with it."

"God didn't train us," Smyth said irascibly. "The army did."

Mai set free a tired smile. "He's got a point."

"Lighten up," Drake said, letting the Japanese woman go. "You'll end up with an ulcer before we're home, mate."

"That's Smyth's one redeeming quality," Romero said, amused. "His cheery demeanor."

Smyth glowered all around.

Drake stared speculatively at the trees. "You taken much of a gander?"

Mai shook her head. "Thought I'd get shelter and rest first. Scout around in the morning." Her gaze swept the men. "No fires. No noise."

Smyth snorted. "Goes without saying." He threw himself down on a patch of ground.

Romero took a minute to shake hands with her. "Thanks for looking out for us."

Mai nodded.

When the marine had walked away, Drake reiterated his comment. "You couldn't have known we were out there."

"I didn't. But what else was I going to do? Stay shipwrecked alone? I know you. I had hope."

"Shipwrecked? More like *plane*wrecked. If the Koreans did make the decision to shoot us down like that, then they must be hiding a bloody good secret."

"Hibiki told us as much in his message."

"About a secret?" If Mai trusted Hibiki then Drake's own faith in him was unshakeable. "That's why we're here officially, but I would have come just for you."

"I know our history, Matt." Mai smiled, her features softening with memory. "Do you realize that we never truly split?"

Drake led her away and sat so their backs were against a clump of thick, thorny shrub. From here they could both survey the clearing whilst their companions slept. "We didn't?"

"You men, you know nothing," Mai said wistfully. "A woman. She thinks of everything. She remembers everything. Her life. . .is rounded. Full."

"Not everyone has that ability, Mai." Drake brooded. "Sometimes—we'd rather forget."

"Perhaps. But drinking an excess of alcohol is not the way."

"We don't all have your strength."

Now Mai regarded him curiously. "But you do. You have so much strength it sets you apart from other men."

Drake shook his head. "In battle. In war, maybe. My hands are drenched in so much blood it anesthetizes me against the horror of it all. But with my women"—he looked down—"I'm made weak through failure."

"The two you lost weren't failures."

"Three," Drake whispered, voice choked with pain. "I lost three."

Mai remained respectfully silent for a minute before continuing. "I'm just saying. . .it doesn't have to be over between us."

"My track record. . ."

"I'm not going to die," Mai blurted before taking a second to evaluate their situation and their livelihood. "At least, not in a way that puts the blame on you. I know the risks. I play the percentages every day. People like you and I, Drake, we're not candles. We don't flicker and shine and then fade away. We're fireworks. We explode with brilliance, we blaze, we light up history and legend before quickly being snuffed out forever and probably forgotten. For pity's sake, take a chance."

Drake stared at her, taken by the passion in her eyes, the commitment and depth of feeling in her expression. He glanced beyond her, at the darkness that surrounded them and what might lie beyond their insignificant refuge.

"Let me sleep on it. Give you an answer in the morning."

And Mai responded instantly with a playful slap. "Fuck your damn Dinorock, you dense Yorkshire pudding. Now I know." Her smile flickered again. "Now I know."

Drake drifted in and out of sleep for a few hours but was wide awake and energized when first light began to creep across the skies. The four of them checked the Zodiacs, secured them a little tighter, and then set about exploring the island. It didn't take long. Within a couple of hours, they had traveled the entire coastline and had picked a landmark from which to venture inland. The rolling seas swept in behind them, surging across the sands and trickling in to lap at their feet as if inviting them back for another bout of *Survival*. They shielded their eyes and stared out to sea every chance they got, but a persistent fog bank hung in the distance, refusing to be burned off. A high mountain rose in the center of the island, its summit cracked and battered. From this angle, it looked like a crumpled paper bag.

"Boy, do I hope we find some food in here," Romero commented. "All I'm seeing as a source so far is fish."

"Oh there'll be bugs in the trees," Mai said, "insects in the ground. Plenty of protein to go round."

She set off, leaving Romero and Smyth wondering if she was serious. Drake followed her, not even sure himself. What little path there was wound about so sharply that they had to abandon it and make their own way. High trees, a leafy canopy and a wealth of intertwined branches raised the humidity and blocked their view. Twice, Mai was forced to climb trees to regain their bearings.

On one occasion, she jumped back down and nodded at Romero. "A few birds up there too."

Smyth sighed at Romero. "We've eaten worse, sir. Remember Thailand? Jeez."

They skirted a lake with high banks and cool, deep water. The far side was taken up by a rushing waterfall, torrents of white water cascading down to destroy the mirror-like surface. Though the lake would provide a good place to wash and its high streams a source of drinking water, none of them paid it a second glance. They'd had their fill of water for now.

A narrow crevice in the land caused a half-hour delay. The bottom was overgrown and treacherous, and the four soldiers were very aware that any kind of injury in this situation could be life threatening. They were careful and took their time, and came at last to the foothills of the mountain.

The slopes were barren. The dark mouths of caves dotted the rocky walls a few hundred feet up.

"Typhoon shelter," Mai pointed out. She checked the position of the sun. "It's getting toward midday. We should rest a few hours and then continue."

"It's not *that* hot." Smyth argued.

"But we're stopping anyway," Drake said. Smyth knew dehydration and weariness were substantial dangers. The marine was just playing the bad-boy role. Mai sank to the ground with her back against a stout evergreen and cracked the top of her last bottled water. Drake dropped down beside her.

"The concern is a lack of food," Drake muttered. "I expected some kind of animal out here."

"It's a small island," Mai said practically. "Besides we're only half way through the interior."

He fingered the small handgun, reassuring himself it was still there. "Be nice to eat real meat tonight."

"We could always roast Smyth."

"Don't tempt me."

Drake studied the tall trees, the green leaves, and the thick vegetation that covered the ground. Forest sights and sounds flittered intermittently past his consciousness; sunlight sparkled and spangled through drifting beams of light.

"There is no immediate shelter near the beach," Mai said. "Which means we're going to have to move inland. Maybe even as far as the caves if nothing else arises. Nothing close to the lake offered any chance of shelter."

"I noticed."

Mai evened out the correct amount of rations. "Almost out. It's nearly time to start thinking about snares and such."

Drake wasn't so worried about the food. Between them, they were four highly proficient soldiers, trained to the highest levels. They could find food in hell if need be. What troubled him was their next move.

"We aimed north for two days," he said. "The current was weak. The prevailing winds were favorable. We can't be far from the Korean shore by my estimate."

Mai shrugged. "Might as well be a thousand miles."

"Well we can't *stay* here. Every day we do brings us closer to death. Survival is out of the question unless we find the mainland, Mai."

The Japanese agent stopped chewing and placed her hand on his arm. "Relax. You don't have to be *that* Drake. The one who makes it all better. Just sit back and we'll see where the next hour takes us. And then the next day."

They journeyed around the mountain and headed back into the forest.

CHAPTER NINE

Alicia watched the geeks at work.

In her heart of hearts, she wished she was anywhere but here. Preferably with her own little geek. Even more preferably with some kind of meaningful life. But fate kept dealing her the Joker card and she kept playing the role. Drake valued her, she knew, and so did most of the others in their quiet way, but life for her was a rolling road to nowhere. It sure as hell wasn't going to stop for long with this team in Washington DC.

The security monitors showed the journalist was back. Sarah Moxley was a bloodhound. To date no one had offered up a single word, but there she was, sniffing around, testing their commitment, chasing an errant firefly that just kept flitting out of her reach. Today, Alicia felt in the mood to give her a word, probably even two.

Still nothing from Drake. Alicia and the rest of the team had to assume their colleague had survived. The last communication said as much. The very fact it was Drake and Mai remained the biggest factor in their favor. And poor old Jonathan Gates, despite his position as the Secretary of Defense, had become embroiled in the political mess whilst constantly banging his head against a North Korean brick wall.

Alicia sighed to herself. *The deeper the secret the harder it was to take seriously.* Their team still remained relatively unknown.

She poured another coffee, her fifth of the day, and replaced the pot noisily. No one looked up. Hayden and her new poodle, Kinimaka, were poring over files sent from the local PD, folders containing information on the perp, Michael Markel, the thirty-five-year-old teacher, and the three people who had died in the botched assassination– the two bodyguards and the Senator's aide, Audrey Smalls, and even Senator Turner himself.

"Problem is," Hayden was saying, "these nut jobs don't need a reason to do what they do. We can't simply put a pin in a reason and hope it sticks."

"Turner will only accept FBI protection for another twenty-four hours." Kinimaka pointed to a nearby screen where an email had just popped up. "And that's only out of deference to the other victims."

Hayden shook her head. Alicia tuned them out. Her gaze fell on Torsten Dahl, sat across the room. The Swede looked bored, anxious and pent-up all at the same time, probably reflecting her own state of mind.

She remembered the moment of Senator Turner's attempted assassination with vivid realism. The blank look on the killer's face, the empty, shark-like eyes, the obvious competence with which the loner teacher, without any sign of a past record, handled a gun.

The answer surely lay buried in his past. Somewhere.

Alicia drained the last of her coffee, now wired up to the max, but with nowhere to go and nothing to do. Even Komodo Trevor—as she called him—had disappeared on another errand, this time without his little girlfriend. She quickly checked her cellphone—no messages. Her biker friends from Luxembourg hadn't been in touch for a few days now. A movement caught her eye on the security camera, and again, that bloody reporter stepped into view.

Alicia smiled. Time to have a little fun and grab a few minutes of distraction. She slipped out of the room unnoticed and padded down the short hallway to the front door, tapped at a keypad and then let herself out into the sunshine.

Immediately, two sets of shoulders spun toward her.

"Miss Myles!" the female reporter was surprisingly quick. "Do you have time to comment?"

Alicia took a moment to study her. Sarah Moxley was a tall, wiry redhead. Flowing locks fell to the small of her back. Wide eyes were hidden behind thin-framed glasses. Her every movement spoke of urgency, as if she was constantly searching for that big story that continued to elude her.

A potentially dangerous adversary, Alicia catalogued the reporter as her training demanded. Sarah was a tiger made to look like a pussycat.

"Why the hell are you people hanging around out here? I mean, it's not like there's bugger all to see."

The reporter advanced a step. "I'm Sarah Moxley. I work for the Post." She proffered her ID, making Alicia smirk.

"Miss Moxley, don't play me for a fool. We both know who everyone is here, don't we?" She focused on the reporter's cameraman. "Except you, pretty boy. Anyone ever told you, you look a little like a younger Matt Damon?"

"Alright," Moxley said without a trace of humility. "Alicia Myles. Ex-British army. Ex rebel. New recruit. Am I right?"

"Not even close." Alicia stepped forward so the two of them were within touching distance. "Miss Moxley, there's no story here. You should look elsewhere."

"Honey, I see ex-army, ex-CIA, and a current Secretary of Defense coming and going all the time." Moxley jerked her head quickly at the team's new HQ. "I somehow think I'm in the right place."

Alicia considered her reply for a moment but then decided to go true to form. "I'd tell you to kiss my arse, but I'm pretty sure you'd enjoy it, and then I'll never get rid of you. So, for now"—she gave a little flourish—"farewell."

Alicia pushed past the reporters and jumped into one of the pool cars. A voice command turned the engine on, and by the time she merged with the steady flow of traffic, her mind was already far away from Sarah Moxley and Washington DC, centered firmly on the whereabouts of Matt Drake and Mai Kitano and what, if anything, she could do to help them.

CHAPTER TEN

They spotted the deer midway through the afternoon. By that time, they had established there were no other people on the island, but judging by tracks, old campfires and a broken-down structure, at some point in the not too distant past, someone had visited and stayed there.

Promising, but not positively uplifting news. They had no idea who the visitors might've been, and no way of contacting them. The foursome had decided to head back to the beach for the night and console themselves with a small portion of their frugal rations, resolving to start setting traps and hunting the next day, when Mai had held up a hand. Shocked, because of the ease of their passage so far that day, Drake had blinked and almost tripped, but soon caught himself when he spied the deer.

It stood alert, ears pricked, nostrils sniffing the breeze. A lovely creature, it appeared far too exquisite too harm, but red meat and protein would soon become the essence of survival for them, so Drake wasted no time in ambushing and shooting the beast. They carried it back, mouths watering, and then laid its body in a patch of barren ground a good walk from their shelter.

"The blood will soak into the ground," Smyth had said, unsheathing his knife. "No point doing it too close to home when we don't know what it might attract."

As darkness fell, they lit a campfire, erected a spit, and roasted the best parts of the deer. Even before it had cooled, they were feasting, fingers burned and dripping, mouths savoring the taste. Drake couldn't remember the last time food ever tasted so good. When they had finished, they all sat around the dying campfire in a comfortable silence.

It wasn't long before they were asleep, Drake lying close to Mai, wondering what tomorrow might bring.

And as the night waxed and waned, Drake found himself half-waking and half-dreaming, all subconscious thoughts centered round Mai Kitano. It all went back to the beginning, back to when they first met.

It had been his second mission as part of the British SAS, in mid-1998. Drake had been twenty-three then, a competent, fresh, deadly special-forces soldier. Their target had been a Chechen warlord, the country's most ruthless. Back in '98 kidnapping was Chechnya's major source of income, and the easy "go to" money-spinner for almost every aspiring warlord. And there were many. But Akhmad Doku ran them all—they could aspire no higher than to grace his boot with their shattered teeth. The new President Maskhadov was making things very hard for the warlords, resulting in some horrendous car bombings against official figures. Normally, the Chechen's would solve matters from within, but Doku didn't run his kidnapping business from inside the country; he ran it from nearby Turkey where the amenities and the lifestyle were a little more suited to his tastes.

Thus President Maskhadov had tugged at an old thread. His education had been through Oxford, his friends graduating into all kinds of business. One of them, a Commander Wells of the British SAS, had been all too happy to send an undercover team over to Istanbul to help eradicate the "Doku germ."

So, a young Matt Drake found himself in the middle of the most chaotic city he'd ever known. And the crowds thronging the streets were nothing compared to the badly repaired houses that massed within and around the city. Space was at a premium, and when Drake saw the palatial dwelling with which the vile Chechen warlord rewarded himself, his blood ran a little hotter, his disgust a little greater. After a few days of investigating, they discovered Doku hosted a weekly party. Drake and another of the team were chosen to pose as guests.

The "prettiest" of the SAS team found themselves gliding along with other partygoers, genuine invite in hand—ripped from the dying hands of Doku's dumbest goon—through a high, arched doorway and into the entrance hall of an ostentatious mansion. Drake didn't like to dwell on the obvious trappings of madmen and murderers—the mock dungeon room; the sealed-off wings; the presence of armed guards; blank, staring eyes of most of the warlord's "escorts;" or the barely concealed track marks on their forearms. Instead, he ventured as far as each sentry's irritation would allow, creating a detailed map in his mind of every entry and egress point, every CCTV camera, every guard station, and the types and quantities of weapons they carried.

Around midnight, he found himself skirting the pool area and, though the evening had cooled a little, the clear waters were crowded with half-naked bodies. At the halfway point, he broke a promise to himself by gawking and almost fell into the pool. But it didn't matter. Almost everyone else did the same.

The woman he later knew as Mai Kitano—she didn't earn her nickname *Shiranu* until the legendary incidents of Y2K at Tokyo Coscon—emerged from the waters by way of the pool ladder. She shook her head as she climbed, sending sprays of water flying from the ends of her long black hair as it whipped around her body. The white two-piece swimsuit she wore drew attention to her perfect body, tanned, curved and flawless in every way. And whilst most people looked away quickly to preserve their decency, one man in particular stood up to get a better view.

Drake now recognized Akhmad Doku, a little, thin-faced weasel of a man who no doubt would serve mankind better as crocodile bait. He bellowed at Mai with that arrogant assurance that tyrannical leaders are known for and beckoned for his bodyguards to help her to his side—just in case she hadn't heard. Drake watched the Japanese woman walk and was instantly sure that she knew how to handle herself. More than that, he was in no doubt that she was military trained. A plant?

He filed the incident away to report later.

The night wore on. Eventually the guests either began to drift away or fall into alcoholic comas. Doku was a benevolent host, allowing them the luxury of staying the night on his expansive deck and terrace. Drake was heading out, feigning drunkenness as the reason for his distance when the Japanese woman again stepped into his sights.

Still wearing the spectacular bikini. Her dark eyes rooted him to the spot. "I recognized you the moment I saw you." Her voice was as soft as drifting snow.

"You know my name?" The young Drake was unnerved, still shaken by this vision.

"No, sir. I meant your type. You are army, I think. And judging by your accent, you're a Yorkshire man. The Chechen president has a tie with your special forces, so I'm guessing SAS. Am I right?"

"I can't—"

"Ah, but you have to. You see, tonight is the night. I've worked on this operation for weeks. I have planned it to the last disgusting detail. I'll get him alone—and end his depravities permanently."

"You're pretty forthcoming to a man you just met."

"No. I'm confident in my abilities, that's all. I know you're British army, ergo you're with me."

Drake cast around desperately for his colleague, but they were alone. "Look. This is a recon. I have no orders to act. I can't be *with you.*"

"My philosophy has always been to take it as it comes or, in Doku's case, more like 'roll with the punches.' I don't need your help, but I could use it. And remember, after tonight, if I fail, you'll never get near him again."

She was right. Drake looked at her and saw the expression of a woman—and an agent—who never failed. He made a quick decision. "What do you need?"

Drake awoke the next morning a little disorientated. The island breeze had chilled his exposed skin; the dreams of Mai had confounded his judgment. It took a little while to remember that he was marooned on an uninhabited island somewhere off the coast of Korea, rather than inside a warlord's house in Istanbul.

When Romero and Smyth marched into his field of vision, kicking at the embers of the dead fire and staring out to sea, he climbed to his feet and stretched out his aching joints.

"Old man," Mai said as she jumped up, "old bones popping like cheap bubble wrap."

Drake gave her the dead eye and then laughed. "Don't you start. Alicia's usually the one with the piss take."

Mai stared out at the rolling grey ocean. The perpetual mist still hung at the horizon, dimming the light of the rising sun. "We need a team to set traps and a team to explore those caves for shelter and surprises. Once that's done, we need to get our heads together and figure out what we're going to use to signal passersby."

They all eyed the mist and the empty sea dubiously. Mai shrugged. "We have to try."

Smyth growled at nothing. "The caliber of passersby around these parts might not be to our liking."

Romero nodded. "Sure thing. Now let's get these traps up and running. You two okay exploring?"

Drake nodded and shook the lethargy away. Safe they might be, but they could not live for long on a desert island. "Keep an eye to that horizon," he said in parting. "It's still our best way of getting home."

Mai stepped lightly ahead as if embarking on a long-anticipated day trip. She used the path they had followed the day before—not so much a real path as a makeshift route that twisted and turned and occasionally doubled back. She moved quietly, aware of the surrounding wildlife and their potential next meal. Drake rubbed his eyes and stared up through the green canopy. The skies were blue up there, studded with drifting clouds. Birds flitted across the roof of the world, chasing dreams that danced among gusts of air. They were a long way from Washington DC, and a lifetime away from Hawaii and the other tombs of the gods. How life could change in a matter of weeks. His body seemed fine, but he was beginning to wonder if his mind needed to catch up. The strain had been terrible since Kennedy died. What they all needed was some down time—some good old-fashioned R and R.

He sighed aloud. Maybe next year.

Mai glanced back. "You bored?"

"A little." Drake shook off the gloom and tried to be positive. "Maybe we'll find an old fighter plane that we can fix and fly to Australia?"

Mai ignored him. It didn't take long to travel into the interior and find the foothills of the mountain. They stared for a few minutes at the small, dark holes that dotted the rising cliff face.

Then Mai was beside him, about a head shorter, pinning him with an intense gaze. "You think this is fate, Matt?"

"It could be just bad luck."

"There's an old Japanese proverb—*to wait for luck is the same as waiting for one's death.* We make our own luck, my old friend."

"I got one too. *Make the best of a bad job.* Not sure if it comes from the motherland, but it hits the nail on the head, I think."

"So you still have nothing to offer? I didn't stay in Washington for you. I stayed for the team and for a better life. For a chance of slipping away from my agency. They'd use me until they got me killed. You know that."

Drake gripped the bridge of his nose. "I know. You did the right thing, no question." He hesitated to touch her, though every fiber of his being wanted the contact. "I'm not one to fritter my chances away, Mai. . ."

She turned on a heel and started to make her way toward the caves.

Drake took a deep breath and followed more slowly, his mind whirling with memory.

"What do I need?" The bikini-clad Mai had laughed at him. "Oh, you'd be surprised. Being undercover this long. . . it makes a girl want to address her values. Or at least take a week long shower. So, soldier boy, what's your name?"

"Drake," he said without thinking. "Matt Drake."

"Ah, as in Bond. James Bond. I like it."

"Well, it has been mentioned. . ."

"You want to take me to bed?"

Drake gawped. "Sorry?"

"To *his* bed. He's waiting whilst I slip into something more comfortable."

Drake took in the white bikini yet again. "I can't imagine what you mean."

"Well, I'm sure that's not true," Mai said with a wicked grin. "But in the interests of expediency, I'll explain. Doku is a freak, a murderer, a pervert and an international terrorist. To you I imagine he's just a kidnapper, but that's enough. Right now he's lying naked on his bed, hands fake-tied, expecting me to climb the walls to his balcony and accost him whilst he's *helpless.*"

Drake shook his head. "What the fu—?"

"It's called role play. You've never tried it?"

"Not like that."

"Well, I'm Japanese. I've done my fair share. Anyway, I can take him out. I can take his guards out. No problem. But to escape alive, I need a diversion." She paused expectantly.

"But why tonight?" Drake suddenly asked, catching up quickly. "You've been undercover for so long. Why now?"

"For the same reason you're here. Doku's become more than a simple embarrassment to his country. And this party at least helps hide the origin of his killers. We won't get a better chance, Matt Drake."

"If he's the kind of man you say," Drake said, "he'll have CCTV even in his room. You know that, right?"

"Of course." Mai presented a silver key. "Plan A—kill Doku and destroy the CCTV room. Plan B—just kill Doku and fuck it. You okay with that?"

"Where the hell did the *key* come from?"

Mai smiled. "A place close to my heart. Now—you ready?"

The Japanese woman leapt lithely onto a nearby marble balustrade. Drake wanted nothing more than to stay and flirt with her for the rest of the night, but forced himself to admit that it just wasn't going to happen. Mai was already grabbing hold of a first-floor balcony, lithe legs swinging, body straining. Drake shot up after her, only then remembering to examine the courtyard and grounds below. The coast was clear, luckily for him, but he had an inkling that Mai had been scouting their surroundings even as she explained her plan.

Some woman, he thought admiringly. There was a woman coming through the ranks of the army, aspiring to the SAS or similar by the name of Myles who the guys were all whispering about. Maybe they were from the same mold.

Mai bounded up the wall. Drake followed. Time stopped for him as she disappeared over a balcony, but she reappeared within five seconds, beckoning furiously. Drake scrambled up the remaining few feet.

And landed softly on the other side, facing a partially open patio door. Through the flimsy drapes, he could see the figure of a man laid out on the bed, a man who could be heard laughing through a silk blindfold and gag.

Mai's eyes twinkled. "Guess what he's about to get." She twirled and tapped on the glass. "Oh, hi. Well who's this fine specimen? All trussed up and so helpless."

Drake watched as the crazy agent strutted up to the bed and straddled the lightly bound man. She actually looked like she was enjoying herself. For a moment he watched, spellbound, then remembered.

He had a job to do. Feeling a little like fresh meat being led to the kill, he leapt from balcony to balcony until he reached the backside of the house. Then, he started to smash glass and throw patio furniture about until it splintered. He shouted and screamed until lights started to come on, not just where he was but all around the house. After a minute or so, he proceeded back, smashing the tall glass doors and on one occasion elbowing one of the shocked guests back into their room.

It didn't take much to cause a distraction. Just noise and an example of violent intent.

By the time he returned to Doku's balcony, Mai was already throttling the life out of the Chechen kidnapper. Drake moved quickly, expecting the door to be kicked in a moment before it actually was.

Three guards shoved inside, eyes registering shock at the scene that greeted them, but no real surprise. Drake understood. Doku was a weirdo. But then the guards saw Drake and brought their weapons quickly to bear.

Too late. Drake crushed the first's larynx with a palm chop, damaged the second's eyes with a two-finger strike, and incapacitated the third by head-butting his nose almost through the back of his skull.

Mai landed deftly beside him. "Not bad, soldier boy. But I could teach you a trick or two. You ready?"

"For what?"

"Me!" She leapt into his arms, screaming hysterically.

Drake got the idea. With a swiftness born of excitement and determination, he barged his way out the door and into the brightly lit hallway. Mai spun in his arms and kicked the door shut behind them. "That way!" Drake carried the sobbing girl past a gaggle of guards, threading a path through milling guests and inebriated hangers-on, listening hard as Mai mumbled directions into his chest. It wouldn't be long before Doku's men found them and then the game would be up.

Mai screamed a bit too loud. Drake squeezed her hard. "Careful."

"Ooo, I like that. But, my new friend, we're here."

"Oh." Drake dropped her and faced a solid wooden door. Mai used the key. The lock turned. Within half a second, they were inside. Several banks of monitors greeted them, all with live video feed. Of course, many were hooked up to the private rooms, but just as many scanned the common rooms and the grounds.

Mai produced a matchbook. Drake stared at her, but didn't dare ask. Her sinful smile said it all. She picked up a chair and proceeded to smash every screen in sight. Drake followed suit. It wouldn't completely disable a state-of-the-art security system, but it would incapacitate it long enough for them to escape. Mai exited the room, flicking a match. Drake tried to keep up. The corridor stretched both ways before them, empty for now.

"Do you want me to pick you up again?"

"Maybe later, after we're clear. But for now stay close."

She pulled him along the corridor, past a series of rooms, some with doors flung wide open to show ornate furnishings and fancy four-poster beds. When they reached the windows at the end, Mai pulled up short. "Oh."

Drake's heart jolted. "Whaddya mean—*oh?*"

"Plan A and Plan B may have become muddled. We ran the wrong way. This was where we ended up at the end of Plan B."

"You mean the *fuck it* part?"

Mai peered through the window. "Yes. The *fuck it* part."

Drake stepped forward. He saw a thirty-foot drop straight down to the swimming pool. Mai was staring at him. "The water's lovely and warm."

Drake heard shouting in the halls adjacent to them. It wouldn't be long. "Plan B," he said for the first time in his life. It wouldn't be the last. Mai ran into a nearby room, a streak of tanned limbs and white designer nylon. She returned a moment later with a heavy desk lamp and launched it through the window with all her might.

"We couldn't just open it then?"

"All locked. No keys. Doku doesn't afford his guests much freedom." Mai flicked away the shards and perched barefoot on the wide sill. "It's been wild, Drake. See you at the bottom." She paused and ran an eye over his clothes. "You stripping?"

Drake coughed, almost choking. "Bollocks to that."

Mai laughed and threw herself backward, a free spirit, crazy-good at her job. Drake wondered how anyone so young could be so expert. Did the Japanese train them from birth? Wasn't that the way they used to train Ninjas? He'd read somewhere that the Ninja clans had all but died out—with only a handful left.

Without another thought, he climbed onto the sill, recognizing that their escape counted on them remaining unseen, and threw himself out into the warm night. A heartbeat of nerve-wracking tension zipped by and then he crashed feet-first into the churning waters, trusting Mai to give him space, shooting down until his shoes clipped the bottom of the pool and then kicking back up as hard as he could.

He broke the surface spluttering, wiping streaming water from his eyes. Mai floated easily beside him, laughing. She pointed to the pool ladder and struck off powerfully. Drake pursued her hard, now laughing himself, and followed her up the ladder. Mai took a second to appraise the area and then sprinted for some nearby trees. By the time she stopped, panting, they were lost among the thick trunks and hanging boughs. Fire blazed from the top floor of the mansion they had left.

Mai pulled him along for a few more minutes until they broke free of the trees and emerged near a shallow lake with a smooth, sandy beach. Moonlight glittered across its flat surface. When Mai's toes touched the lapping waters, she used a judo throw to set him on his back. He didn't resist.

She climbed on top of him. "This is one relationship I think should be consummated immediately, Mr. Drake."

That was his first experience of Mai Kitano.

CHAPTER ELEVEN

The caves were dark, musty, full of cobwebs and debris, dirty-smelling and unconnected. Apart from shelter from a storm, they offered the castaways nothing. After a cursory check, Drake and Mai soon realized their time would be best spent elsewhere. They took some time circumventing the mountain from the height of the highest cave, but even up there, at that time of the morning, the hanging mist refused to relinquish its secrets.

"Bastard gets thicker by the day," Drake said, dubiously. He shielded his eyes, squinting. Mai turned her nose up at him.

"Whoa, you stink, my friend."

"Well, thanks. Guess I forgot my Lynx."

He led the way down the mountain, head still pounding in a turmoil of mixed feelings. He'd become very conscious that Mai had been leading the way since they'd been shot down, much like she had led the way when they first met. He ploughed down the steep mountainside until he reached the foothills and then the forest. Of course, he knew where they were going long before he admitted it to himself. It was a foregone conclusion, had been for some time.

The lake glistened invitingly, sparkling with promise. Mai regarded him innocently from beneath hooded eyes. "Remember the first time we discovered a lake together?"

"Vividly."

She unzipped her jacket, the sound loud in the stillness, and shrugged the heavy material off her shoulders. It fell to the ground with a thunk. With her hands above her head, she stripped off her vest. In another minute, she had unbuckled her trousers and stepped out of her underwear.

Mai Kitano stood before him naked. It was a sight he remembered well, a sight he would never forget. He watched as she turned and sauntered into deeper water, at length turning to face him once more.

"You joining me?"

"Fucking right I am." He rushed into the lake, crashing face forward, not even bothering to take off his clothes.

And when he reached her, it seemed like the past had merged with the present.

CHAPTER TWELVE

Walter Clarke had been traveling for days along what he liked to call his "east coast run." A grueling schedule to be sure but, when finished, a run that gave him three days straight with his family.

He sat inside his car for a minute, listening to the sound of the hard-worked engine tick, and watching the sun settling vibrantly across the Vermont skies. Then, closing his heavy, black briefcase and shoving whatever insurance documents spilled out carelessly under the front seat, he cracked open the car door and climbed out.

Cool, fresh air greeted him. Walter breathed deeply. Time for some wonderful downtime with the kids. He hadn't had this much free time since he'd stayed—

The light footfall startled him. He spun, expecting a playful neighbor or his buddy Chris to be sneaking up behind. But the sight that greeted him made him think he'd inadvertently stumbled onto the set of *The Walking Dead.*

A tall, spare man stood six feet away. Walter gasped. The man's eyes gave him a thousand-yard stare; his movements were robotic, but the big handgun never wavered. Walter stared down the wide, cruel barrel and wondered what he'd ever done wrong.

"You've got the wrong—" he started to say, but the weapon boomed and Walter Clarke knew no more.

Lights went on in houses close by. Curtains twitched.

The residents who dared to peek out forever wished they hadn't. They were front-row witnesses as the zombie-like shooter took his own gun, placed it over his heart, and pulled the trigger.

Hayden rubbed tired eyes, increasingly frustrated by the lack of anything concrete in this case. Both she and Kinimaka were starting to wonder if Senator Turner's attempted assassination had indeed been the random act of some nutjob. But other elements of the case didn't add up. Chiefly, Dai Hibiki's forewarning. Drake's unofficial shooting down. The perp's demeanor. An autopsy had found no chemicals in his body, no puncture marks in his flesh, no signs of foul play.

A mystery. Much like another mystery they had all contemplated frequently over the last few weeks—why the hell had Russell Cayman removed Kali's bones from the third tomb of the gods in Germany? Despite a huge effort, the man and the bones were nowhere to be found. But he'd resurface, they all agreed. He'd resurface with a plan.

Hayden sat down, momentarily stumped. She was just about to announce her intention to take a couple of hours off when all hell broke loose. Ben squawked and Karin hit her desk hard. "Red flag," she cried. "Putting it up on the monitor."

Hayden stared as a police report flashed up on screen. A man in Vermont has been shot dead about an hour ago. *Nothing unusual there*, she thought. But what did raise the hairs on the back of her neck was the description of the shooter. The same MO, the same appearance, the same outcome. If Hayden hadn't recently seen Michael Markel lying on a slab, she'd have thought he might have reanimated and done the deed himself.

Fire shot through her nerves. "Mano. Alicia. Dahl. Take a look at this. Looks like it's about to kick off big time."

CHAPTER THIRTEEN

The mist lifted on the sixth day.

Drake and Mai, Romero and Smyth, immediately hotfooted it to the mountain and scrambled as high as relative safety allowed. The rockface was crumbled and shale-strewn, but offered several sturdy ledges to use as viewing platforms. They each took a side.

When Drake stopped, he took a deep breath and then stared hard out to sea. He saw something that almost made him stumble and fall off the mountain. Vestiges of a hanging fog bank still clouded the view but there was no doubt about what he was seeing.

"Here!" he shouted. "And hurry the fuck up!" Within minutes, they joined him, panting and looking expectant.

There, a few miles distant, stood a second island. This one clearly larger, but still hard to make out. But it wasn't the island especially that made them all gawp.

It was the large warship docking in its natural harbor.

Drake watched intently. The warship wasn't all that big compared to, say, an American aircraft carrier or *Arleigh Burke*-class destroyer, but it looked capable nonetheless. And without being up to scratch on his languages, it was also pretty clear that the long red banner with the glyph-like white characters stretched across its rails, and the hanging red and blue flag with the red star, that this baby hailed from Korea—of the northern variety.

Romero whistled. "Now there's a fly in the ointment."

Mai pursed her lips. "Not really. That's the island we were aiming for initially." She smiled. "The mission's far from over, my friends. Hibiki is on that island along with everything he spoke about."

"And now we have a ride." Drake eyed the warship.

Smyth grunted angrily. "We have to get there first. And then overpower a shitload of the little bastards. Not quite that easy, SAS."

Mai shook her head. "For you, maybe. Now, get your gear and pack up whatever food and water we have. Hide the Zodiacs. We should do this before our strength gives out. We should do this now."

"And when we get there?" Smyth grumbled.

"That's when the fun starts." Drake winked and started to make his way down the mountain. "It's a long way home, guys. Time to stop tossing it off and get hustling."

CHAPTER FOURTEEN

Hayden stepped out of the new HQ for a breath of fresh air. Unfortunately, she stepped straight into the path of Sarah Moxley, pain-in-the-ass news reporter extraordinaire.

"What do you have to say about the random murder in Vermont?" The redhead thrust a mic in Hayden's face. "The similarities to Senator Turner's attempted shooting are uncanny."

"I don't know what you're talking about."

"We know your bloodhound was on site when the shooting happened, Miss Jaye. We know more than you think."

My bloodhound? Hayden wondered. Then she thought of Alicia and gave the woman a pitying glance. "Piece of advice—I wouldn't say that to her face."

Moxley blinked. "Point taken. I've met her. Colorful to the point of garish."

"You won't get me talking, Miss Moxley. If you'll excuse me—"

Hayden stalked back inside. She'd forgotten about the goddamn reporter who'd made it her life's mission to harass the new agency. What the hell had Alicia been saying to her?

The control room was full of conversation for a change. Mano and Dahl were discussing the poor insurance salesman and tracing the route he'd recently taken up and down the east coast. Problem was, it didn't overlap with Senator Turner's—at least not yet.

A senator and an insurance salesman, Hayden thought. What on earth connected them?

Ben and Karin were delving into the background of the shooter. A man of thirty-one—Calvin Torrance was a bus driver and a loner, a respectable member of a nearby Vermont community who had never put a foot wrong in his life.

"Juvey record's locked," Karin commented. "Just like Markel's." The blond turned toward Hayden. "I think we should bring some pressure to bear. That's two out of two and pretty much our only link."

"There's a reason they lock a kid's record, sis," Ben said. "It's to protect them."

Hayden agreed with Karin. They had found a link and it needed pursuing. Trouble was, their own agency didn't have any clout yet. "I'll call Jonathan."

But then Karin's eyebrows shot up and she started to stare oddly at her screen. "That's odd."

Half a minute passed. Hayden tried not to throttle her. "*What's* odd?"

"Sorry, boss. Senator Turner's name just jammed up the airwaves. Our red flag system has gone friggin' crazy. I can't—" Karin tapped furiously, like a woodpecker on speed. "Can't pinpoint the source. Give me a few."

Hayden moved behind her. Dahl looked across from his perch. "I'm smelling some action."

Karin isolated the source in less than a minute. "Crap," she said. "Unbelievable. There's a bank robbery in progress. In D.C. Something's fucked up 'cos there's reports of live fire. And the shooter..." She started to chew on a nail. "To quote a police officer from the scene: *another one of those freaks who tried to kill Senator Turner. . ."*

Hayden felt a chill deeper than fear, deeper than terror, something that ran through her bones and into race memory. She managed two words. "Mount up."

CHAPTER FIFTEEN

The area around the bank was a war zone. Torsten Dahl began to feel right at home. This was his stage, at last. He quickly threaded his way through a dozen haphazardly parked cop cars until he reached the front line.

A cop stared at him. "Who the hell are you?"

Dahl whipped out the brand new I.D.

"SPEAR?" The cop shook his head. "What will they come up with next?"

"Do you have a situation report, sir?"

"Yeah. We have fourteen hostages in there, a dead guard and a crazy perp. Damn bitch is shooting every few minutes. Situation's going straight to hell, man. That's my report."

Dahl rocked back on his heels. "The shooter is a woman?"

"Yeah. Of the female variety. 'Sup, you don't get 'em back in Blighty?"

"I'm not English." Dahl related his findings through his throat mic.

"Special Tactics are here." The cop pointed to a newly arrived vehicle. Special Tactics were DC's equivalent to SWAT.

"You want me to handle this?" Dahl asked Hayden. "Or leave it to SWAT?"

The cop considered him more closely.

"We need the shooter alive." Hayden's voice crackled in Dahl's ear. "And preferably the person she came to shoot. Whoever that might be."

Karin's voice then joined the connection. "One thing's clear—the person she came to shoot is still alive. Otherwise, she'd have killed herself by now."

"We have to get in there, Dahl." Hayden decided. "Now."

The Swede just nodded. He didn't have to check to know Alicia had his back. When he turned back to the cop, the man actually backed away. "I ain't going anywhere with you, bud. You both got that crazy in you. My ole bud, bless his soul. He was the same, plain—"

Alicia shushed him. "Listen, *bud*. How did you know?"

The cop pulled a face. "What?"

"That this bogus bank robber acted the same way as Turner's shooter?"

"I was there, miss. I saw it all. A lot of us did."

"But how have you seen *her.*" Alicia gestured at the bank building.

"Oh. She's been wandering about the place. Staring out the windows. Checking rooms and offices, according to the spies in the sky. Who knows what else? Seems like she's searching for something."

"Some*one,*" Dahl corrected him. "When's the last time you saw her."

"Before you got here. Maybe ten minutes."

"This is a rescue mission," Dahl said. "Check with your lookouts now. Do they see her?"

The cop took out his radio and looked up at the surrounding buildings. "You guys. You seen any activity in there?"

"Not a damn thing."

"Negative. Been a while—"

A shot rang out from inside the building. The Special Tactics team looked like it was gearing up for action. Dahl didn't wait. He vaulted the police car, sprinted the hundred yards to the front door and pressed his face to the glass. Alicia kept pace.

Inside, the bank was a scene of desperation and confusion. Several people were knelt with faces to the floor and hands on heads, others were standing hesitantly, still more were walking uncertainly toward the doors.

Dahl wrenched them open. "Move it. Get out of here!"

He pushed inside with Alicia. The Englishwoman stopped the first group. "Where's the crazy bitch?"

A young man with slicked back hair pointed in the direction of the open offices and interview rooms. "Back there."

"She with anyone?"

The man nodded, a guilty look flashing across his face. "Chased Michelle back there a few minutes ago."

"Who's Michelle?" Dahl said as he tore off.

"Just a teller," the man said with bewilderment. "She's just a bank teller."

Dahl crossed the open floor in seconds. At that moment, he saw movement ahead—a woman stepping into the open and holding a gun as if she knew how to use it. Dahl launched into a forward skid, feet first, bringing his weapon around as he flew across the polished floor and placing a few pounds of pressure on the trigger.

"Stop!"

But the woman fired reflexively. The bullet flew past, striking a nearby desk. Dahl hit the woman's shins at speed, knocking her legs out from under her faster than she could think. She hit the ground even as he shot by and he grabbed her—going for her hands and the gun.

She twisted like a dervish, pulling away, and delivered a solid strike to his temple that made him see stars. She had been trained, this woman, no doubt in his mind. As he shook it off and went in again, she rolled away from him, three, four times, until she'd gained a little distance.

Brought the gun up in front of her. . .

. . . and then turned it toward her heart and pulled the trigger.

Dahl clicked his tongue angrily. When he looked around, Alicia was emerging from the room back there, her face a cheerless mask.

"One dead body in there," she whispered. "Nametag says 'Michelle Baker.' Shot in the head at point-blank range."

There was the sound of someone choking, and then bursting into tears. Dahl looked up to see the man with the slicked-back hair standing a few feet away.

"That bitch hunted her." He sobbed. "She wasn't interested in the bank or the money or any of us. She knew something. She came here hunting for Michelle on her first day back from vacation."

Hayden made her way over to where Dahl and Alicia seemed to be comforting one of the bank tellers. A bit odd, but then you never knew what those two were going to do next. She reached the conversation just as Alicia was querying as to the dead clerk's recent holiday destination.

What?

But the broken down man answered immediately. "Atlantic City. That's where she always goes. Saves her money up for a whole year and then hits the best east-coast casinos. One big blowout."

Hayden looked around. The bank hadn't been damaged in any way. *A bank teller?* She whipped her head around as one of the lead cops said: "You won't believe this."

His colleagues looked over. The cop indicated the dead body of the assailant, hand still wrapped around the barrel of the gun she'd turned on herself.

"She still has her ID. Name's Leanne Prowse. A registered nurse."

With the mystery deepening and no clues forthcoming, the team took their leave of the scene and headed back to HQ. Ben and Karin were already scrutinizing the backgrounds and lives of both Michelle Baker and Leanne Prowse. Dahl and Alicia were explaining how the woman, a local nurse, had fought, albeit briefly, like a highly capable, trained operative. Hayden was fielding calls from Sarah Moxley and, more importantly, Secretary of Defense Gates.

The minivan behind them went unnoticed. Its blacked-out windows concealed a wealth of surveillance equipment, some of which had been put to good use at the bank, and some of it right now.

Track carefully and don't engage, were the instructions from on high. *And locate their HQ. The plan is going well.* No one knew where this new covert team sprung from, but they needed to know everything about them.

The new team was becoming more famous by the minute.

CHAPTER SIXTEEN

Mai kept a careful eye out as the men stowed away a good proportion of the food they'd accumulated so far. They had decided to leave a small percentage on their island in case they were forced to return at some point. A quick inventory showed they had one small pistol between them, enough food and water for a few days and their basic survival gear.

Mai thought it ample enough equipment to make the island, discover its secrets, contact Dai Hibiki, and steal the warship. She'd done something similar before, back when Matt Drake was married.

As she made ready, Mai thought back on her life. Before now, or before the "Odin thing," the only good thing in her life had been her sister, Chika. From an early age, Mai had known nothing but strife, adversity and training. Learning the art of war meant throwing your entire mind, body and soul into your education. It meant maintaining ultimate focus—no distractions. For a girl as young as Mai had been, it should have harmed her, maybe broken her spirit, but with hardship also came chance and fortune—the Japanese girl had nothing else to compare her life to. Not until she left the clan anyway.

Chika embraced life differently. Not because she chose to, but because the clan that sheltered Mai only had room for one sister. Torn apart, even at that early age, the trauma never subsided. Mai sought Chika out at her earliest opportunity, and now the sisters were each other's best friend and soul mate, all that remained of their once joyful family.

Mai had a faint recollection of her parents. Nothing more than shades of grey flickering in her mind, but impressions of a happy family, nights of stories and cuddling and laughter, just enough to scar her heart in the deepest way.

Now Mai studied the rolling waters that lay between them and the Korean island. It appeared to be a fast, easy swim, but they all knew that even the calmest of waters could be treacherous. Hidden tides, swirling eddies and lurking inhabitants were just some of the dangers awaiting them. She thought about her sister and about all the miles between them. Chika was better off where she was, safe amongst the quieter streets of Tokyo, working for a promotional company.

And that brought her full circle to Drake. Mai wasn't a woman to fall back on old ground, but the Englishman was one of the few who'd gotten under her skin. The man was an emotional wreck, but worth trying to salvage. She secured her pack one last time and was the first to enter the sea. At first, the playful waves lapped at her feet, but as she waded deeper, the heavy tide began to pull at her invitingly. She leaned forward and struck out softly, the new island before her, charting a course around to the west of where the warship had docked and patches of dense vegetation obscured any sign of a beach. There was always a chance that every square inch of the island was under surveillance, but Mai and the others doubted it. The North Koreans, whilst very capable and seemingly well-armed, were unlikely to assume a group of soldiers might swim up to their secret island in the middle of nowhere.

Mai swam with the current as much as she could. Sea water stung her eyes. Rogue waves doused her and pulled her under. The swells beneath her ballooned and deflated with every passing minute, hampering her progress, but she shut the negative thoughts out. All that mattered was progress, no matter how little.

Behind her she could hear the progress of the three men. They were soldiers and marines; this shouldn't be hard for them. It took a couple of hours to gain the island, but Mai had the ability to compartmentalize and, before long, she was pulling herself out of the water and into a dense thicket of trees. The men joined her within minutes, shivering now that they were dripping wet and standing still.

Drake broke the silence. "If Alicia were here, she'd suggest we all strip and dry each other off."

Romero coughed. Smyth looked a little annoyed. Mai ignored him and studied the lay of the land. "Warship's that way. I'm guessing the facility's nearby." She swigged her water. "You ready?"

Mai headed out. The untamed and undisturbed appearance of the undergrowth told her no one had bothered venturing this far out from the base. It was hard going for a while with the forest reluctant to give up its stranglehold. Mai shimmied up a tree to make sure they didn't stray off course.

When she came back down, a half-smile ghosted about her lips. "Ground rises for half a mile or so," she reported. "Should give us a bird's-eye view of their compound and the docking area."

They all nodded grimly. It was about time they caught a break. Cautiously, they started forward again, pushing their way through the brush, starting to sweat a little as the ground took on a gentle rise. Mai signaled a silent halt when the sound of voices reached her ears.

Drake was right behind her. "They're drifting on the wind."

"I know. I'm trying to hear what they're saying."

Drake gawped. "They must be more than a mile away."

"My Korean's rusty to the point of being dangerous." Mai acceded, misreading his surprise. "All I can make out are the words *doctor, prisoners* and *the general.* They're speaking fast. Seem to be in a hurry."

Drake appraised a nearby tree. "Looks like we're going up, guys."

Mai scampered up like a monkey. Drake followed a little more serenely, less confident in his abilities now than he'd ever been, despite taking down the Shadow Elite and regaining the third tomb of the gods. The death of Kennedy Moore and the revelations about Wells and Alyson would bleed a deep shadow into his heart and mind until the day he died.

Mai waited for him near the top, and then they inched their way along separate boughs until their eyes and noses cleared the leaf cover. There, spread out before them was the secret North Korean facility that Mai's old friend, Dai Hibiki, had warned them about and a weapon heavy, surveillance-strong warship at anchor in the bay.

The facility appeared to be a permanent site. Many trees had been razed and cleared to make way for several low-slung buildings. Some of the structures looked like makeshift houses, probably home for permanent residents like doctors and guards. The guardhouse itself was clearly noticeable, a two-story structure with high towers that spanned the entrance to the site. What gave it all an incongruous and obsolete look was that there were no walls around the site. The whole place was wide open, as if it had been dropped into a cleared space and left there. Some of the walls had trees brushing against the windows, as if the forest was trying to claim back what was rightfully its own. Most of the clearings between structures were overgrown and being reclaimed by the island.

Mai felt a sense of relief, only tempered when she took into account the amount of men a warship held. Add to that the complement already present on the island, and they were dealing with a formidable enemy force, easy access or not.

"So we're well outnumbered." Drake read her mind. "Could be worse."

"We need to find the communications room, liaise with Hibiki, and find out what the sneaky bastards are hiding." Mai counted off the tasks on her slight but deadly fingers. "Failing that..." She eyed the warship. "We need to get the hell off this island."

Drake grinned appreciatively. "I knew there was a reason I kept you around."

CHAPTER SEVENTEEN

Now there were three murders, and no practical clues. The team reviewed the facts for perhaps the hundredth time, still finding no noticeable link. Michelle Baker was not an obvious target—her job as a bank teller, whilst it may attract the dumber kind of criminal hoping to be able to pressure a woman who potentially handled hundreds of thousands of dollars a day, was not a reason to hunt and kill her. Even a disgruntled customer surely wouldn't go to those lengths, though Alicia tended to disagree. When everyone stared at her, she turned away. It was her duty to be the awkward one, wasn't it?

Michelle Baker's single outstanding feature was that she had recently returned from vacation. Every year she hit the east coast casinos and stayed in the same hotel.

Hayden brought her details up. "Alright. Atlantic City. Seems she preferred quiet nights and busy days. Her hotel is several miles away from the fun, on the outskirts of Atlantic City. A secluded and expensive little place called The Desert Palms." Hayden paused. "Way out of her price range."

Dahl cracked open a bottle of water. "The fellow back at the bank did mention that she saved up for a big blowout. So she treated herself one week a year—good for her."

Hayden pursed her lips. "Maybe. We have three victims. Three complete strangers. Three murderers. Three complete strangers. The only link is that two of them have sealed juvey records. Karin—did you have chance to check on Leanne Prowse yet?"

"You're not gonna like it." Karin chewed on a lock of hair. "Leanne Prowse was normal in every way. No records of any kind. No file. Nada."

Kinimaka was pacing up and down the office, part of his recovery routine. "So what does a senator, an insurance salesman and a bank clerk have in common?"

Alicia clucked at him. "Sounds like the start to a bad joke."

The Hawaiian stared at her. "What are you doing anyway? You're nose hasn't been out of that cellphone since you got back here."

Alicia raised an eyebrow. "Careful, Mano. Just 'cos we shared a last night together doesn't mean I won't spank your arse in front of your new girlfriend."

Kinimaka cringed. Alicia grinned to see Hayden and Ben suddenly become mightily interested in the screens before them.

"We spent a night *drinking*." Kinimaka stressed.

"But I'll tell ya anyway, 'cos I'm nice like that. Been texting me some bikers."

Komodo looked over at her. "The ones you met in Luxembourg? I've heard of that biker gang, you know. Their kind of notoriety doesn't come by attending Grand Prix's and coffee bars. They're hardcore."

"So am I," Alicia said sweetly. "But thanks for the friggin' concern, Trevor."

Ben looked up then, his eyes serious. "An email from Gates just came in. Says they still haven't worked anything loose with the North Koreans. Any action at this point would be a sign of aggression and not viewed lightly in certain parts of the world."

"So we just leave 'em there?" Alicia was suddenly in the conversation. "We should send a small covert unit. Me."

"The Koreans have already detected one of our 'secret missions.'" Hayden told her. "Best not to risk another. And Drake's last communication did say they were ok."

Alicia jabbed at her cell with such ferocity that Hayden could easily see her breaking one of the buttons off.

Karin sat back in her chair, narrowing her eyes as her brain worked overtime. "There is one other thing that links all the victims." She mused. "Though it's barely worth mentioning. Probably nothing at all."

"What is it?" Three mouths asked at once.

"Travel." Karin made a noncommittal face. "Senator Turner. The salesman and Michelle Baker. They were all planning on or had recently been travelling."

CHAPTER EIGHTEEN

Shaun Kingston stared at the seated figure before him and wondered how the hell anyone so obtuse, so gross, and so self-serving could ever rise to the rank of general.

But then, he thought. We are dealing with the Goddamn North Koreans here.

"My good friend," he said aloud, "whisky?"

"As if you need ask, Mr. Kingston."

"Your English." Kingston always buttered them up first. "Is excellent, General."

"Of course it is. I attended an English boarding school. And no doubt better than your Korean."

Kingston allowed an ingratiating nod rather than ask about North Korean boarding schools. The final payoff was worth a little self-effacement at this stage.

Kingston poured the drink. "I assume you. . .dispersed. . .the delicacies we sent you for Christmas?"

"Of course."

"Do you remember the name of the village?" Kingston couldn't resist.

The general's face didn't even crack, or wobble, as the case would have been. "I forget."

Kingston passed over the expensive looking tumbler, noting the attentiveness of the general's bodyguards when he leaned toward him. "Do you foresee any barriers?"

The general sipped his drink and wobbled his jowls. "There are new developments, Mr. Kingston, as you are aware. At this stage, Korea does not believe the island has been discovered. We believe the flight was random, off course maybe, or speculative."

"And why do you believe that? Did China tell you?"

"China is our ally," the general spat. "Not our leader. Our struggle can be achieved with or without their aid." A moment of silence followed, during which the big man clearly took hold of himself. "The Americans are making no real noise of this disappeared plane. It does not seem high on their priorities. We believe it is of no consequence to them."

"Good." The last thing Kingston wanted was the Stars and Stripes putting an end to the brokering of the biggest deal of his life. His eyes flicked for a moment to his PC, open before him and displaying his company's striking logo:

Kingston Firearms International, the world-renowned and acceptable face of his business. But not enough.

Never enough.

"I don't mind saying—I thought it a risky deal you employed with the sleeper system," he said. "But one that has paid off. So far."

The general went still. "Korea can never know," he muttered. "The risk is beyond your reckoning. It is the brainchild of decades, the procurement chain extends across the globe, and we use it for ourselves." The man shuddered now. "Pray we don't get found out."

"The Russians are making noises," Kingston told him. "About some enormous archaeological find. It's big enough to divert their attentions from making money, which says a lot."

"The Russians are always making noise." The general dismissed Kingston's comment. "It's how they sleep at night. Our inspiration in Korea comes through the confidence that our certain victory is assured. We always do what we say we will do."

Kingston ignored the speech. It sounded too much like Korean propaganda and he had personal issues to organize.

"So the spring cleaning is going well?"

"Three down, two to go," the general said. "No issues."

"There is one issue," Kingston reminded him.

"The secret team?" The general raised eyebrows like the thin wisps of a snake's tail. "Your men are dealing with that, yes? My own men might get too. . .enthusiastic."

Kingston watched grim smiles appear on the bodyguards' hard faces.

"We are on American soil, after all." The general laughed, not a sight a man wants to see before lunch. Even a sumo wrestling match would be easier on the eyes.

Kingston wondered if he should share his findings about the new team with the general. That they were indeed a crack outfit, and had been behind the recent discoveries of the existence of old gods' bones and artifacts around the world. Kingston zoned out for a second—*was the new Russian find linked with that?*

He decided not to share his knowledge. The last thing he needed was a bunch of trigger-happy Koreans running around DC.

"We're watching them." He nodded. "We know where they live. So to speak."

The Korean general smiled expansively. "Good. Good. Now tell me more about these weapons."

CHAPTER NINETEEN

Mai Kitano stood at the edge of their makeshift encampment, watching the sun sink over the horizon. She used the quiet moments to compose her mind. She watched the sea catch fire, and then the water boil, and then the light was gone.

She adjusted her gaze toward the enemy base, waited a few moments more for her eyes to adjust. It was darker down there, shrouded in shadow with deeper wraiths already settling in. Her kind of darkness. The darkness of predators and hunters.

Drake had floated the idea of one person attempting a deep reconnoiter. Mai had stepped up instantly. Not only was she the best person for the job, she had an ally on the inside. Or so they hoped. No one challenged her.

Now Mai crept deep into the forest, making her way around to one of the camp's blind spots she'd marked earlier. The loamy undergrowth gave to her passing without sound, the trees barely whispered as she crept by. Nothing moved. She gained the tree line in less than thirty minutes and stood silently, staring at the rough sides of the buildings, a shadow amongst shadows.

Nothing stirred in the camp. No sounds could be heard, save those that hailed from the anchored warship. Mai stayed low and crept toward the building until she could touch its weathered side. She rose carefully beside the window as a faint noise reached her straining ears.

The building must be soundproofed. How strange—here—in the middle of nowhere and on a secret base. Even the seamen, it seemed, were not a party to what was going on. Of course, Dai Hibiki had said as much in his message.

Mai took a quick glance, saw an empty room, and then allowed herself a longer look. She was peering into a small, rectangular stone-walled room that gave onto a wide hallway. Through the open door she saw banks of lights hanging from low rafters that illuminated a long corridor. Closed doors ran down each side, most with letter-box like openings at their base.

Prison cells?

Gently, Mai pulled at the window frame. Nothing budged. No such luck. But there was another window a little farther along and more around the other side. She sank into the shadows again, low against the wall. As she did so, an almost silent footfall came from her right.

Her eyes flicked, nothing else. A large shadow stood there, barely visible in the dark. Then his arm moved, travelling toward his pocket and Mai readied to spring, but it returned flicking absently at a lighter, the flame short and sharp, and lighting up his hard, severe features.

Could be a doctor having a time-out, Mai thought. The man carried no weapon that she could see. After five minutes, the man sighed, spat on the ground and walked away. Mai wasted no time in sneaking to the next window along and taking another glance inside.

Same view, from another angle. This time she could clearly see the cell doors. She watched as the man she had just seen strolled down the corridor, tapping his fingers lightly on the walls as he walked by. He disappeared out of her sight.

She tried the window. Again, it didn't budge.

She pushed harder. This room, away from the corridor lights and what might be the Operations Center, was her best chance of sneaking inside unseen. With a grunt she took a hard grip and heaved. The window frame gave a little. One of the catches slipped open. Complacency had to be second-nature in a place like this.

Mai pushed again. This time the window eased open a crack. She waited half a minute before sliding it all the way up, climbing inside and then closing it after her.

Then she crouched in the darkness, listening.

Now inside, she could hear all the telltale signs she had expected. Forlorn shouts echoing from behind closed doors. Intermittent screams shooting from farther away. The shouting of angry men. The cajoling of others. The whine of instruments. The constant hum of machinery.

This was a hell-house to be sure.

Mai inched toward the door and peered out. Stark rows of cells marched away. She counted at least ten to either side, doors standing amidst bright white walls. Beyond the last cell, she spied rows of windows and two men peering through whilst talking to each other in Korean.

What she heard made her shiver.

"He isn't succumbing. The drug is rejecting him. Our efforts are useless with this one."

"Sometimes this happens, Kwan Lee. It has happened before."

"Yes. But it is a waste. And now we are one short."

The second man hung his head. "The general will not be happy."

"The general does not control this operation. If the manager knew we were being forced to replace these assets. . ."

"But he will never know," the second man said with vigor. "Will he, Kwan Lee?"

"No."

"It is not just your life. It is all our lives."

"I know."

"And more will come."

"They always do."

At that moment, a door opened behind the man and out stepped a third. Mai blinked rapidly. It was Dai Hibiki, the man who had started Drake and her on this journey with his warning communication.

One of the men turned to him. "Is our new patient comfortable, Leading Seaman Hibiki?"

"She is, *Seonbae*. Fed, watered and strapped down."

Mai felt as though she'd had her heart doused with a bucket of ice. Why was Hibiki using the honorific address of *Seonbae?* The word meant *teacher,* or *mentor.* Which meant Hibiki was this man's student.

It was possible he was faking. Hibiki was deep undercover. But still. . .a little niggle of doubt ate at her. It wasn't just the word, it was the tone, the way he spoke it, the subservience, the awe.

"You are proving a useful beast, Seaman Hibiki. And quite suited to this work. We are always short a pair of hands here. Perhaps you could stay when the ship leaves us?"

Hibiki dropped his gaze. "That is up to my commander, *Seonbae. "*

"Of course, of course. But, they rarely perform a head count, Seaman Hibiki. And our successes all glorify the general's victory. Our dedication will make possible Korea's superiority over its arch enemy."

Hibiki remained silent, head down. The doctor dismissed him. "Go now. Think on it."

Mai slunk back into the shadows as Hibiki came walking toward her. Her hiding place was bare. No cupboards, not even a desk or a chair. She fancied it was an interrogation room of sorts. If she had been sure about Hibiki, she would've given him some kind of sign as he clumped past, but Mai stayed hidden, heart and mind heavy with worry.

As he passed Hibiki's eyes flicked toward her. But Mai was stood so deep in shadow, he couldn't discern her shape.

Mai lingered. She had what she needed. The majority of the Koreans remained on the warship with the island crew being little more than a smattering. But there would be other guards that she hadn't seen yet.

The temptation was to check the cells and then the rooms beyond. She wondered what lay behind those banks of windows and what made the captives scream. She wondered why they needed strapping down. The communications room, if anywhere, would be at the far end or possibly in the guards' quarters.

But she could best help them by staying free. She crossed over to the window and exited the lab building, dropped to the soft grass and crouched in silence. She was about to move away softly when the crunch of heavy footsteps sounded nearby.

"A heavy bastard," someone muttered in Korean. "This should not be our job."

"Stop complaining. Our leader says it is our job. Then it is our job. You never complain when it's a woman."

A throaty chuckle made Mai's blood boil. She knew immediately what was happening. Judging by the footsteps and grunting, there were at least three guards dragging a captive along between them. The captive sounded barely alive, grunting when the men kicked him. Most likely the man she had heard the two doctors discussing.

Mai let the guards find a forest path that they'd obviously trodden before. On stealthy feet she followed, closing in with every step. By the time the guards reached a small clearing dominated by over a dozen irregular mounds, she was a fast leap away.

The complainer let go of his captive's head, letting it smash to the stony ground with a thud. He laughed, then out of the corner of his eye, must have seen a shadow move.

Mai didn't hesitate. The guards might well be missed, but Drake, the marines and this poor man were her priority, and what she'd already seen proved that they needed to quickly escape this island.

She lashed out with her foot, caught the complainer right in the jugular. He gurgled, coughed, and fell to the ground hacking, but with his windpipe crushed, he wasn't about to be more of a problem. The other guards spun toward her. Mai ran lightly, leapt off the ground and connected solidly with the first's chest, sending him tumbling head over heels across the terrible mounds he had no doubt helped build. The third reached for a weapon, but again Mai was lightning quick. She stepped in close, caught his wrist and snapped it. To his credit, the man did little more than grunt and brought up a knee that caught her painfully in the lower stomach. Mai twisted away, making space for herself, and sent the man spinning to the ground. She stomped his groin, his solar plexus and his neck in two seconds and then returned her attentions to the second man.

Who was just picking himself up from behind one of the small, rocky graves.

"Where did you come from? The ship?"

It was all he had time to say. His neck snapped seconds later. Mai respectfully skirted the dozen or so graves as she made her way quickly back to the captive. He was lying in the dirt, head to one side, breathing shallowly with a look of such hopelessness branded into his features that Mai knew it wasn't just from being held and tortured in this place.

This man's life had been hell.

Mai cradled his head. The man's eyes gained focus for a second before he died. It was only after his last breath had expired that his eyes lost all semblance of pain and his haggard features at last smoothed out. In death, Mai saw, he had gained an inner peace.

Her thoughts turned back to the present. Quickly she surveyed the forest, fixed Drake's position in her mind, and took off at a fast pace. The bodies needed hiding, and fast.

CHAPTER TWENTY

Drake almost jumped out of his skin when Mai descended on their camp. The Japanese woman was moving quickly, her every movement screaming urgency. It took but a few minutes to relay her information.

Romero and Smyth were up and ready to go. Drake grabbed his pack and said, "Lead on." They filed into the deeper forest, following Mai. The moon offered a scant glow, the sea breeze distracted them with its urgency. When Mai stepped into a clearing and stopped, Drake quickly summed up the situation.

Of course, she was right. "Time to get off this bloody island."

They dragged the bodies away from the clearing and into deeper undergrowth. There was nothing they could do for the poor, dead captive, so they concealed him with the guards. It did cross Drake's mind to make it appear as though he had recovered and killed the guards himself, but on listening to Mai's account of his debility, he quickly dismissed the idea.

It was time to fly.

They crouched among the creaking trees. It had taken some time to hide the bodies and dawn was already streaking the skies. Drake was beside Mai, their bodies touching.

"Hibiki?"

"Too early to say. We can't risk alerting him."

"Why else would he send the message?"

Mai breathed a heavy sigh. "He's good, okay? That's my instinct. He's good."

"Only way off this island is on that warship."

"But somebody has to stay behind to shut this damn base down faster 'n crap through a goose. We can't rely solely on our escape attempt or any kind of rescue." Romero put in from behind.

"Unfortunately," Drake said. "I agree. Bollocks."

"So." Smyth sounded impatient. "You and Maggie Q here got any plans on how to persuade the ship to leave?"

"There is only one way," Mai said confidently. "The person in charge of it must believe he wants to leave."

"Oh yeah? Where's that from? The Art of War?"

Mai turned a steely eye on the marine. "I think we have our teams, Matt. Romero and you take the ship. Smyth and I will take the island and meet you on board."

Drake had already guessed as much. The rising dawn amplified the fire in Mai's gaze. Smyth might well regret his choice of words.

"Use Hibiki only if you're convinced about him. Otherwise. . ."

"I know."

"A simultaneous attack?"

"Yes. We'll hit the base and go for the ship's Captain. When we do that—" Mai paused. "You need to be on board. Just in case."

Drake frowned. "We could help by—"

"Best if you're on board," Mai said softly. "No mistakes." She met his eyes. "Besides, it won't be a problem. You have your work cut out finding a place to hide and then leading us to it. And we're more than likely going to land in North Korea, *if* we survive the trip."

"Piece of piss," Drake said quickly. "North Korea. China. Russia." Drake counted the places off on his fingers. "Europe. Washington. Like I said—"

"A cellphone would be good too," Smyth said drily, but with a rare smile. Maybe he was looking forward to working with the legendary Mai Kitano. Maybe he thought she really was Maggie Q.

Drake hunkered down and rummaged around for food and water. "Right then. Let's thrash this out. We want to be ready for tonight."

As darkness invaded the land, Drake and Romero crept among the thick trunks, staying as close to the tree line as they dared. The warship was a large, ugly chunk of steel sitting at ease among the calm waters of the natural harbor a short swim away. The decks were quiet, seamen lounging around as if bored. This may well be a regular, monotonous trip for some of them.

The two men found a flat piece of earth to dig into near the water's edge and secured their weapons. All they were waiting for now was Mai's signal.

Mai crouched alongside Smyth, waiting for the shadows to creep even farther over the guards' quarters. They had decided to strike at them where they felt most comfortable—the place they rested, the place they slept. The weapons they had lifted from the dead guards were held loosely in their hands, two Dragunov SVUs and a Bullpup sniper rifle. With a sound suppressor and special muzzle-break to help absorb a large amount of recoil, it was perfectly suited to their needs. And interestingly, it was Russian made.

At last the darkness was enough. Mai strode toward the main door with Smyth watching her back.

"Go, Maggie," he said as she neared the entrance.

She paused and looked back. "Have you got a little crush on me, Smyth?" Without waiting for an answer, she opened the door and stepped inside, straight into a communal room complete with a widescreen TV, several loungers, a big sofa and a round table pockmarked with knife scores.

Several men stared at her, stunned.

Mai opened fire without mercy. There wasn't a man on this base worth saving. She believed that as much as she believed in herself. Bodies pounded back into the walls or tumbled over the sofa. Mai allowed a man to scramble out the open window to raise the alarm and bounded across the hallway.

Into a kitchen. A Korean guard was running at her in mid-flight, checking his weapon whilst still clutching a mug. His mistake. Mai sent him and the mug's contents against the window, smashing the pane and staining it red.

Smyth fired behind her.

She stepped back into the hallway. Enemy guards were jumping into the line of fire, clearly dazed and unused to action. Maybe at one time they had been a crack force, but today, they were cats in a barrel.

But then, the entrance door behind them, the one Smyth had closed, suddenly crashed open. Mai heard a cry of *"Get them!"* before a bunch of troops swarmed toward her.

Drake heard the gunshots and prepared to slide into the water, but at that moment, the warship erupted with activity. All hands hit the deck running and the great engines began to turn. Was it coincidence?

Never mind. Drake dove forward, hitting the murky waters with a splash and cutting through the waves with a strong stroke. As he swam, he saw both the warship's boats cast off from the dock and rev their engines.

He trod water for a second. Romero rose beside him. "What gives, man?"

"They're heading back to the ship."

"Not even a Korean with his ass on fire could get to the boats that quickly."

"Agreed. It's coincidence. But look—they're not changing course."

"They have orders," Romero reasoned, "from their high command. Shit, man, we'd better hurry it up."

"But Mai—"

"Ain't gonna make it! Come on!"

Mai fired around Smyth, then turned back to the hallway. A few bodies still twitched, but otherwise, the coast was clear. She raced forward then dropped to her knees and skidded, twisting her body as she did and shouting at Smyth to move.

The marine backed toward her, firing carefully. Bullets whizzed around him. At one point, he half-twisted and yelled, but it was only a bullet tearing through the sleeve of his jacket, nothing to really shout about.

Koreans fell at his feet. But more came. It soon became apparent that he wasn't going to make it.

At least not alone.

"Damn!" Mai waded in. Jumping among her enemies, she sent one tumbling against the other so they fell hard to the floor. She smashed heads against heads, turned rifles inside out and disengaged their firing barrels with a deft turn of the wrist. She ripped a handgun from a man's hand, turned it on him first and then shot two of his colleagues in the blink of an eye. She caught a knife a hair's breadth from her throat, having allowed it time to get that close to dispatch another enemy, and then wrenched it away from its owner.

"Here, have it back," she muttered, burying it through his sternum.

He was the last.

Smyth stayed on one knee, eyes sweeping the bloody mess for survivors. "Jeez, lady," he breathed. "If I didn't have a crush on you before I sure as shit do now. That was—"

A booming gunshot drowned out his words. The bullet nicked his ear. Smyth whipped round calmly and fired. The guard collapsed noisily.

"Grab some weapons," Mai said without stopping. "And light these bastards up. There's more outside."

Drake allowed the current to take him closer to the big, steel-hulled ship. They had been waiting for the distraction of Mai's fire to use the ropes they had salvaged from one of the Zodiacs. A rough plan to be sure, but then a man from the north of England prided himself on being rough around the edges.

Now it was a bigger gamble. The warship's own dinghies were already back in place and the great anchor was rising with a savage clanking sound, as if all the ghosts of purgatory had risen at the same time. Drake heard shouts from up top. Even the Naval Officers were sounding shocked. Mai and Smyth had set something alight alright.

"Now or never." Romero pushed him. "Do it."

Drake set his jaw. Mai could still make it. He set his sights to the back of the ship where several taut lines had still to be cast off and above that, where the depth charge rails were. Hand over hand he climbed up, facing the skies, listening only to the sounds of Romero aping him on a nearby line and the tramping of feet above. Once, when the sound of voices became too clear, Drake froze, hanging in mid-air, praying for a stroke of luck. Then more cries struck the air. Drake scurried up the last few feet like a rabid monkey.

The Korean staring over the ship's rail got the shock of his life, but before his eyes had widened to more than a saucer's diameter, Drake snapped his neck and hurled him into the waters below. Romero nodded as he alighted to his left.

"Good work."

Drake made to skulk over to the starboard side, but Romero grabbed his heavy jacket. "We should get below. Our mission can't fail now, bud. She's on her own."

Drake angrily shook the marine's hand off and moved stealthily onward, but then stopped. "Balls," he whispered.

Romero was right.

CHAPTER TWENTY-ONE

Lauren Fox didn't like to think too hard about what her next client might enjoy or fantasize about. Like any girl, she had her hang-ups, but they weren't overly plentiful. The way her clients looked or dressed didn't matter. They had been vetted by the agency. They weren't serial killers or cops or wives or private investigators. Actually, one of her best clients *was* a private investigator, but he was an old friend and harmless, in all aspects. All things said, she was an easygoing girl—which was just as well in her profession. But some requests were just plain *wrong.*

Lauren climbed out of the shower, dabbed herself dry with a luxurious towel and crossed over to her vanity. Expensive perfumes and after shaves lined up like willing suitors, eager to play. She checked the discreet carriage clock. Her next client was due in twenty minutes. Still time to tidy and prep, and turn herself into the high-class, two-thousand-dollar-an-hour call girl he was expecting.

She dabbed on a little Notorious, dressed quickly in sexy underwear and styled her hair. If a client ever saw her getting dressed, they wouldn't believe it was the same woman who controlled them so easily when she stripped. But they never would see her. Even with the overnighters and the weekenders, she retained a measure of privacy.

Ten minutes to go. Lauren shook off the everyday world and put on her game face. It was almost fantasy time. The new client—a guy called Quinn—hadn't requested anything specific, but sometimes they were the nastiest ones—the ones that couldn't quite explain themselves over the phone.

No matter, she thought. There were protocols in place and she'd already discovered she was none too shabby with an improvised weapon. Lauren Fox was streetwise to the max, quick-witted and smooth talking. All abilities that helped evoke the false veneer that she treated her rich clients to every day.

Nightshade.

The buzzer sounded and she checked the little monitor out of habit. Guy looked okay, but so had Freddie White, the one she'd had to subdue with a toaster whilst naked and standing on one leg because he'd been trying to eat the other.

She still bore the teeth marks.

The toaster still stood like a trophy in her kitchen, dented, but still usable. This guy—Quinn—didn't look anything like Freddie. He looked more like an all-American football player, a fraternity jock, a rich kid enjoying daddy's money. She hesitated for a second, finger poised over the lock-release button, wondering why he hadn't looked up.

"Come on in," she said sweetly, but still he stared at his feet. Of course, many of her first-timers did. Most of them were call-girl virgins, or at least high-class call-girl virgins. It took several sessions for the shyness to wear off.

They were the best ones, of course. The sweet, shy ones. And the agency had already vetted him. Lauren jabbed the button and waited to hear footsteps outside her door. A lightning check of her attire, a glance in the mirror and she flicked the lock open.

Quinn stood outside, and now he was looking at her.

"Hey? You okay?"

She could tell immediately that he wasn't. The question was a way of stalling, of gaining precious moments to think. And the bulge that ran down the trouser leg of his tight jeans? That shape was definitely all wrong.

Lauren threw the door back in his face as hard as she could. He caught it, making the frame shudder. She backed into the apartment, unable to tear her gaze away from those dead eyes. The eyes that saw her, knew her, but stared at her with the coldness of a shark or a crocodile assessing its prey.

Quinn advanced stiffly into the apartment, lacking even the presence of mind to close the door behind him. Lauren backed up until she felt the base of the bed at her heels. Her cell phone lay on the bedside table. The agency would already be wondering why she hadn't dialed the special support number, the one that approved the client. But they would wait a few minutes before acting. And, right now, that was a few minutes too long.

Quinn lunged. Lauren flung herself across the bed and reached for the phone. Quinn's hand closed over her ankle. She screamed and lobbed the phone at his head, making him flinch. So much for that idea. She leapt for the kitchen, but he blocked her path and came on. Again, she was backed up against the bed. She jumped onto it, feeling wobbly and unsafe. Quinn's emotionless eyes tracked her every movement. For a college kid, he moved like he knew how to handle himself in a fight.

And that's just what you're gonna get, asshole, Lauren thought. No way would she give up easily. Every day of her childhood she'd had to fight tooth and nail not to be bullied or cut or raped. Those days still lived strongly with her. This crazy mother had picked on the wrong girl.

She launched herself off the bed, catching him by surprise. Her thighs locked around his head and her weight sent him crashing to the ground. She landed on his face and neck, wishing for once that she was a little heavier. She heard his nose crack, maybe the sound of his jaw breaking. His grunt was lost in the flesh of her thighs and ass.

"Not quite the treatment our clients usually have in mind," said a deep voice from the open doorway.

Lauren looked up, instantly relieved to see Arnie standing there. Arnie was an awesome guy, a bouncer, a broken-nosed boxer, a friend to all the girls. The way he looked had given him his nickname. But not a girl at the agency ever forgot to lay one on him every chance they got.

Now Lauren rolled off Quinn, slightly surprised when he climbed straight to his knees. Asshole was probably on some serious shit anyway, eyes like that.

Blood from his broken nose spattered across her expensive white rug.

"Oh, for fuck's sake."

She saw his hands were down his pants. She heard Arnie approaching. Then she remembered. "Shit, he's got—"

But by that time, his hands were free, gripping a small 9mm pistol. Lauren hit the carpet, but Arnie never even saw it coming. He walked straight into the first round, looking shocked when his right ear exploded in a gout of blood, and staggered when the second round slammed into his gut. The third bullet thudded into the meat of his shoulder, spinning him around and the fourth imploded the back of his head.

He collapsed, dying fast, eyes staring hard into Lauren's with a glint of blame. Her brain screamed at her. It was fight or flight. She had seconds to decide. . .

No decision necessary. To run was to die. Had always been the case for her. She kicked out, striking the weapon and sending it arcing high onto the bed. When Quinn went for it, she grabbed his ankles and pulled hard. Again he fell, landing on his nose. His scream shattered the almost silent cocoon of exertion that had surrounded them. The young man pushed up off his arms, blood now coating his face and the front of his clothes. He swung a haymaker. It glanced off her temple, making her see stars. She reeled back, settling on her heels.

End of fight, time to die. Quinn was six inches from the gun. No way to reach him in time.

So Lauren did the only thing she could—for the first time in her life, she chose flight. But not toward the open door. Instead, she sprinted for the window. It was always left slightly ajar, secured on its hinge-clip. Now she hurled her entire body at the frame, smashing the hinge and crashing through the window, glass shattering all around her. The apartment was three floors up.

She hit the concrete floor of her balcony, still rolling, and slammed firmly into the thin, iron railings. The entire row of balconies shuddered, but held. Twisting her body she looked up just as Quinn fired. What remained of her window smashed outward in an explosion of glass and splintered wood. The bullet whizzed past her, whining like an angry wasp as it went, half-destroyed by the impact.

Quinn advanced across the bed, lining her up in his sights.

Now what? The leap had gained her seconds. The gap to her neighbor's balcony looked like the Grand Canyon. And not only that—she couldn't hit it running, she'd have to jump atop the railings and then make the leap from a standing start.

No good choices left.

Scrambling forward, red silk kimono untied and flapping behind her like a cape, she grabbed hold of the bars as another shot rang out. The bullet pounded into the concrete a hair's breadth from her right knee, digging up sharp shards and dust and spraying her with metal fragments.

Lauren climbed onto the railings, bare feet slipping across the cold metal. She had nothing to hold onto, but leaned against the brick wall. The wind whipped at her. The terrifying drop lay before her, three floors straight down to the street. She swayed, and suddenly understood what people meant when they said "my heart climbed into my mouth." It was the undiluted fear of imminent death.

She waited, not even considering the jump.

When Quinn strode over the destroyed threshold of the window frame, Lauren lunged at the hand holding the gun. Time stood still as Quinn held onto it and turned the barrel toward her, but Lauren fell at his feet and heaved her entire body in the air, sending his shot high into the sky and loosening his grip on the trigger.

Sirens filled the streets below.

Quinn didn't react. With the gun dangling loosely from one finger, he sought to subdue her with his free hand. Not a chance. Lauren, seeing one more opportunity, seized his wrist and upper arm and spun as hard and fast as she could. He spun with her. When she let go, the momentum she had built up sent him smashing into the railing.

And as his upper body leaned backward, she leapt at him, both feet hitting his torso hard. The force of the blow sent him cartwheeling into space, free falling soundlessly all the way to the street. Lauren landed hard on her shoulder, almost crying with the pain, but shocked and relieved and happy to be alive.

Her seventy-year-old neighbor now poked her silvery head over the adjacent balcony. "Not like it was in my day," she said with a dry crackle in her throat. "Back then, a man respected a girl. Even if he had just paid for an hour on her ass." She chuckled. "Bastard."

Lauren shook her head. Her neighbor, Miss Finch, was a reluctantly retired prostitute who Lauren had made the mistake of confiding in one drunken, wretched night. She'd regretted it ever since. Now she hung her head and crawled away to meet the cops.

This confrontation promised to be just as hard as the last.

From below, a gunshot rang out.

CHAPTER TWENTY-TWO

Mai hurried away as the kitchen began to burn. Flames were already leaping over the surfaces and would soon start capering up the walls to the ceiling. It was the signal Drake needed, in more ways than one.

The unspoken possibility had lurked like a disgruntled poltergeist between them all day. The chance that the teams might become separated, forced to go on alone. Mai and Smyth would have to continue as if the worst had happened, whilst hoping for the best. Same for Drake and Romero. There was no other way.

She followed Smyth to the rear of the building. The marine grunted. "Thought you might like to see something I found earlier." He pointed to the floor.

Mai's eyes followed his fingers. The rough frame of a trapdoor lay beneath a hastily upended bed. The door was closed.

"Thoughts?" Mai's mind worked overtime, never stopping evaluating their situation.

"Don't look like anyone made it down there." Smyth kicked at the dust that coated the frame. "They're waiting for us outside. We no longer have the element of surprise. I'd say—" Smyth stamped lightly on the frame, watching it judder. "Take our chances."

"And hope it's not a basement? A torture chamber? A storage room?"

"Sure. Ya got a better idea?"

Mai glanced up at the darkened windows. It wouldn't be long before someone seized the guards' attention and forced them back into shape. They might yet attack, despite the flames.

"Damn." She bent with Smyth and together they hauled the door upward. Cold, fresh air washed past their noses.

"Good sign," said Smyth, lowering his body down first. Mai took a moment to improvise two torches out of hardy bed sheets and shattered table legs, and hopped onto the ladder.

Hungry flames ate away the darkness to reveal a room no larger than the kitchen upstairs. Ripped apart boxes were strewn across the floor. Mai almost started straight back up the ladder before she saw Smyth gesticulating toward a corner.

"Breeze's coming from that way." The marine hurried over. Mai clung to the rungs, holding the flames away from her face. There was a sudden crash from upstairs.

"Fire's spreading," she said. She jumped down. Smyth turned, a look of cheeriness on his face.

"A tunnel."

"Stop smiling, Smyth. It doesn't suit you."

Quickly, they traversed the short tunnel, Mai handing over the second torch and gripping hers as long as she was able. It turned out to be just long enough. A solid rock wall soon faced them, the only way up a well-made wooden ladder.

"From the direction I'd say it's going to bring us out in the lab." Mai sighed. "At one time this could have been a way to transport patients unseen, or get the guards in and out during a typhoon. Crafty Devils, these Koreans."

Smyth studied the Japanese agent for a moment. "Still trust your friend, Hibiki?"

"Do you trust Romero?"

"It isn't the same."

"Are you sure? What exactly do you know about Hibiki and I?"

Smyth's face twisted back to its customary scowl. Mai smiled at his back. "That's what I thought you knew."

The marine scrambled up the ladder. Mai listened but heard no sounds of pursuit. In another half second, she was directly below Smyth as he inched open the trapdoor. Mai recognized the shadowy room immediately. It was the same room she had hidden in earlier, listening to the conversations of the doctors.

"Slowly." She hissed. "This room was clear earlier."

Smyth eased up the door until he could clamber out. Then he was up with a quick cat-like movement, weapon ready. Mai writhed her body after him with a fluid grace any middle-eastern belly dancer would have been proud of.

They crouched in darkness, listening.

Then, from behind them a voice whispered. "Don't shoot."

Mai recognized the voice. Quickly she stayed Smyth's hand. "Hibiki?"

"I saw you earlier, Mai. I have been here for some hours, hoping you might return."

"Ya got fuckin' lucky there, bro," Smyth sputtered. "In more ways than one."

"Or we Japanese are better than you allow," Hibiki said without inflection. "But Mai. What are you doing here?"

"Long story that started with a message. From you."

"Ah. I was not sure it got out."

"It got out alright." Smyth hissed, with one eye on the half-open door. "To half the world's intelligence agencies."

Mai hung her head. "I must apologize. He is not with me." She looked up. "Not for long, at least. Hibiki—" she said insistently. "Dai. What is going on here?"

"I don't have long," Hibiki said. "They will soon miss me. But the truth is—I don't know. Not exactly. It is a long-term op. Very long term. Worth keeping my cover for." The Japanese agent hesitated. "Do you see?"

"I see," Mai said instantly. Inwardly, she worried about the fervent light in her old friend's eyes. "Dai, listen to me. Are you alright? This has already been a long op."

"Nothing like yours." Hibiki hit back. "When you took down the Fuchu triad. That was legendary, Kitano. Legendary."

"I know," Mai said. She didn't need to brag. "But this. . .it worries me. More importantly the *endgame* worries me."

"More reason for me to stay in." Hibiki nodded. "Until we know."

"What *do* you know?" Smyth asked, shifting position.

"The patients arrive by warship." Hibiki flicked his eyes in the direction of the harbor. "They are collected *en masse* in North Korea, but originate from Europe. I believe they have an abduction chain that stretches from Germany to Russia and through China. I have heard all the places mentioned, and more."

"Quite an operation." Mai mused, then looked hard at Hibiki. "And quite a coup. For the agent who takes it down."

"Naturally." Hibiki inclined his head.

"Tell me more about the patients."

"It's not good for them. They are already broken—most of them. Men and women from the streets. But the transformation is breathtaking. I have seen a down-and-out slob of an east-European, a broken-down wreck, turned into a fine American in months. The accent smooth with a Yankee twang—" Hibiki now couldn't resist goading Smyth a little, it seemed. "Fit. Strong. Confident. Assured. And terribly obnoxious. The process must include a form of advanced brainwashing, I'm sure."

"But then what happens to them?" Mai asked.

"Six months later. . .they're gone. I don't know to where."

"Is it always Americans?"

"No. But mostly."

"Answer's fuckin' obvious." Smyth swore. "They're gone to America."

"They would fit right in." Hibiki raised an eyebrow in the dark.

Mai pursed her lips. "It seems a bit of overkill. Most people *fit* in America. It's a country of many cultures."

"It is," Hibiki said. "There is an angle somewhere. And a new operation has started from this end. I mentioned the American senator in my message. Something is happening right now."

"You need to learn more," Mai said to him. "You need to stay in the craziness. You need. . . to take risks."

"Agreed."

"We're going nowhere." Mai indicated the island. "We'll be around until you're ready to leave."

"They will be hunting you, Mai."

The Japanese agent and the marine turned, smiled and spoke in unison.

"I hope so."

CHAPTER TWENTY-THREE

Hayden was as pleased as she could be under the circumstances. Recently faxed through, they had received the schedules, movements and itineraries of the previous three victims and now they had what appeared to be a fourth attack, and a survivor.

Lauren Fox appeared in the doorway of the conference room. Hayden saw immediately the woman was in need of more than just a Band-Aid. She offered a hand. "Cops're busy," she said, coming around the table. "And don't like taking orders."

"Ditto." The woman said. "Now where the hell am I?"

"We are a. . ." Hayden experienced a momentary loss of vocabulary. "*Different* kind of government agency. Has a doctor seen you yet?"

"They sent some guy to my cubicle, who prodded and poked around for a bit. Think he was a doctor."

"Nothing broken?"

"Nothing physical." The woman now turned a pair of intelligent eyes onto Hayden. "Look, lady. I'm not stupid. I know my rights and I know when I see a lack of procedure. Now. Where am I?"

At that moment, bless her soul, Alicia Myles walked into the room. "This the hooker?"

Hayden shook her head and walked to the head of the table. "Sit down, Miss Fox." When the woman hesitated, Hayden repeated her words with more force. "Sit *down."*

The woman complied, clearly understanding that even now she walked a fine line with the authorities. Alicia plonked herself down in the chair right next to her, leaving nine other chairs empty.

The woman took a deep breath and then turned to Alicia, meeting her gaze with a mix of conviction, smarts and venom. "Ya got something ya wanna know?"

"Two grand an hour?" Alicia asked. "Really?"

"Ya brought me all the way here—dressed like this—to ask me 'bout my earnings?"

Alicia shuffled her chair back and peered under the table. "Nice legs, but two grand? I'd have to see the rest of you without the mac."

Hayden felt her control snap. "For God's sake, Myles. Can it. Look, Miss Fox, I can only apologize for our. . . lack of attention. . . as to your attire, but this is an urgent matter."

"And it's not like you're not used to wearing so little," Alicia added helpfully.

"Jeez. Do you guys wanna hire me or something?"

"Maybe later." Alicia smiled. "But, for now, we have lots of questions."

Kinimaka and the rest of the team filed in. Hayden noticed right away that the only person missing was Ben. "Lauren," she said, grabbing the woman's attention. "It's mainly about the man who tried to kill you today. Steve Quinn. Did you know him?"

"Nope. And he wasn't a regular either before you ask."

"Ever seen him before?" Kinimaka prodded. "Anywhere. Post Office? Coffee shop? Supermarket?"

Hayden watched closely as Lauren Fox tried to evaluate the situation. The woman wanted to know more, wanted to be put at ease, but Hayden had no intentions of fulfilling either wish. Not yet. She needed answers right now.

"So," she said quietly, "take your time. Make sure you answer truthfully. I sure don't want to have to send you back to the cops, Miss Fox."

The woman's expression showed she understood. Here was a survivor, hardened by experience and making a tough but shrewd living out of staying alive.

"Let's start with the obvious." Dahl spoke for the first time. "The man who tried to kill you committed suicide *after* falling three stories onto the concrete pavement and breaking most of the bones in his body. Why would he do that?"

"Four stories," Lauren said softly. "And over here they're called sidewalks. You English should do your research better. Pity the asshole didn't break his trigger finger."

"I'm not English," Dahl began, then blinked. "Never mind that. Why do you think he tried to kill you?"

"I don't know. Aren't you guys listening to me? Read my lips. I didn't know him. I hadn't seen him before. To my knowledge, I haven't pissed anyone off lately. Okay?"

"You told the police that he handled himself like he knew what he was doing. What did you mean by that?"

"The cops asked if I noticed anything unusual about the guy. 'Yeah', I said. 'He knew how to fight, knew how to hold a gun, knew how to shoot it.' Like that."

"And what makes you the expert?" Hayden asked.

Lauren shrugged. "I've seen all kinds. I grew up partly in foster homes and partly on the streets. I know the difference between a bully and a man with skill. You need to learn stuff like that fast to survive."

Dahl sat back in his chair, clearly impressed with her. Hayden heard his cellphone chirp and saw his eyes wander. The Swede had been spending a lot of time talking to the wife and kids lately—becoming more homesick by the day. It hurt her to think it, but she didn't see the Swedish warrior sticking with the unit much longer.

Hayden checked her own cell when it began to ring. The caller was Jonathan Gates. "Excuse me," she said. "I have to take this."

Outside the room, she answered quickly. "Sir?"

"This woman. What's she like?"

"Lauren Fox? We've only just got going, sir. Off the top of my head, I'd say she's clever, capable, and knows how to take care of herself. Streetwise, would be the word."

"Good to know. Well, be sure to keep me up to date."

Gates ended the call. Hayden frowned at the screen for a second. It was good that Gates wanted to know as much as possible about the only survivor of this weird killing streak. Gates' wife had been murdered mere months ago. The poor guy still continued to struggle through an ocean of grief and, at times, Hayden wasn't entirely sure he'd make it.

She walked back into the room in time to hear Dahl ask about the woman's whereabouts during the last two months. This was it. She quickly crossed to her chair and opened a sheaf of papers.

Somewhere along the line, these four strangers had to have crossed paths.

CHAPTER TWENTY-FOUR

Matt Drake felt his stomach roll alarmingly as the old warship crested another rolling swell. "This is worse than being cast adrift in a bloody dinghy," he complained. "With Smyth."

Romero gave him the stare. "Thought you were tough, SAS man."

"I used to be," Drake told him. "But then a diet of daytime TV, rush hour traffic and alcohol turned me soft. Now, I just wing it."

Romero studied him as if trying to gauge how much of that was actually true, then gave up with a sigh. "You English and your sense of humor. I'll never understand it."

"Neither do we." Drake shifted to relieve a cramp in his leg. Both Romero and he had been sitting in the dark for hours. More though good fortune than skill, they'd located the holding cells where the "passengers" were kept when the ship sailed for the island. The rooms were dingy, dark and strewn with rubbish. Perfect for concealment as long as the voyage didn't last too long or more "passengers" were picked up. In either case, Drake and Romero were prepared to disembark as soon as the ship docked.

"Wonder how they're getting on?" Drake said yet again.

"That Mai, she's something else, man. Where the hell did you find her?"

"She found me," Drake answered obtusely.

"What's her story?"

"You wouldn't believe me if I told you."

"We've got hours, dude. Try me."

"It involves black assassins. Kidnapping. Ninjas. Clan warfare. Child trading. And the end of something legendary. Are you sure?"

"Damn. Wish I had some butter popcorn and a bag of Twizzlers. Sounds entertaining."

"And that's why you'll never know. We're talking Mai Kitano's *life* here."

"Aww, dude, I didn't mean anything disrespectful."

Drake nodded. "I know. But the Japanese, they take these things ultra serious. Family? History? If Mai heard you talk that way about her past, she'd kill you, mate. Colleague or not."

Romero opened his mouth to speak, but at that moment, they both felt a sudden change in the ship's momentum. Drake shifted again. "Is it slowing down?"

Romero nodded. "Better eat and drink up, Englishman. It's time to bug outta this bullshit cruise."

They rose, stretching. Drake checked his jacket and supplies, his weapon. They crept around the stacks of rubbish and paused by the unlocked cell door.

"Clear."

Romero inched his way out, still shrouded in darkness. The crew hadn't ventured down to this level during the entire voyage. No need to, Drake guessed. No need to assault their senses with the feral stink of unwashed bodies mixed with strain, fear and hardship that permeated the place.

Above, they heard the sound of boots hurrying around the deck. Something was definitely going on. The two men retraced their steps of earlier. With a gesture Romero signaled that they should wait for the sudden activity to die down. Drake nodded and the two men crouched for a while, not speaking, not moving, seemingly unfocused and oblivious, but in reality, coiled and fully tuned in, listening intently in the way only Special Forces soldiers can for that unwanted footfall or creak that would tell them they had company.

It never came. After about half an hour, the commotion subsided. Romero looked at Drake. "You ready? I'm gonna gamble on this one. A dollar bill says we're docked outside Monaco."

Drake smirked. "I'll take that bet, pal. My pound's on Saint Tropez."

Romero cracked open the hatch and peered out. It was full dark outside. Lightning flickered across the horizon. A light drizzle infused the air. As Drake climbed higher, the surroundings began to piece themselves together, inch by inch.

Romero let out a breath. "This sure ain't Europe, bro."

The dark curves and jagged edges of high mountains encircled them. Both land and sea rested in pitch-blackness, apart from several rows of static lights to the left that appeared to mark a nearby town or village.

"That there." Drake pointed. "That's dry land. Nothing matters more for now."

A cold wind sent a shiver through Drake's bones as he clambered out onto the deck. But that was nothing compared to the sudden ratcheting of a gun being cocked and the sharp bark of command at their backs.

"Jeongji!"

Drake turned slowly, raising his arms. "And the same to you, my friend."

A lone soldier stood there, soaked to the skin, hair plastered to his skull as if he'd been using superglue for hair gel. Drake guessed he'd been left behind to guard the ship, a solitary man in a lonely port where there was no enemy.

Romero stepped away so the man would have to shift to see both of them. "We're port security, dude. And please keep the noise down. We don't want the entire port to hear you jabbering away like that."

The Korean jabbed the air with his rifle. *"Ani iyagi!"*

"Yeah, yeah, I like Psy too." Drake glanced at Romero. "If we start dancing Gangnam Style, do you think it'll fool him?"

"Not really." Romero looked horrified, as if he thought Drake was serious.

The Englishman drifted forward another half-step whilst talking to his colleague. The Korean, angry, gestured again, stepping into range. . .

. . .straight into a palm thrust, which sent his head back until his neck creaked. Blood sprayed from his broken nose. Drake twisted the rifle away instantly from his grasping fingers and Romero stepped in to finish the job. The Korean went overboard with barely a splash.

Drake scanned the horizon. "Looks good. See across there?"

Romero nodded. "A group of seamen walking toward a. . .barracks, I think. Soldiers going home."

"We'll follow them," Drake said. "And select one lucky fellow to explain where on Earth we are."

Drake was feeling bone tired by the time the pair had reconnoitered the barracks area and pinpointed a likely victim. The target was one of only a handful of soldiers who spoke English and came across as a leader of sorts. Romero grabbed him in the middle of a leisurely cigarette break and the two of them hauled him, kicking and mumbling, away from the barracks.

Romero trained a gun on him whilst Drake took the lead. "Hey," he said. "Hey! You tell me where we are. You tell me!"

"Changjon. Near."

"Where in the *world*?" Drake thought it appropriate to punctuate his request with a punch and watched the man's head slam back into a tree.

"Korea." The man gasped. "Kangwon-do province."

Drake considered that. "How far from China?"

"Five hundred miles."

"Alright," Romero muttered as if realizing he'd just won the bet. Drake ignored him.

"And this?" Drake waved at the barracks, the warship, the faraway island. "What's the story?"

For the first time, the Korean looked scared. The guns hadn't scared him, neither had Drake, Romero or the punch in the face. But this question sent a shadow of fear blooming across the man's features.

"I. . . don't know," he said haltingly.

"That's a big fucking gun, pal." Drake made sure the Korean saw it. "Rammed anywhere, it's gonna hurt. Question is—how much pain can you take?"

"I have a wife," the Korean mumbled suddenly. "I have a child. Please don't kill me."

Drake stared, taken aback. Romero chuckled. "Who gives a fuck?"

But Drake waved the American away. He stared at the Korean soldier as if seeing him for the first time. "You'll see them again," he said. "If you tell me what I want to know."

"Just a base." The man's arm trembled as it pointed toward the barracks. "For soldiers. The ship takes us to patrol. Sometimes we are at sea, sometimes in another province. And sometimes. . ."

"The island?"

"Yes. We take on board many prisoners and deliver them to the doctors. Then we leave. That is all I know."

"You don't collect them later?"

"No. I have never seen one leave."

"They must have another way off the island," Romero said.

"There are graves," the Korean volunteered. "All over the island. We are ordered to bury many bodies. Most of the prisoners, I think, never leave."

"How long?" Drake asked quietly. "How many years has this been going on?"

The Korean searched his memory. "Past my time. I don't know."

The man looked thirty plus. Maybe older. Drake thought hard. "How do they *get* these people?"

"They use the Russians. There is some kind of chain across Europe. A child is kidnapped in Spain. Within hours, he has been swiftly transported through a handful of checkpoints—houses situated in Germany, and then Russia. From there to China and, later, to Korea."

Romero whistled. "That's sophisticated stuff, my man. An op that big. . .we're talking serious brass, and serious leadership."

"And serious payoff," Drake added, thinking of Dai Hibiki's original message. Something about advanced weaponry. They hadn't seen any signs of it on the island. "Tell me—where is the HQ?"

"The island."

Drake shook his head. That wasn't it. Couldn't be. The chain of command would stretch much higher than that, but then a soldier wouldn't be privy to that kind of information. He tried a different tack. "Okay. Where is the *European* HQ?"

"Germany." The Korean spat the word out. "But I know most about the smaller houses in China and Russia. The big one, the important one, is in Germany, but now everyone talks of the Russian one because they have made some fantastic discovery. Something about gods and ancient towers. Something so big they say it makes the island operation a tiny speck. "

"And the rest of the HQs?"

"I'm sorry. Please don't kill me."

Drake listened as the man reeled off addresses in China and Russia, then shot Romero a look. "We could do worse than heading to China," he said. "We need to get out of Korea pronto. China is as good a place as any round here."

"Better than South Korea?"

"We don't know how far this thing reaches," Drake said. "This guy's already mentioned Spain, Russia and Germany. Who knows where else?"

"And in China?"

"We could pay a visit to their little *house*. Maybe learn some more."

"Sounds like a plan. What about him?" Romero jerked the barrel of his gun sharply.

The Korean soldier began to shrink back, as if he might be able to squeeze into the tree at his back. "Please. I have a wife. A child."

Drake stepped forward and buried his knife through the man's heart.

"So did I."

CHAPTER TWENTY-FIVE

Hayden put the phone down after another odd conversation with her boss. Gates had just rung to inquire about Lauren Fox's mental state. Now the secretary had told her he was on his way to meet the woman. Hayden had warned him about the news reporter, Sarah Moxley, who continued to hang around but her boss seemed unperturbed.

The man had changed since his wife died. The fast-thinking, clear-talking, inspiring leader had been replaced with something cloudier. Something more suited to politics perhaps, but not something she could stake her career on anymore.

A situation that needed reviewing, but not yet. The high-class hooker, Lauren Fox, had been rumbling on about going home for the last twenty minutes.

"You should stay for your own safety." Kinimaka was telling her, the huge Hawaiian looking out of place as he sat next to the small, pretty woman, dwarfing her. Hayden found a smile flitting around the corners of her lips as she stared at him, seeing his discomfort like no one else could, knowing him so well after their long working relationship, and wondering more and more often how the other kind of relationship might get started.

Lauren waved at him. "I already proved I can look after myself."

"Your assassin was one of many, Miss Fox. You are the fourth victim in a few days. Sorry, *attempted* victim." Kinimaka coughed. "We don't know the scope of this thing yet. If you could help by giving us your movements—"

"I already told you! I get about. My job calls for some travel every now and then, alright? I gave you my movements."

Trouble was they didn't match up to all the previous victims. Not yet anyway. Kinimaka was studying the paper she'd written on. "How about early January? Let's try that."

Hayden thought about the previous victims. All dead because, as strangers, they had crossed paths with someone dangerous. And they had pretty much travelled in the same areas. At least, that was the theory. How they fitted in with suicidal, faceless assassins was a mystery that had them all beat.

"I have clients," Lauren was saying. "If you're not gonna charge me, at least let me contact them. My business is my livelihood."

Kinimaka looked surprised. Alicia, still sitting next to the feisty woman, brightened up. "Tell you what, Foxy. I haven't had a shag in months. How 'bout I spend a few days standing in for you?"

Lauren was about to answer when a shout rose from the control room. Hayden sped off immediately, Alicia a step behind.

The banks of monitors were flashing. Both Ben and Karin were standing. Torsten Dahl was buckling into a bulletproof vest.

"Move!" the Swede cried. "Fifth attempt in progress! The victim and the cops're holding the assassin off at a friggin' service area not thirty minutes from here!"

CHAPTER TWENTY-SIX

Torsten Dahl leapt out of the big Dodge SUV even before it stopped moving. A row of cop cars sat before him, lined up outside the entrance to a small service station. A dozen pairs of world-weary eyes swiveled toward him.

"Who the hell are you?"

Dahl ignored them, considering the black SUV classification enough, and not caring for their tones or surly looks. He sized up the scene himself within a minute.

Several bodies lay strewn across the grassed area in front of the station. Dahl guessed these were innocent bystanders, caught up in the madness when the assassin tried to reach his target. It was after this that reports had started coming in of a shooter behaving very much in the manner Hayden and Kinimaka had flagged with every US agency. After that, the shooter's target—a truck driver—had apparently produced a gun, escaped and barricaded himself in an alcove the service station used for a game room.

"We need to take this bastard alive." Hayden breathed in Dahl's ear. "If possible."

Beyond the wide glass doors, Dahl made out the shelves and bright lights of the shop. Foregoing subtlety, he dragged one of the cops over. "What's the layout of this place, my friend?"

The cop blinked for a moment before catching the look in the Swede's eyes. To his credit, he was wise enough to know it was time for some straight talk. "Doors open onto an entrance hall. Shop's off to the right, game room down a bit and to the left. Then the restrooms. We think the shooter's past that, roaming the small food court and the fast-food area."

"Civilians?"

"You better believe it, buddy. Restaurant staff and day-trippers. Some got away when the shooting started, sure, but it'd be a mistake to think everyone made it."

Dahl grabbed Hayden's arm. "If he's anything like the other assassins, this man will be hunting the truck driver to the point of obsession. He won't be watching the exits or entrances. He won't be watching the people in there." He paused, looking between Hayden and Alicia, quickly deciding on the least caustic and embarrassing of the two. "Sorry, Mano. Your girlfriend's mine for a while."

*

Lauren Fox, watching events unfold on the big screen monitors, saw the camera swerve and sway as Dahl and Jaye moved swiftly around the building, heading for the rear entrance. She was intrigued, despite herself. One part of her wanted to get the hell out and salvage whatever remained of her clientele; the other was most definitely caught up in the excitement.

And a deep, wiser part of her knew that staying put was the safest move. For now.

The Secretary of Defense had joined them a few minutes ago, given her an appraising look, and then gone to talk to Ben and Karin Blake and their bodyguard, the big dude they called Komodo. Lauren noticed his eyes lingering on everything—from the field cams of Dahl and Jaye and Kinimaka to the surveillance cameras that protected the building's perimeter, to the toned curves of Karin Blake's body.

There was an interesting dynamic running through this group, she thought. She saw loyalty and compassion running alongside the capacity for instant violence and ruthlessness. Lauren knew how to read people. It was a quality that had kept her alive most of her life. She saw Ben Blake's despair. His sister's delight. Komodo's happiness. And Jonathan Gates' utter desolation.

Of course, she had heard about his wife and how she had died. The entire country knew. Lauren had already connected the dots and figured out that this was most likely one of the teams that had taken down the Blood King. The Russian criminal, Dmitry Kovalenko, was currently languishing in some secret hellhole, awaiting trial.

What the hell had she landed smack dab in the middle of?

And why? Her mind flicked back over the last several weeks. Nothing unusual jumped out at her. The photographs of the three dead victims rang no inner bells. Hayden had told her to focus her mind on any recent travel but she traveled almost every day. Now if the blond agent had specified *outside New York*, that might narrow the field a bit.

She hadn't, but Lauren ran through it anyway. *Three times*, she thought. Washington DC. Boston. Atlantic City. Each time a ritzy but far-flung hotel.

On the monitors the action had started. She wasted no time concentrating on Torsten Dahl's field-cam.

Dahl strode boldly through the kitchen of the resident Popeye's until he could see the food court area. Once there, he grabbed Hayden again, held her close, and ducked down behind the counter.

"See anyone?"

"Unfortunately not. Come on."

Dahl rounded the counter and then sat with his back against it. Hayden cuddled into him, playing the scared girlfriend. Now they saw several pairs of scared eyes staring back at them from between table legs and even from underneath booths. Dahl picked out two bodies splashed with blood.

Then came the sound of fast footfalls. Dahl looked up in time to see a broad-shouldered man wearing a blue Abercrombie and Fitch zipper top and black khakis stride into the food court. Again, the Swede saw those staring eyes, the blank expression, and the competent manner in which the assassin moved. The gun he carried was held loosely, but still in a way where it could be used in half a second.

"These are what all the assassins have been like?" Lauren asked. "These are the guys who are trying to kill us?"

Jonathan Gates rubbed his eyes tiredly. "You got it, Miss Fox. You still want to be returned to your apartment?"

Lauren made a face. "Not really."

"Then sit still and watch."

"This team you got. How good are they exactly?"

Dahl held off on the charge. It wouldn't do to get an innocent hit by a stray bullet. Plus they wanted this guy still breathing. The Swede held his natural urge in check—that of mayhem and destruction—and instead, concentrated on the man's gun.

"Pretty standard." He breathed to Hayden.

"Problem is when he recognizes a threat or nears the end of his mag he's gonna go ballistic," the ex-CIA agent murmured into his chest. "Suicidal tendencies do that."

"I got him covered." Dahl's hand rested near a concealed weapon.

"Geez. He's *holding* his gun. Just how fast are you Dahl?" Hayden sounded awed and a little worried.

"I haven't yet met an equal." As usual Dahl's tone was matter of fact. The man didn't know how to boast. Hayden believed his claim without question.

"Decision's yours."

Dahl was waiting for the squeaky clean assassin to turn away when all hell broke loose. The truck driver, it seemed, had made a similar assessment about the killer and must have been running low on bullets. A heavy grinding sound preceded the hammering of work boots against the tiled floor and, as the assassin turned, the truck driver flew into view.

Both men fired at the same instant. The assassin from the hip, the truck driver as he dove forward. Both bullets shot hopelessly wild. Dahl drew before

Hayden could blink. The truck driver skidded helplessly across the polished floor, gun skittering away as he landed heavily. The assassin set his sights carefully.

Dahl had no choice. He fired in a heartbeat, saw his bullet strike his target's bicep and shatter through bone. The gun pinwheeled away. The man's body half-turned, but he kept his attention on the truck driver lying right before him.

The assassin, right arm hanging in a bloody ruin, continued to focus on his prey with a terrifying single-mindedness. His good arm flew out, striking the truck driver hard on the face. His hand closed around the man's throat, squeezing.

But then Dahl was on him, ripping him away and hurling him against a wall-size neon advertisement. The light fizzed and then went out.

The truck driver collapsed in pain and relief.

Hayden slid to his side. "You alright? Are you hit?"

"Nah. Nah, I'm good. I got a permit for my gun, miss. I ain't part of no militia."

"That's good. That's fine. We need to talk to you."

The truck driver made an effort to pull himself together. He sat up and cast a rheumy eye over both of them

"You guys don't look like cops. He doesn't even look American."

Dahl smiled and raised an eyebrow. "Thank you."

"Didn't say it was a good thing, buddy."

Hayden held up a hand. "Please. We *really* need to talk."

CHAPTER TWENTY-SEVEN

There was no comfort for Matt Drake. Not physically or mentally. His developing feelings for Mai were very much tempered by the self-hate and blame he nurtured for Kennedy's death. Inner turmoil tore him apart, emotions ripping at his heart and his mind, making his stomach empty and his soul more than hollow.

The recent revelations about his old boss, Wells, weren't helping. He found no closure in the fact that the man he had trusted and defended so long had turned out to be his enemy, and one of the catalysts behind the murder of Alyson and Emily—the car accident that ended their lives.

Arranged by an operative who went by the codename *Coyote*. Man or woman, group or corporation, they would pay. The Shadow Elite had paid dearly, but Drake knew even now it would be a mistake to think they were gone. The Shadow Elite had thrived for untold years by being part of a family. You didn't destroy four families by chopping off their heads. It was the source that caused the festering, the root of the evil. And sometimes the root could be an entire network, or a single entity.

Some part of them still nestled in the shadows, spinning webs, he was sure.

And then he thought of Russell Cayman. The shadowy agent had not been heard of since he walked out of the third tomb of the gods carrying Kali's bones. Was there a reason he had taken them? The Goddess Kali had been a manifestation of the worst kind of evil, sometimes associated with the Devil himself. It was interesting that Cayman chose her. And was he now being sheltered by what remained of the Shadow Elite? Didn't really seem their style, but Drake assumed even they would have to restructure after losing their figureheads.

Now he jounced up and down in the covered-over bed of an old truck. Occasionally, either he or Romero lifted a flap of canvas and peered out, but the bleak, hilly brown and green landscape rarely altered. Sometimes they heard the sounds of workers toiling in the fields. Once when they looked out, a fine, drizzly mist had settled over everything. The man they had paid from the wedge of dollars in their packs had taken little persuading. This despite the harsh sentences handed out by the North Korean authorities to anyone helping Westerners, or indeed any of their own people who were caught trying to cross the border to China or repatriated as refugees. Most of these people faced harsh punishment, possibly torture and imprisonment in labor camps.

Still, many North Koreans escaped the impoverished country every day. The border might be well guarded, but desperate men always found a way.

Drake and Romero kept an eye on their driver, but every time they checked, all they received was a world-weary sigh from a face that was deeply creased by years of hardship and eyes that had long since forgotten what joy felt like. These were people born into toil, used and forgotten except by their own families. Six hours into the journey and they were still only about half way through. Drake found his thoughts drifting again—this time toward his old roommate and friend—Ben. The lad hadn't matured as Drake had hoped. Despite facing death and captivity and somehow landing a girlfriend as hot and capable as Hayden Jaye, the young man had barely developed beyond the introspective super-geek he'd always been. It worried Drake, but he just hadn't been in a position to help Ben. Nor had he known how to go about it.

One thing was clear; Ben was badly affected by the death of the soldier in the third tomb. Getting blood on your hands always made it seem more real, even if whizzing bullets still passed you by. Hayden had tried to help, Drake knew. She was a good person and wouldn't intentionally harm anyone who didn't deserve it.

But help only worked if it was accepted, taken on board. The recipient had to participate. Ben clearly wasn't.

Carry your load. An old Dinorock tune. But it wasn't necessarily true. To trust and to share was to half the burden, wasn't it?

Drake took into account his own burdens. In addition to his women, there was the death of Daniel Belmonte and his protégé—Emma. Drake hadn't yet found the time to visit her father, and even that fact wore him down.

He needed a bloody vacation.

Well, he thought, been on a deserted island, a sea voyage and to North Korea in the last week or so. What more could he ask for?

Before the truck jostled and rebounded its way to the border, the truck stopped and the driver shouted. Drake and Romero popped their heads into the front cab.

"We here?"

The driver pointed. Drake understood. The border was across the dank hills to their left. They managed to get from the man that this was a relatively easy, but still manned, crossing point, which was perfect. They needed to get across sure, but they still needed transport on the other side.

Outside it was soggy and damp and hot. The two soldiers put their heads down and began the hike to the top of the nearest hill. The truck drove noisily away behind them. Within an hour, they had carefully crested the rise. Helpfully, the mist receded a bit as they shuffled across the top.

Below them, patchy grassland led to the Koreans concrete wall, wide enough to accommodate several men walking alongside each other. Beyond that lay about thirty feet of overgrown and untended no-man's-land, perfect cover, ending where China's crisscross patterned wire fence reared a little farther on.

A straggling line of ten or twelve troops marched in time along the Korean wall, heading for a distant checkpoint.

"Seems pretty low key," Drake said. "We'll cross and double back to the checkpoint. Borrow a vehicle tonight."

Romero began to crawl down the wet hillside. "Sounds good to me."

Another three hours and they were nearing Harbin. The Chinese city was a surprising mix of ostentatious historical architecture and modern commercial office buildings, reflecting the changing face of not only the city, but the country as a whole. Harbin overlaps culturally with European designs amidst a distinct Russian cityscape and a new scenic waterfront combined with modern road systems. But instead of appearing haphazard and pretentious, the mix of old and new celebrates the past whilst fully embracing the future. Drake drove their battered old vehicle down a wide, increasingly busy road, feeling more conspicuous by the minute.

"Ah, shit," Romero voiced his concern. "Why the hell did we think Harbin would be a backwater village? Ya know, at a glance, this place could be any big European city."

"Outdated western perceptions." Drake nodded. "Still hold strong. We should ditch this junker and find us a map."

Romero pointed at a universal sign. "Train station," he said. "Best place we could go."

Drake made the turn and they parked the vehicle in as unassuming a position as they could find. It was a moment before Drake and Romero shared a look.

"Balls. You think we might stand out from the crowd?"

They studied each other. "Lose the vest," Romero said. "Loosen the shirt. Buy a backpack. You'll pass."

"Me?"

"There are Europeans all over." The American gazed out the grimy windows. "But not a soul from the good old U.S. I can see."

"Alright." Drake quickly made ready and then climbed out of the car. The streets were clean and bright. Even the old architecture appeared newly washed. The Chinese filled the pavements and the wide-open plaza that fronted Harbin Station. Cars whizzed by. Streams of workers flooded up and down the nearby subway steps. Drake put his head down and headed for the station.

Protocol dictated they contact Washington, but Drake concluded it was too risky at this point. Better they flush out the Chinese part of the operation and continue on to Russia before making the call. At least in Russia they might find allies.

He walked right through the entrance underneath a big black-and-white clock and cast about. Wide, vaulted ceiling, train times, and entrances were dead ahead. Shops to the right and a terrace of windows to the left. Drake headed for the nearest shop, seeking out civilian backpacks, jackets and a map. He also bought food and water after exchanging his American dollars at a nearby *Bureau de Change*.

Once equipped, he made haste to vanish, heading back to Romero and then walking away from the tiny minivan they'd appropriated from the border.

They walked into the city, purposely losing themselves whilst studying the new map.

"Once it gets dark," Drake grated, "the Chinese part of this human trafficking op won't know what hit them."

The bright lights of Harbin lit up the night. Drake and Romero paid a taxi driver to take them within three blocks of the address they wanted and stepped out into a neighborhood of relative dark. Dogs barked. Hushed conversations pinpointed those hidden in the evening gloom. Speed was the westerners' ally as they followed a predetermined route directly to the address the North Korean soldier had given them.

Assuming he remembered correctly, and had been telling the truth.

Drake trusted the information, but even so, it still needed confirming. The house in question blended in with the rest of the row, perfect camouflage for any kind of den of iniquity. The locals would be warned and brutalized, the authorities paid off. No city in the world was free from this kind of poison so, conceal it as they might, the criminal fungi still spread its malicious tendrils through all of society wherever it could find root.

With little time to waste, the two westerners chomped at the bit as they realized the only way into this building was through the front door. The covert option was negated by endless rows of darkened windows overlooking the street and rear. The hours ticked by and the night had grown colder, silent, and more fearful as the men became ever more conscious of their overstuffed backpacks, hidden weapons and conspicuous presence even crouched in the pitch black.

"Maybe this wasn't such a good idea," Romero whispered.

Drake nudged him. "You think?"

A shadow moved in the doorway of the house. A half-dressed man moved into view, taking some air, leaving the door ajar behind him. Drake moved fast, rushing out of the night like a white devil, locking the man into a chokehold before he could utter a word.

Romero checked him over. "I'm likin' this." The American held up his pistol. "You belong to a Triad? A Tong?"

Drake's captive twisted. Well-formed muscles and experience enabled him to free his head before the Englishman recaptured it in an even stronger hold. "Okay. Guy's a fighter. Let's do this."

Earlier, they had decided that if any of these guys came up as smelling like anything other than roses, they were going to chance a raid. There was simply too much riding on the outcome for them not to risk it. The senator in Washington, Dai Hibiki, Mai and Smyth, not to mention the island captives and the Europeans and Americans being kidnapped every year. The odds screamed for a chance to be taken—and Drake never shied away from a battle.

Quickly he snapped the guy's neck, and then followed Romero to the door. The marine wasted no time squeezing through the small opening and then padding down a short, unlit entryway. Its far end was shut off by a big, four-panel, carved Chinese screen, antique in appearance but of modern design. A white light illuminated the upper panels. Shadows moved to and fro.

Romero took firm hold of the screen and swung it back hard along its runners. Drake slipped into the revealed room, almost struck immobile by the scene of abhorrence and chaos beyond.

The room had been cleared out so that it resembled nothing like the interior of a house. The brick wall was bare, the rear-facing windows painted black. Thick chains had been fixed to the wall, to which at one time human beings had clearly been attached. Open handcuffs lay on the floor. Scraps of clothing were scattered everywhere—shirts, blouses, pants. An open toilet lay in the middle of the room, dug down into the house's foundations and emanating a foul stench. Luckily, there were no captives today, just Chinese men clearing up.

Drake slammed the butt of his gun into the nearest man's face, rendering him unconscious. The second he threw into the latrine. By that time, Romero had rounded him and was firing on the few who drew weapons of their own. A third man came at Drake wielding a wicked dagger like they did in the movies, rolling the deadly weapon around his thick wrists and letting it slice through the air. Drake let him strike, moving in close so the arc of the weapon caused the blade to pass over his shoulder, and head-butted him into submission.

Again, surprise became the third member of their team. These men had never thought to be raided, not here in their own province, in the carved-out niche of what they considered their own city. Whilst Romero cleared the upstairs rooms, Drake roused and interrogated the three men he'd knocked out.

Only one spoke English. He confirmed the next address in Moscow, and that the main HQ was in Frankfurt, Germany, but nothing more. By the time Romero returned, Drake had already made sure every man there would never support human trafficking again.

"Quick," he said, gathering up the cellphones, wads of money, pistols and ammo he'd taken from the bad guys. "Clock's ticking, mate."

Mai was relying on him. No way would he let her down.

CHAPTER TWENTY-EIGHT

Drake and Romero quickly executed the next stage of their plan, both feeling a somewhat immature excitement as they neared the time when they would contact Washington. They stole a battered, white minivan from Harbin Station—one of literally hundreds—and started on the long road that led to Vladivostok, Russia. From there, they would board a plane to Moscow. Soon, they wouldn't have to make their own plans anymore.

Soon, the American government would pave the way for them.

Drake watched as Romero drove. The winding road opened before them, murky, deserted and split only by their headlights. He sorted through the cellphones he'd collected, choosing the newest and most advanced looking—a Sony Ericsson.

"Hope they're in."

He tapped out the agency's number and waited for the connection.

"Yes?" Karin's voice, suspicious and reserved as it should be.

"It's Drake. I guess you'd better put me on speaker."

Karin emitted a few expletives, shouted across the office, and almost burst Drake's eardrums as she shuffled excitedly around and then came back on, sounding breathless.

"You're   on!"

Drake gave a situation report and their position in as few words as possible. Even then it took him fifteen minutes with Romero chirping up all the time. He didn't mention it, but was relieved to hear everyone sound so happy to hear his voice. He made a point of stressing Mai and Smyth's tricky situation on the island.

"Let me get this straight," Hayden repeated his last words. "You and Romero are heading back to Washington—across Russia and Europe—and on the way you're taking down a human trafficking ring. That right?"

Drake shrugged in the dark. "What else would you expect?"

"Alright, well, we have a situation of our own right here." Now Hayden began to talk, explaining about the mysterious American-bred assassins with their blank eyes who were taking their own lives as well as that of a single target. She told him that they now had three survivors including the Senator and that they were about to try and find a link between the five victims.

"How does it connect to the island?" Drake's immediate thought.

"Through Dai Hibiki's original message. The first intended victim was Senator James Turner, though they missed him and hit his staff. Since then, same kind of assassins, same MO."

"High profile hits?"

"No. Civilians. No clear link."

"Second attempt on Turner?"

"Never happened."

Drake pulled the phone away from his ear as a double-beep sounded. "Damn. Bloody thing's running out of battery already. Listen, I'll contact you again soon, but first I need to speak to Alicia. Is she there?"

A moment's pause followed. Then a voice said, "Right here, Drakey."

His lips curled upwards. "Missed me?"

"Hmm. . .not half as much as your little sprite friend. You really trying to say you were marooned on a desert island with her?"

"And two other men."

"Lucky bitch."

"Listen. I have a job for you. One you're definitely gonna love."

"Oh yeah?"

"You remember that biker gang? The one we used in Luxembourg?"

Alicia didn't speak for a moment, then sounded bored. "Vaguely."

"Would you fly over there and enlist their help again? Then you all ride to meet me in Frankfurt, Germany. We have a big, bad HQ to take down and I think we're gonna need some help."

Alicia cheered. "*Now* you're fuckin' talking!"

CHAPTER TWENTY-NINE

Hayden tried to quell the feeling of elation and concentrate on the problem at hand.

The truck driver—Mike Stevens—sat across from Lauren Fox at the conference table. The rest of the team sat or lounged around. Stevens, to be fair, still looked shell-shocked and awfully intimidated. Lauren looked bored.

Hayden knew she had to take charge if they were to head off any more attempts. Drake and Mai were safe. In fact, for now, they were all safe. And Alicia had retired to an interrogation room to call up her buddies in Luxembourg.

So, no distractions.

"You two are the key," she said. "I get it. You don't know each other. You've never seen each other. Never crossed paths. But—" she held both their gazes. "You have."

She indicated the big monitor at the head of the room. "Watch this. I have uploaded the other victims' movements for the last few months up there. Believe me when I tell you, guys, strangers or not—you've all met recently."

Ben Blake hit a button. "We hope," he muttered beneath his breath.

Hayden felt a rush of anger but ignored it. The "chance meeting" was all they had. Other than that, it was all random, indiscriminate. These murders had been orchestrated by a single man or organization. It stood to reason that it wasn't just chance.

A picture of Senator James Turner came up first. Mike Stevens sighed. "Well, I can sure put this to rest straight away. I ain't never met that guy. Not even by accident."

Mano Kinimaka leaned forward. "How do you know? Do you think when Nicole Kidman hits Wal-Mart, she goes out dressed like she was in *Titanic*?"

Stevens and Lauren stared. Even Dahl looked confused. "Was she even in *Titanic*?"

Hayden took a hold of it before it degenerated any more. "What Mano's trying to say—badly—is that you and Turner may have crossed paths without even knowing it. Just give it a chance."

Stevens nodded. A list of Turner's movements appeared on screen. "I sure done some o' those places," the truck driver spoke up. "Washington. Maine. Baltimore. New York."

Now Lauren Fox sat straighter. "Me too, I guess. New York. Boston, Atlantic City and Washington in the last three months."

"I done A.C. too."

The monitor continued to flow, flicking pages like a book, now having gone past the intended victims and on to the unintended casualties of all the shootings. When the picture of the Senators aide—Audrey Smalls—flicked by the truck driver jumped so hard he banged his knee.

"Wait," he spluttered. "I sure as hell know her."

CHAPTER THIRTY

Drake and Romero hit the streets of Moscow at 4 a.m., January, 26th. Without being the safest city in the world, Moscow was, at least, safer and more accommodating to the two Westerners than, say, North Korea or even China.

Still running on adrenalin and travelling light and fast out of necessity, Drake and Romero barely had time to breathe before a pair of aloof and restrained CIA agents slipped them guns, money and credentials along the *Koltsevaya* metro line that encircles Moscow. A quick trip to a hotel room, a nap, and they were ready to travel into one of Moscow's most notorious districts—Vykhino—an area in the industrial south east with a high crime rate and the dubious honor of being situated close to Lyubertsy—the area whose residents used to control and intimidate the entire city.

"We take everything with us," Drake said. "No stopping now until Germany. It's essential we hit that place whilst they're still unsure what's happening. Agreed?"

"We have to take out the Russians first." Romero coughed. "Let's focus on one enemy at a time."

"Done it before." Drake hefted his pack. "Do it again."

"You mean Kovalenko, don't you? The Blood King?"

"Never heard of him."

"Don't be a dick. Half the army still thinks he's a legend and that the whole Bermuda Triangle, Hawaii, thing was made up. Nothing but propaganda surrounding these tombs."

Drake shook his head. "The government has a lot to answer for. Let me put it this way—if a civilized government knew it had cocked up, maybe overlooked a terrible criminal who took many innocent lives and almost started his own war, would they broadcast his existence or let it die down into legend?"

"Point taken."

"So let's go."

Moscow was just starting to wake up. A wan light bled from the cloud-strewn skies, casting a faint illumination across the sprawling city. Drake and Romero took the Metro to Ryazansky Prospekt, the closest point to the address they'd been given. But this was a bad neighborhood. Not even the bravest tourists came here. Once outside they quickly located a vehicle and promptly stole it.

Now mobile, they wouldn't stand out from the crowd.

Drake gripped the wheel as they crawled by the address they'd been given. His eyes met Romero's. This was different. Here was something that resembled a Russian timber yard, a merchant of sorts, complete with tall, wide racks, a counter sales cabin and an extensive warehouse.

"Easy access," Romero noted.

"Maybe," Drake mused, looking in vain for CCTV stanchions. "Or if they know were coming. . ."

"Death trap."

"There's too much in motion to back out now." Drake thought about Mai and Smyth, fates unknown, and about Alicia on her way to Luxembourg. He thought about Hayden and her difficult investigation back in D.C. The men and women still being held captive on that island.

The marines who had died on the airplane. The pilot. And so many more.

"So far. . .we haven't stopped," he said. "And it's served us well. We've still a long way to go so. . .fuck it."

He swerved the car, revved the accelerator, and tore toward the shabby gates. Metal shrieked as they smashed apart, bolts and hinges sent skimming across the roughly concreted yard. The car crashed through. Part of the left hand gate caught on its luggage-rack, flapping to and fro and scraping across the trunk.

Drake blasted toward the main cabin.

Hayden stared at the truck driver. "You know Audrey Smalls?" Could it be coincidence?

"Yep. Lovely woman. I met her at the Desert Palms hotel in Atlantic City. She didn't mention what she did for a living I can't believe she's dead."

"Wait." Now Lauren sat rigid. "The Desert Palms? That's where *I* stayed. Bit ritzy for an ordinary trucker though. No offense."

"Well, offense taken. So fuck right off, lady. The place offers a discount to regulars like me. "

"She's no lady. . ." Ben must have agreed with the trucker, but Hayden held up a hand that immediately stopped his flow.

"The Desert Palms." She stabbed a button, progressing the information at a fast pace until Walter Clarke's schedule came up. A tremor of delight shot through her.

"Our insurance salesman did his east coast run that week too." She pointed though she didn't have to. "Stayed at the Desert Palms on January 10th. He was victim number two."

"Dunno when it was," Stevens said. "Sounds good. And yes, I remember Walter too. Tell me, is the next victim a bank clerk named Michelle Baker? She used to visit A.C. once a year for a big casino blowout."

Hayden stared, dumbfounded.

The truck driver looked sad. "I think I know what this is all about."

Drake skidded the car to a sudden halt. The swinging gate gained momentum and flew from the top of the car, hitting the cabin doors with a loud bang and breaking windows. Glass shattered and cascaded to the gravel-strewn ground as Drake and Romero jumped out of the car, leaving the doors open and the engine running. Drake prepped his gun, a PKM variant Kalashnikov, 7.62 caliber, modernized for light use. Not the best weapon, but not bad at short notice.

He hit the steps, Romero at his side, and kicked the door hard. It buckled immediately, locked from the inside. Another kick and it flew open.

A man was running at him, bloody wood saw held high.

"Fuck me." Romero breathed.

Drake blew him away with a quick burst. His body shot backward, slamming against a jam-packed rack of shelving. Screwdrivers and packets of nails rained down nosily. Hammers, tape measures and boxes of screws hit the floor and landed on the dead man. Drake hurried through an open archway into the back of the cabin. Three short rows of desks faced him. Beyond them was a big office, its walls oddly papered with what looked like old maps and diagrams.

Big men in leather jackets and jeans were squeezing though a small door, hampered by their size. Once through, they came running at the intruders like huge grizzly's, arms spread wide, mouths screaming above their bushy black beards.

Behind them, an even bigger Russian appeared, stripped to the waist, more hair on his chest than any 80s rocker had on his head, flexing muscles and growling with disdain. Drake blasted the first wave. Romero stepped to the side and picked off the stragglers. Men fell everywhere, some landing right at Drake's feet through momentum and just plain toughness, able to take more bullets than an armored car and still keep coming.

One of them landed a blow. It glanced off Drake's shoulder, but still numbed it. More men piled out of the office. Now, past them, a great round table could be seen as well as the man strapped to it. Arms stretched unnaturally, head pulled right back to expose the throat. The man was in agony. Blood dripped from all his limbs. Arranged around him were yet more men.

Drake emptied his clip. A Russian tackled him around the waist, dead before he even hit the floor. But Drake staggered back and found himself stabbing at his next opponent with the barrel of his gun. It was a good prod, taking the man in the windpipe and making him double over, gurgling. Romero picked off the next two.

The way forward was open, albeit littered with dead and half-dead bodies. Drake and Romero made it to the office door, at the same time trying to make sense of the strange maps that papered the walls, before the hairy Russian ambled out, grinning like a maniac.

"So!" he rumbled. "The famous Matt Drake. Like your James Bond, no? Why you come to Mother Russia?"

"You know me?" Drake faltered.

"Like I said. You famous man. Bang, bang." He made the motions of firing a pistol. "You take down Dmitry, am I right? You take away his dream as well. Don't worry, Matt Drake. You are famous here. For that, I only kill you a little."

Drake sidestepped as the hairy Russian lunged, but the man was amazingly fast. One huge, meaty paw grabbed a handful of Drake's jacket, and thumped him sideways against the flimsy wall. Drake hit it so hard the plaster caved in, sending white puffs of spray into the air. One of the ancient maps rolled down over his head.

Drake's gun clattered to the floor. Romero was busy holding off two more Russians as the monster came on, reaching for Drake.

"Name's *Zanko!*" The Russian sounded like the announcer at a circus introducing a new act. "Most days I eat an American for breakfast but for you. . ." A shrug made the crazy physique ripple and swell alarmingly. "I make exception."

Enormous hands grabbed the front of Drake's jacket, lifting him into the air until his feet left the ground. Drake, still winded, could do nothing as the Russian pinned him to the wall. "Vladimir!" the man bellowed. "Vladimir! Bring me my hammer and nails!"

Gunshots split the air as Romero took out his opponents. A third hit him hard, riddled with lead but still coming strong. Romero went flying across a desk, his gun clattering to the floor. They were hopelessly outnumbered, Drake thought furiously. This wasn't a fucking satellite drop-off for a trafficking ring. It was the base of a major operation. Most likely the base for several major operations. Strength flooded back into his body and he started to struggle. The Russian, Zanko, knitted bushy brows that met in the middle.

"You English," he scoffed. "I could still hold you there with one hand. See?" And Zanko switched grips, now pinning Drake's body with just his left paw, a grin stretching his face that went from ear to ear.

Drake evaluated the situation whilst waiting for Vladimir to find Zanko's hammer. The office at the back was clearly the hub of the place, the O.C. The tied and hopelessly stretched out man still lay across the table, panting shallowly. Half a dozen Russians still stood around his body, no doubt discussing methods of interrogation or assessing information already gleaned.

Since the room had emptied somewhat, Drake could now see a grizzled old man sat right at the back below a heavily barred window, watching proceedings without movement but with sharp, hawk-like eyes.

The eyes locked on Drake as if sensing the attention, but nothing changed in the face, not even the faint folding of a cavernous wrinkle. The old man's exposed neck was a mass of dark tattoos.

Two more big men stood at his side, assessing matters right along with him. Drake revised his appraisal of this place. Maybe it was *the* HQ for this organization. It certainly appeared important, what with all the old maps and diagrams everywhere. He noted now even more ancient-looking scrolls spread out over the desks. Something was definitely being investigated here. He recalled the Korean soldiers claim about the Russians making some great archaeological discovery lately. Something about the gods and ancient towers, something immense.

Now Zanko shook him as if noticing his inattention. "It will get a little more interesting in just one minute, small man."

Romero groaned to his right. Drake saw a high spray of blood. Grief knifed through his gut. *No!* The marine was a good soldier and a good man, caught up Drake's run of bad luck by mischance alone. He didn't deserve. . .

Then Romero rolled out from under the desk holding a knife, face and hair dripping. It was he who had struck the blow. He pulled a pistol and aimed it at Zanko.

But the monster Russian was quicker than either of them gave him credit for. Without even looking—perhaps watching the reflections in Drake's eyes—he swung out and backhanded Romero across the face. The marine literally flew, legs and arms flapping, the width of the office and smashed into the far wall.

There he collapsed, unmoving.

Drake began to kick wildly. He swung at Zanko with both arms, landing a strong blow across the jaw.

A man came up to them carrying a well-used hammer and a packet of four-inch nails. "Here you are, Zanko. Don't take too long. We're due to open for business in one hour."

Zanko grinned even wider. "I only need one minute."

Hayden blinked at the truck driver. "You know what this is all about?"

"Well, some of it, I guess. I met those three, your first victims." He said the last word in a whisper, as if scared it might spell out his own doom. "We ran into each other one night, all complete strangers, in a bar at the Desert Palms. It were one of those once in a lifetime connections, ya know? Total strangers meet and bond and have the night of their lives. Done some good nights in my life, guys, but nothin' like that 'un."

"What happened?" Kinimaka asked.

Stevens stared into space, thinking back. "Y'know. Nothin'. Nothin' bad anyways. It were all about the conversation, the jokin' around, the beer. The stories. We didn't barely leave the bar."

Hayden considered it for a while, then turned to Lauren. "Why don't you tell us your story? Maybe we'll get a link."

Lauren brushed her hair back. "Well, sure. The agency booked the gig, if you know what I mean. We don't do names, except stage names. For this I was Nightshade, a kind of dominatrix."

No one spoke. Lauren hurried on. "There were two clients. Not unusual. I was treated well and driven home the next day. The only remarkable event was that I was treated with complete respect by both men and nothing sleazy happened."

"Nothing sleazy?" Ben sputtered. "You just said you were a dom—"

"That's business." Lauren interjected. "It's expected. But there are rules that should be followed. Safe words. Guide lines as to procedure, tolerance and, frankly, when to stop. Usually. . ." She sighed. "They want to take it further than the parameters allow. They want nasty things which I ain't about to go into. They push for more and it can get ugly. *That's* sleaze."

Hayden glanced at the secret video camera that had been installed in the conference room high up in a corner. She knew Gates was watching from his office on the Hill. His interest in Lauren Fox was a little odd to say the least.

Hurriedly, she quelled those thoughts. "Tell us more about the two men?"

"Nothing out of the ordinary. Both rich. One an American, the other Chinese, I think. The American was tall, well-built. The Chinese guy short and wide. One time—" She half-laughed. "As our session became more in-depth, another Chinese guy barged into the room and asked a question. It sounded like a request, you know? When the first guy answered—totally breaking character—the second saluted and rushed away."

"Wait." Dahl held up a hand. "When you say Chinese. Could he have been Korean?"

Lauren made a face. "I guess."

Hayden caught Ben's eye. "Bring up a list of prominent Korean officials."

"Oh God." Stevens suddenly began muttering. "Oh dear God. That's it."

Kinimaka glanced toward Hayden before addressing the truck driver. "That's *what?*"

"It were earlier that night. Some kid told us 'bout a free private dining room. Hotel normally charges a bundle for 'em. We was drunk and happy enough even by then to think it a good idea. So we went looking." Stevens sniffed. "Didn't think nothin' of it at the time. We barged into this room—a well-dressed American and a chinaman—or mebbe Korean. The Korean was wearing a jacket full of medals. Looked pretty official like, I dunno, an officer maybe? They seemed shocked when we rushed in. A few bodyguards herded us out like goats. We laughed about it, then went back to the bar, giving up on the idea of the private room. Oh crap. Is that it?"

Ben turned his laptop around, the screen partially filled by a man's face. "That him?"

"I'm pretty sure that's the Korean dude. Yeah."

Lauren stared. "Yes. That's him. Is he important?"

"General Kwang Yong, of the Korean People's Army, is leader of the Special Operations Force. The KPA consists of five branches, with this being the most obscure. Naturally."

"What's he doing in the U.S.?"

"Well," Dahl said, "he's the leader of an important branch of the largest military organization on earth. Take a bloody guess."

Drake watched as Zanko waved one of the dull, galvanized nails before his eyes.

"Hold still, Mr. Drake. The first nail? It will only tickle."

The point dug into Drake's palm. Zanko fumbled with the hammer, his outsize, fleshy hand too big to maneuver it quickly and hang onto Drake at the same time. "Vladimir!" he cried. "*Bystro!*"

Zanko nodded at Drake. "Just be moment, my friend. Did you know. . .?" His voice took on a matter-of-fact tone. "That I once did smother a man to death using my armpits?"

He twisted his body so one was revealed. Drake almost gagged at the sight of thick locks of matted hair, glistening with sweat and hanging from his arm like a gelled-up sheepdog.

Drake felt the pain of the nail being placed in the center of his palm. Vladimir pulled back the hammer. Romero rose behind him, shaking his head. The marine stared blankly, looking confused.

But his presence distracted Zanko. Vladimir struck with the hammer. Drake shifted his hand aside as Zanko looked to the side, conscious of the enemy at his back. As the hammer hit Zanko's smallest finger, Drake struck like a snake, grabbing its handle and twisting away, turning, and in one complete move buried the claw in Vladimir's shoulder.

The man screamed. Zanko grunted. Romero's eyes began to clear. Drake might be a battler, but he knew a bad fight when he was in the middle of one.

"Go!" He swore when Romero, still slightly befuddled, ran in the direction of the back office, toward even more trouble. Using every ounce of energy, he leapt free of the corner and put a precious few feet between himself and Zanko. The mountainous Russian roared at his heels.

Drake ran hard for the office door and then suddenly stopped, flinging himself to the side. Zanko, fast but still unable to stop his freight train body fast enough, hit the frame like an elephant hitting a brick wall. The entire cabin shuddered, its far end disturbed so much it fell entirely off its brick supports, crashing to the ground and upending everyone in the office.

Romero shouted. "Window!" Drake paused though, just for a second. A sixth sense told him a minute spared here might save them hours or even days of trouble later. He looked at the walls, really looked at them, trying to digest and divine some kind of meaning.

A more recent map showed Iraq and its borders, its roads and towns. An older one showed ancient Babylon, mapped out by historians and experts, with several areas highlighted. Drake could make out the words *"gate,"* and *"swords"*, with the rest being obscured by a garish Post-it note covered in Russian scribble. A place called the *Ishtar Gate* was circled.

Still another picture was an ancient representation of something called *The Tower of Babel*, an old legend Drake was barely aware of. Far back in time, didn't the people and the priests try to construct a tower of stone high enough to reach God?

Romero's shouting and crashing tore his attention away. Zanko was already picking himself up off the floor, but his body was currently blocking the office door. The old Russian boss just knelt among his men, fixing Drake with an emotionless stare that made the Englishman shiver.

Such detachment in this situation was unreal.

Then Romero smashed the window and Drake dived out after him, bullets strafing their heels.

"So, the five of you stumbled across a Korean general on U.S. soil. The man never appeared dressed as a soldier to you, Lauren, giving you no reason to question him. You shouldn't have mattered. That changed after Stevens and the other victims saw him. A decision must have later been taken to tie up all loose ends." Hayden glanced from eye to eye. "Sound about right?"

"It most certainly does." Dahl clicked his fingers. "But who's the American?"

"His host." Hayden turned briefly to the hidden eye. "An influential man, I presume."

The conference phone rang immediately. Hayden answered and Gates spoke. "Time is of the essence, Jaye. Get them to make a photo fit of this guy. If the Koreans are here on U.S. soil trying to make a deal. . ."

Hayden flashed back to Dai Hibiki's original message. "This could be all about arms, sir. Futuristic weapons."

"It usually is, Jaye. It usually is." Gates signed off, sounding weary. Hayden tapped the desk. "Lauren. Stevens. We need a picture of that American and we need it last week. Ben will help you with the photo fit. The rest of you—the Korean general clearly gives us a link to the island, but what about the strange assassins? They're American—no doubt. And how does it fit in with Drake's kidnapping ring? If it is somehow tied to the Koreans then why draw attention to themselves?"

"The deal on the table," Kinimaka offered. "Might be humongous."

"Then God help us."

Outside, Romero threaded between big packs of timber. Hundreds of cubes of the stuff sat in the Russian yard, waiting to be picked over and sold, and the marine used the bulky, piled-high pallets as cover. Drake followed a step behind. Bullets sent wood chips flying in all directions; sharp splinters littered the ground.

"Go left!" Drake cried.

Romero ducked down an aisle, heading around the back of the big office now and toward their car. The shooting had momentarily stopped as men piled out of the broken window behind them. Romero jumped through the open car door without touching the sides. Drake looked up to see Vladimir, hammer still hanging from his shoulder, pushing out of the cabin door.

Just got time. . .

Drake leapt over the car hood, sliding off the other side and landing right in front of Vladimir. The Russian looked pained and surprised. "Off to the doc were you?" Drake took hold of the man's jacket and threw him against the car. Vladimir hit the hard metal wing with a metallic *clunk* and screamed. The hammer wavered as blood poured from the wound.

Romero revved the car's engine.

"Hold yer friggin' horses."

Vladimir groaned. Drake punched him in the nose. "I don't give a shit about this place." The Englishman hissed. "Seriously. I have no interest in you or God-Zanko or your creepy bloody boss. But give me the address in Frankfurt. Give it to me now. And I'll let you live."

Vladimir looked momentarily confused. "The traffickers? Your business is with them?"

"Just them." Drake sounded convincing even to himself. "Be quick. I still have time to take your Russki head off with that hammer, Vlad."

"That is small time for us. We don't need that anymore."

"Then give me the address."

Vladimir quickly reeled off an address that sounded German. Drake lingered another moment as Romero started to reverse the car.

"If you're lying to me. . ."

"Why would I lie?" Vladimir shrugged, making the hammer bob up and down. "As you say—you have no interest in us."

Drake ran for it. Men wearing leather jackets and lethal-looking frowns were pouring out of the timber aisles. Drake dived headlong into the car as Romero forced it into a yawing one-eighty-degree turn. The second Drake's head hit the dashboard Romero slammed the accelerator through the floorboard. Tires squealed and the smell of burned rubber stung the air. Sparks flew from the bodywork as bullets bounced off the chassis. One of the wing mirrors exploded. Drake fell back into the passenger seat.

"Nice work."

"You too."

The car shot out of the timber yard, slewing dangerously as it joined the main road. "Close one." Romero ventured.

Drake shrugged. "Could've been worse. We could've both been smothered by that monster's armpits."

Romero made a gagging noise.

Drake reached for a cellphone. "You know something? The CIA surely knew that timber yard was a major HQ. And they said nothing."

"Welcome to the CIA. If they feel overlooked or ordered around, they ain't gonna help you, dude. Crisis or not."

"Hayden was CIA."

"Nah. Not fully. Hayden Jaye was the CIA liaison to the Secretary of Defense. Different beast."

"We'll need to deal with that later." Drake tapped out a number. "But for now—I wonder how Alicia's doing with that gang of bikers."

CHAPTER THIRTY-ONE

Shaun Kingston had heard and seen enough. "Your 'sleepers' failed." He spoke softly, without the slightest hint of a threat, but still his words were menacing. "Your island has been attacked. It could be compromised. Even now, they don't know if the enemy have vacated, are dead or are in hiding. This whole operation could be falling apart, General."

Kwang Yong shrugged. "Or your propaganda is just that, Mr. Kingston. I have heard nothing so dreadful. The victory will still be ours. The Republic does not fail."

"It'll fail if you don't get my weapons," Kingston shot back before he could stop himself. *Goddamn.* Where was his usual reserve? *Blown to hell*, he thought. Along with all his dreams of unlimited wealth. But maybe not yet. And he couldn't exactly suggest to the general that his own men were probably keeping schtum because of the time honored 'shoot the messenger' syndrome.

"You would do well not to threaten me, Mr. Kingston. We Koreans do not respond well to threat."

Kingston nodded, accepting the rebuke. "Window's short," he said. "But we still have a play here." For once, he was glad he'd included his bodyguards in this conversation and in particular his primary muscle—a man called Germaine. Tall, thin, built like a knife and just as sharp and deadly, he was a born killer. Easy to underestimate and almost impossible to hurt, he prided himself on always being that one lethal step ahead of his enemy.

Now Germaine stood at his side, two other bodyguards by the high set of windows at his back. They faced the seated Kwang Yong and his own assembly of personal guardians. To Kingston it felt like a stand-off.

"A play?" The Korean chewed on the phrase as if it had been delivered hardboiled. "What do you mean?"

"A balls-out finale. Anything goes. We have a good team in place—all ex-military who are willing to kill. We have to accept that since our spotters saw the hooker and that damn truck driver being taken into this new HQ, the team within are well on their way to figuring this whole thing out. Don't you think?"

"We do have more sleepers." Kwang Wong grinned. "It is just the matter of a phone call."

"I know you enjoy destroying these people's lives with a mere sentence, General, but please…" Kingston faltered. "Things have moved on."

"We could bring an army of sleepers. An army of brothers."

Kingston considered that for a moment. He hadn't realized there were so many. An army might be useful one day. "Not now," he said. "But be ready."

"Sir." Germaine spoke at his side. The whip-thin man wasn't one to request attention unless action needed to be taken, so Kingston instantly acknowledged him. "Yes?"

"Two of them just left the HQ. The woman, Jaye, and her CIA partner. The Hawaiian."

It was the first enemy movement since the truck driver had arrived hours ago.

"Shit."

"Actually that's perfect, sir. Divide and conquer."

Kingston had never been able to think like a killer. He envied Germaine sometimes. "Alright. Time to put our affairs in order. General, this is my game now." He turned to Germaine once more. "Give the go ahead. Take every last one of the bastards out and destroy everything."

CHAPTER THIRTY-TWO

Hayden felt a sense of excitement as she and Kinimaka left Washington alone. It wasn't just the investigation or the new sense of purpose, or even the recent breakthrough—it was being with Kinimaka.

Alone.

Odd, in a way. They'd worked together for years, mostly alone. But now it felt different. Now it *was* different.

"Wonder if there's a Hard Rock in Atlantic City."

Hayden had forgotten about his fetish for collecting shot glasses. "You mean you don't know?"

"Actually I do. It's on the boardwalk."

"Not on our route, Mano."

Hayden felt a twinge as she shifted in her seat. The knife wounds were still far from fully healed. Her discomfort made Kinimaka press a hand to his own ribs.

"Still sore?"

"My mother sent me a traditional remedy. *Lau Lapauu,* she said. Some kind of healing herb, compounded with traditional remedies."

Hayden laughed, knowing what was coming. "Still sore, then."

"For sure."

"At least she cares." Hayden thought back to her childhood days when her father had always been absent. The job always came first for him. Maybe that was why he'd been so good.

The skies darkened into early evening. They continued the small talk for a few more miles and then Kinimaka finally manned up.

"You and Ben are finished then?"

"Yeah, he's. . .young."

"He says his band want him back."

It was the first Hayden had heard. "The Wall of Sleep? I thought they had a new lead singer."

Kinimaka shrugged as he merged onto I-395 North. "Point is. . .you're single."

"Well, for now." Hayden hid a grin by staring out the window. "I've had to field a few calls. You know how it is."

"Sure I do. Those hula girls never leave me alone."

Hayden snatched a quick glimpse out of the corner of her eyes, but couldn't tell if the big man was teasing her. Before either of them could say another word, her cell rang and Ben Blake came between them.

"Hi. We've checked out the hotel. I managed to hack into its database. The most expensive rooms were registered to 'VIP guests' on Thursday, January, 10th. No names. Our victims were all registered there. The VIPs took an entire wing, most likely for bodyguards and stuff."

"Thanks, Ben." Hayden sounded unhappy. "Listen. You don't need to hack anything anymore. We're official now."

Ben clicked his tongue. "Then why the hell do you need me?"

The line went dead. Hayden turned to Kinimaka. "Sorry."

"You don't need to apologize for him. It's not—"

The tones of her cell blasted out again, a standard ringtone to help formalize their new agency. "Yes?"

"Karin here. What Ben forgot to tell you was that Drake just rang. He hit the Russians, got nothing from them but bruises and an address in Frankfurt. He's en route there now." Karin paused, breathing heavily.

"What is it?" Hayden sensed more and braced herself.

"Something he said sounded whacko. He told me to start researching the ancient city of Babylon and the Tower of Babel. He wondered if there might be some kind of link to the tombs of the gods."

"He asked you to do that *now?*"

"Well. Not exactly. He said *if I get chance.*"

Hayden opened her mouth, but Kinimaka's low growl silenced her. "We're being followed."

Hayden didn't move. "How many?"

"At least two. Hard to say."

"Karin. Track our position and call out the local PD. Looks like we got some company."

"Consider it done. I'll stay on the line."

Hayden opened the glove box, took out two fully loaded Glocks and filled her pockets with extra ammo. Quickly, she tied back her hair. She'd purposely let it hang loose for Mano's benefit.

"Cops are on their way."

Kinimaka's eyes were fixed firmly to the rearview. "This ain't gonna wait, boss."

Hayden felt the jolt as a vehicle rammed them from behind. Kinimaka wrenched at the wheel to keep them straight, but even then, their car slewed across two lanes.

"There." Hayden pointed out the upcoming off-ramp and, below it, a row of flashing   lights.   "Go!"
Kinimaka twisted the wheel again, this time toward the interstate's exit. The chase vehicles followed suit. By the time they realized Kinimaka's intentions, he was already among the approaching cop cars.

Chaos ensued. Kinimaka jerked the wheel and came around. A black SUV clipped their wing, coming to an abrupt halt. Another SUV squealed to a halt behind it. And there, beneath the stark light offered by the high off-ramp lights and swinging traffic lights, men and cops piled out of their vehicles, armed to the teeth.

Cops ducked down behind their doors and tires. Men dressed all in black and wearing full face masks leapt over obstructions, advancing with terrible force, loosing bullets in a non-stop, deadly wave. Hayden rolled out of her door as their windshield cracked and disintegrated. She hit the ground a second before Kinimaka, the big Hawaiian almost breaking his back as he twisted in an effort not to land on top of her.

With no time for thought, Hayden scrambled behind the big rear tire. The cop cars to their left were getting shredded, ragged holes being torn through hard metal and glass, safe havens being demolished. The cops hadn't even dared raise their heads yet. The fury of the onslaught was stunning, razing all hope from the entire area.

"How many?" Hayden shouted above the blitz.

"Ten. At least. All armed." Kinimaka bellowed back.

Hayden heard Karin's voice over the car's Bluetooth cell system, calling in air support. *Good move.*

Hayden squeezed herself into as tiny a target as she could as bullets even began to fizz off the road beneath the car, skimming like rocks thrown at still waters. "We have to do something. We're gettin' killed here!" Kinimaka grunted. Without ceremony, he laid his gun down and tackled a nearby road sign, hitting it hard and upending its thick, metal pole and rough concrete base. Hayden gawped. Kinimaka hefted the sturdy sign and literally *threw it* over the roof of the car straight among the ranks of the approaching enemy.

"What the fuck, Mano?"

The Hawaiian shrugged. "You called it, not me."

The gunfire wound down for a moment, replaced by the gruff cries of shocked and wounded men. Hayden risked a peek through the nearest shattered window. Scenes of disarray met her eyes. The signpost had flown true, actually hitting the enemy soldiers and knocking some of them to the ground. The shock of the moment had destroyed the focus of the others. Maybe their leader had been hit.

"Go."

She motioned furiously and brought her gun up. At the same time, a dozen cops imitated her. The sound of police issues and Glocks barked at the night, not as imposing as the machine-gun fire, but just as deadly. The enemy line crumbled, men falling to their knees, pin wheeling or scrambling for cover.

Hayden slipped around the rear of the car, Kinimaka in her wake. The full face masks and body suits of the enemy gave no indication as to their identities. Hopefully, if they left someone behind, that might. But as Hayden pressed forward, squeezing her Glock and maintaining a deadly accuracy, the retreating force scooped up their injured and dead and laid down a hail of covering fire.

Hayden hit the dirt again. No matter how much she wanted to know who she was dealing with, she couldn't disrespect the kind of firepower these guys had brought to the fray. Someone sure as hell wanted both Kinimaka and her dead. Some of the cops tried to match hardware with the enemy. Bullets clanked and sparked and fizzed off cars, Kevlar and signposts.

The Hawaiian hunkered down beside her. "There they go. What now?"

"We check out that friggin' hotel, and quick." Hayden told him. "And warn the guys back at HQ. If these soldiers came after us, they might just try to hit our base next."

Kinimaka grunted. "Bad luck for them if they do. The caliber of people back there—"

Then the radio squawked. It was Karin's voice. "Hey, Dahl. Komodo? You seein' this? I can't believe the base is under attack."

Hayden dove back into the car, amazed that the Bluetooth system still worked and offering up a prayer. "Don't fuck about!" she cried. "These bastards are fully loaded, believe me. Just kill 'em all!"

CHAPTER THIRTY-THREE

Matt Drake hadn't seen Alicia for some time, but the moment when they reunited in Germany contained no more emotion than two workmates meeting at a coffee shop, a bit of backslapping, a few innuendos about Mai, and many leading questions. Drake did his best to field them all. Alicia did spare a handshake for Romero and the look in her eyes spoke volumes for how much she appreciated him helping keep Drake and Mai alive.

"Trouble with this team," she told him privately, "is it gets under your skin. You don't wanna let go. Keeps me awake at bloody night."

"One day," Romero told her, "I hope to meet the rest of your team."

"Can't see why." Alicia turned away. "They're a bunch of boring bastards."

Drake surveyed the area. Alicia had organized the meeting. It was an empty airfield situated about two miles out of Frankfurt. Most of the place was overgrown, brown grass and barren trees were whipped by a stiff wind out of the east. A broken down hangar stood like an imposing old man, barren and desolate against the bloody dawn. A weed-strewn, pitted runway was the only road out.

"Forget something?" Drake turned to Alicia.

But the Englishwoman was already texting. Drake shook his head. "Next thing you'll be a Facebook celebrity."

"Always been a social media flirt." She smiled a little. "Now I'm just a social whore."

Romero turned to Drake. "Did she mean to miss out the word *media* at the end there?"

"Believe me, mate, *nothing* Alicia does or says is by accident."

Then the roar of many engines starting up made a mockery of the quiet morning. Drake watched as a stream of big bikes poured out of the hangar's open doors. Like a gleaming metal torrent, it twisted and snaked around until it came alongside them. Then, as one, every engine shut off, leaving nothing but a tremendous, overwhelming silence.

Alicia stepped up to the lead biker, leaned over and placed an arm around his big shoulders. "Meet Lomas. My newest friend."

Drake nodded. "We've met before."

"The big guy there's called Tiny. That's JPS. Fat Bob. Knuckler." Alicia pointed the first few ranks of bikers out with a grin. "The lady there's called Whipper. Oh, and this is Dirty Sarah."

Drake didn't know where to start. He knew enough about bikers to know how they got their nicknames. Generally it referred to a person's attitude or character, sometimes to their physical appearance. So a big guy became Tiny. A fastidiously clean woman became Dirty Sarah.

But Whipper?

"Thanks for helping out," he managed, feeling a little bit spotlighted before the two dozen bikes and riders.

Lomas, their leader, removed his sunglasses, fixing Drake with bright, blue eyes. Drake saw a hardness there that had nothing to do with life on the road. "Gig pays well," he said in a British accent. "Or so I'm promised."

Alicia whispered something in his ear. The biker tried hard not to smile. Romero leaned in. "I'd love to know what she's saying. Even the guy's beard's twitching."

Drake made a warning face. "Cos I like you, I'll say this just once. My advice—stay clear of Alicia Myles. I'd tell the bikers the same thing but we need their help."

Drake turned to the assembled men and women. "We're talking about taking down a criminal headquarters. A human trafficking ring. If it's anything like the last one Romero and I just saw in Russia, it could get messy." Nobody moved a muscle as he looked them over. "Just so you know what you're letting yourselves in for."

Alicia came over, unzipping her jacket and pulling out a sheaf of papers. "Lomas and Tiny printed off some Google maps." She winked. "We've already planned the attack. Question is, Drake, you ready to saddle up with the Slayers?"

Drake trusted her skill and training without question. "So long as I don't have to join the bloody gang. The name's not the most original I ever heard."

Alicia shrugged. "Your choice. It's actually short for Bitchin' Motherfuckin' Hellslayers. But they couldn't fit the whole thing on their business cards." She slowly climbed astride Lomas's Ducatti Monster. "Life's a twat, sometimes."

Drake and Romero followed the biker pack as they came through the hills and down into the streets of Frankfurt. Drake, in the passenger seat, checked out the weapons Lomas and his gang had brought for them, grunting a sigh of approval as they neared their target area. Quickly, he tried calling the Washington HQ, but the call failed. Perhaps the lines were down at their end.

The address proved to be one of the many buildings and warehouses that littered the train yard and container yards around Frankfurt's railway station. He wondered briefly if these people somehow manipulated space on various trains, but then the procession of Moto Guzzi's and Ducatti's and Harley's pulled up, its riders reluctantly climbing off their mounts, most already looking eager to get back on. For a biker, life was about the journey and the ride, everything in between was mere chaff and static.

Alicia strode up to the car. "Ya think anyone noticed us?"

Romero laughed. Drake was used to her and rolled his eyes. "Don't encourage her."

Lomas and his second-in-charge, Tiny, strode up, leathers creaking. "One thing you can be sure of. . .getaway's gonna be right pretty."

Drake felt a stab of guilt. "Seriously, if you have good friends or loved ones here, you might wanna consider giving them a pass. At the very least we're going to get in a firefight. The Russians might have warned them we were coming. I can't guarantee everyone's safety here, and I won't promise to be able to save them if they get in any major trouble."

"Message understood, SAS." Lomas grunted, sharp eyes again betraying the scruffy, disheveled-looking exterior. "We know the risks."

"And I ain't SAS," Drake mumbled, though for some reason he flashed back to Alyson and her hard-spoken certainties that he would never be anything other than a soldier.

"Bah. You guys are like our gangs. Once a brother always a brother. No mind. . ." Lomas held out a hand. "Let's go fuck up some kidnapper's day."

Drake shook it. The leaders threaded back through the assembled gang and walked right up to the open gates of the business, ignoring the amazed stares of a few passersby. Drake stopped by the gates. The front yard was small, just an acre of bare concrete for parking cars and dominated by a large Portakabin. He glimpsed the top of a gantry crane rising above the Portakabin and guessed the rear yard was where the bulk of the business lay.

"Balls out?" Alicia suggested.

Drake shook his head as Romero choked, clearly not understanding the phrase. "It's still not entirely clear we have the right address. There's not even a sign in the yard stating their alleged business." He eyed Lomas. "You two up for a stroll?"

A minute later Lomas and Alicia wandered into the empty yard. Together they walked boldly up to the cabin door, leaning on each other to help hide weapons and create an innocent appearance.

Alicia reached out to turn the handle, then stopped suddenly. With a quick body shunt, she hit the deck, pulling Lomas with her in an awkward heap. "It's *wired!*" There was a moment of expectation and then a relative anti-climax as a small blast sent the door flying outward.

Problem solved, Drake thought. He signaled the charge. The ex-SAS man, the marine, and twenty-two leather-jacket-and-blue-jean-wearing bikers tore across the parking lot, pulling weapons from every pocket, pouch and waistband as they ran. Following a quick signal, they split into two streams, going left and right down the side of the cabin.

"Assholes must be waiting in back," Romero said as Alicia and Lomas joined them.

No one responded. They all pealed around the side, ready now. Drake got a glimpse of railroad tracks, big containers and a few small cranes, and then the entire vista opened up into an enormous yard. Myriad train tracks and a few old carriages dominated the scene, but the huge blue gantry crane to the right and the steel girders stacked below drew the eye. Drake immediately saw movement on the gantry walkway and in between the girders and yelled a warning.

But it was the man standing ahead with legs apart and aiming an RPG in their direction who really bothered him.

The weapon clicked, and the missile took flight with a supercharged hiss. Drake flung himself headlong, firing as he scraped along the ground to make sure the man didn't let loose any more rockets. The RPG went high, slamming into the surrounding wall and exploding. The only damage to the biker gang came from bricks landing on their hastily covered shoulders and heads.

"Cover me!"

Alicia scrambled across the ground, spying the discarded rocket launcher and a spare shell. Drake immediately opened fire on the girders, seeing his bullets spark and clang off the rusted metal. He bought Alicia half a minute, which was all she needed to load, aim and fire the weapon.

The rocket hit hard, exploding and smearing fire all across the face of the iron. Big girders caromed left and right, stacks toppled over, landing on top of those sheltering behind and below. The screaming began.

Drake slipped behind a container, running its length, Romero and several others at his back. Near the far end, he got a good view of the gantry crane and spotted a man in a suit running up its integral ladder.

He raised an eyebrow. "That's strange."

Romero peered around him. "Ya know what? I bet the Russkies told 'em there'd be just the two of us. They're not expecting a mini-army. Explains the small door charge and the man with the RPG. Rush job."

"Kudos to Mother Russia." Drake sprinted forward, firing at anything that moved. "Clear the yard, but leave me some alive!"

He raced up the metal steps two at a time, at first surprised by the instability of the crane structure, but then ignoring it. The suit climbed ahead of him, overweight and puffing. Drake caught up rapidly just as the man reached the top.

"Sit down." A club over the head with the rifle butt made the man do just that. Drake viewed the length of the gantry, saw half a dozen kidnappers sitting among the struts and aiming guns at his friends below. The height momentarily disoriented him, but then his training took over. He peppered the platform with bullets. Kidnappers yelped in surprise, most losing their grip and tumbling to the yard below. Others fell dead. Only one stood defiantly, aiming his weapon back at Drake.

"I got your boss." Drake rolled his eyes in the direction of the groans. "Give it up, pal."

The man shrugged, ponytail falling across one shoulder. "He's not *the* boss."

Drake advanced across the metal bridge, ignoring the slight sway of the structure, and the noise of the creaking, swinging crane. The two men stared down the V of their sights at each other.

"Come to think of it," ponytail said, "I didn't like the bastard anyway."

He squeezed the trigger. But Drake was ready. With anticipation born of superhuman ability, he threw himself off the gantry just as the kidnapper pulled the trigger.

Alicia fired from below, winging the guy and making him fall to his knees, gun clattering.

Drake fell through space. The jaws of the crane came up quick. He let go of his weapon, reached out and grasped the cold steel as his body rushed by. For a second his hands gripped, arresting his fall, but then with the smooth surface offering no purchase his fingers simply slipped away and he continued his fall.

Straight down to the hard concrete.

With milliseconds to prepare, he curled his body, realizing his back was about to take the brunt of the fall. The distance from the crane to the ground wasn't that far but. . .

. . .then he hit.

Alicia saw him coming. Lomas, Tiny and Dirty Sarah were pounding up the gantry steps toward the kidnappers, so she fixed her attention on the falling man. When he landed, she held her arms out and slipped her body under his, letting the impact be absorbed by the both of them.

It still hurt like a mother.

Drake groaned against her chest. After a moment, Alicia realized she wasn't badly hurt and neither was he.

"Fucksake, Drake," she whispered. "You should know by now. There's easier ways to get on top of me."

Drake was well enough to chuckle into her breasts. "Yeah. But I was all out of Nutella."

As always, time was against them. The area around the girders had proved to be the main hiding place for the kidnapping gang's hierarchy. When the RPG destroyed it, most of the men had died, but a few wounded and dying still lay crying in the dirt.

Drake found no compassion in his heart. Whatever small consideration for enemies had existed inside him had been cleaved away the day Kennedy Moore died. Now, he threw one wounded man against the other and ignored their pleas and the aching of his own bruised bones.

"I know you kidnap Europeans and Americans," he said. "Adults. Some homeless, some down-and-outs. If I find out you kidnap kids, I'll bring a fucking army down on you and paint the earth with your blood and crushed bones. Do you understand me?"

The men lying before him blinked. Before this, these men had been tough, brutal and dangerous. Now all they could feel was their torn and crushed flesh. All they could see was their own slaughter. The men nodded. One of the two suits they had rounded up wailed; the other sat with blood pumping from his thigh, trying to maintain a ruthless expression on his face.

"Alright. I want to know all about this kidnap operation. The entire chain. Where the orders come from. Your feeding grounds. The whole lot." He checked his watch. "Oh, and I want it in the next four minutes."

He glanced up at Lomas. "Prep the bikes. We'll be leaving in six."

CHAPTER THIRTY-FOUR

Dahl flung his body headlong down the passageway that led to the arms room as armed gunmen burst through the front door. The others were ahead of him. He'd sent them there a few minutes ago and then waited to arm a few "surprises."

Bullets slammed into the new plaster-coated walls around him. Boot heels pounded the freshly laid floorboards. Doors were smashed in. At this rate, their new HQ was soon going to become their old HQ.

Dahl rolled to his feet. Komodo passed him a prepped weapon. "We have about four seconds," he said. "Get your damn vests on" His eyes bore into Ben and Karin especially. When his eyes fell on Lauren Fox and Mike Stevens, the truck driver, he sighed. "Wrong place, wrong time, people. Sorry."

Then he turned, fell to one knee, swiveled and fired as the first of the enemy came to the corner. His bullet sent the man reeling backward. Blood sprayed the walls by his side. He dove forward. The next man tripped right over his sliding body. Komodo finished him off with a headshot, aware that even civilians wore vests these days. Dahl slid his body around on the polished floor, hitting the far wall with his legs and then pushing off hard. . .

. . .coming back onto one knee, gun nestled comfortably on his right shoulder, firing with care and precision.

Bullets thumped through walls all around him. One even nicked his vest, but his aim didn't waver. He was a big man, an expert soldier trying to balance his courage with skill, and set forth making a mess of the approaching enemy team.

The black-clad enemy force collapsed in the narrow hallway, men in front falling and tripping men behind. Some were compelled to clamber over their dying colleagues. But at last, one of the stragglers took a chance and hurled his body straight at the Swede. Both men grappled and smashed through the plaster wall, making a ragged new hole into the interrogation room.

Komodo stepped up. The corridor was littered with Dahl's victims, but there were still half a dozen men struggling forward. Komodo let them come, destroying the first's face with a devastating elbow, twisting the second around in a headlock and breaking his neck, at the same time taking a round in the vest that jolted him, but only succeeded in putting extra fire and venom into his actions.

Then, the unexpected happened. The plaster and timber wall that separated the arms room from the main OC was kicked in. A merc crashed through, black armor covered in white powder and wood shavings, and was now behind Komodo, among the civilians.

Ben scrambled back on his hands, face suddenly a mask of terror. The kid was lost, reliving something dreadful. But not this moment. He was back at the third tomb with the blood of the dying soldier on his hands, traumatized and unable to act.

It was Lauren Fox who stepped forward, closely followed by Karin as she saw the merc's weapon swiveling toward Komodo. Lauren grabbed the arm that held the gun, expecting the man to jerk the weapon toward her. She released her hold when he did, letting his momentum swing the barrel harmlessly past and jabbed at his throat with stiffened fingers.

He gurgled and staggered, but the man was no pushover. Luckily, Lauren didn't expect him to be. She already had a follow up planned. A swift knee to the groin. But her attack struck something hard and strangely rubbery.

Shit, she thought. If that's his balls, he's a freakin' alien.

"They protect those." Karin stepped past. "But not from this." Pressing her body against him, she fired three swift shots with a handgun pulled from the arms cache. The merc went limp, slipping to the floor.

Lauren turned around. "Give me one."

Komodo twisted, taking the weight of a merc who'd launched himself at the ex-Delta man. With a shrug of his muscled shoulders, he sent that man on his way right into the external wall this time—the one made of bricks and blocks and solid mortar. The crunch was sickening. The man bounced back, still twitching.

Dahl reappeared through the ragged gap into the interrogation room. Hanging shards of plaster collapsed all around him. He peered up the corridor.

"Well. That's that sorted," he said matter-of-factly. "Anyone fancy the cinema next? I hear the new *Die Hard*'s previewing."

Komodo's eyes were only for Karin. He pulled her in a tight embrace. It was Lauren who stepped over to Ben.

"Hey, kid. It's over. It's done."

Ben's eyes took on a little focus. For a second his jaw worked but no sound came out. "He. . . he died in my arms. I have. . . his blood on my hands. Right here." And he held both hands out, palms up, shaking like a man with epilepsy.

Lauren back away. "Kid, I ain't no shrink. But I'll tell ya this—you're in the wrong damn business if you can't handle a freakin' gunfight."

Karin pushed her way past. "He's been through a lot," she whispered. "He'll be okay."

Dahl fixed Komodo with a stare. "You know what, my friend? They're still building the escape route out of here. Not finished. There's only one way out."

Komodo started picking his way through the tangle of arms and legs and pools of blood. Dahl followed, motioning for the others to follow but at a distance. Karin and Stevens had to drag Ben up from the floor to get his legs moving. The haunted look still sat like frozen death in his eyes.

As he walked, Dahl constantly patted the pockets of his dead enemies. He didn't expect to find wallets, IDs or any other kind of credentials and wasn't disappointed. He called Hayden on his cell.

"We're okay," he said in answer to her quick question. "You?"

He listened as she related her own experience. "Alright. Well, we need a safe house now, Hay. You got one lying around anywhere?"

Her answer surprised him, but shouldn't have. Hayden Jaye was among the top half dozen operatives he'd ever worked with.

They passed the OC, checking the space carefully for any snipers or stragglers, but the enemy had either given up or were all dead. Dahl found it difficult to believe they'd seen the last of them. There was only one reason an enemy force would be sent against a new government facility.

Someone with power, money, and a stomach full of guilt was getting scared. The game was now well and truly on. This could only be their endgame.

Outside, the traffic flowed and the day moved past as if nothing had happened. Dahl stopped abruptly when he found Sarah Moxley lying unconscious or dead on the grass. Two other bloody bodies lay next to her along with a shattered camera and discarded rucksack.

Komodo moved ahead to fetch the vehicles. Dahl dropped to his knees. Sirens wailed as they approached the HQ. The woman's eyes began to flutter.

"You okay, miss?" Dahl patted her gently.

The woman glared up at him. "I missed it, didn't I? Three weeks!" She sputtered. "Three Goddamn weeks I've been camped out here and I friggin' missed it."

Dahl held her as she struggled to sit up. "I wouldn't do that yet—"

But she had already seen them. "No. Are they. . .? Oh no."

"I'm sorry." Dahl pulled her close as the sobs wracked her body. For now, there was only grief, but soon would come the terrible guilt.

But it was all random, all chance. Happened all the time. The merc who dealt with her had simply smashed her head with a rifle butt instead of slitting her throat with a knife. The rhyme and reason of it never even entered the equation.

An ambulance pulled up, followed by a phalanx of cop cars. Komodo sorted the classifications and red tape out whilst Dahl held Sarah Moxley, Karin held Ben, and another day of maneuvering and intrigue began in Washington.

CHAPTER THIRTY-FIVE

Mai Kitano had been alone with Smyth on the Korean island for over four days. She came up with the phrase "alone with Smyth" and smiled to herself, relishing something for the first time since Drake left. It was bad enough being left alone with the irascible marine, but being alone after her recent time with Drake, and with the nuisance of being hunted all over the island, elevated the problem to "thorny."

In truth, avoiding the Korean patrols wasn't a hardship for either of them. They were both trained well beyond the level of their hunters and found no trouble in leaving no signs of their passing. The island was big enough to accommodate all of them.

Now, however, Mai had decided enough was enough. They had gotten nowhere in four days of waffling with Dai Hibiki and it was time to confront and take down this entire operation.

"Just you and I?" Smyth had growled.

"I'll do it myself if I have to." Mai had strode off among the trees, mind made up, already planning her route back to the lab and what she would say to Hibiki at their loosely prearranged meeting.

They could no longer sit by and wait for something to happen. It was time to act.

Now, Mai and Smyth lay on the cold, hard ground, concealed amidst a thorny tangle of brush, casting their eyes over the facility they had come to know so well. A stiff breeze whipped spray and sea salt over them like so much frosting.

"There." Mai saw Hibiki ambling over to the trees, cigarette in hand, and shuffled forward until he came into earshot. "Staying safe, *nakama?*"

"Something has happened." Hibiki took a long drag and then flicked ash at the breeze. "All hell has broken loose in the U.S. it seems. The big players are getting out."

"Right now?" Mai gave a proverbial nod to Hayden and Dahl, Alicia and Drake. It had to be them. "Then this island needs wrapping up," she said firmly. "To be handed over as one big, neat present."

"Too risky," Hibiki said, echoing Smyth's own argument.

Mai took a moment to ensure Hibiki met her eyes. "Is that the same man who helped me through the hell that was Tokyo Coscon speaking? Or his broken shadow?"

"No. It's his older, wiser self. This island's days are limited, Mai."

"Agreed. But every hour that passes means sixty minutes more agony for the captives behind you. It means another hour when we don't know what the hell is going on, when we could find out something that may help our friends. And it means the North Koreans have more time to destroy this place, wiping out all the evidence."

"To do that they'd have to sink it into the ocean—" Hibiki began, slightly scoffing, and then suddenly stopped talking. "An act well within their capabilities."

Smyth had joined them by now. "Sounds like Mai has a point."

Hibiki flicked his cigarette away as Mai and Smyth emerged from the undergrowth, weapons at the ready.

"Follow me."

Hibiki led the way inside the facility, confident that at this late hour the doctors and guards would be sleeping. Even so, he assessed every corner and corridor before he led them on and utilized every blind spot he'd exposed in the surveillance system.

At length, the three soldiers entered the main lab, Mai and Smyth for the first time. Several observations hit them at once.

The machinery was state-of-the-art, brand new, gleaming. The startling scent of sterilization fluid stung their eyes. The patients were all strapped down to their gurneys, but shuffling and twitching as if locked in some nightmare they could never escape. Unknown instruments were scattered everywhere, some on metal tables, others balanced on wheeled trolleys, some humming and others gyrating. A snaking web of rubber and plastic tubes stretched from machine to human like a horrifying snare, a dreadful trap designed by madmen and exploited by psychotic dictators.

At the far end of the lab, a large, metal wheel marked the doorway to a vault.

"Weapons room." Hibiki followed their stares. "And when I say *special* weapons, I really mean it. I've seen some of them now. The AICW? Prototype rifle? It's now called the Xm-25. A computerized multiple grenade launcher and it's not a prototype anymore. And there's a tested railgun in there, just for fun, and the blueprints to the DREAD silent weapons system." He paused, noting their lack of recognition. "We're talking one hundred and twenty thousand rounds a minute here."

Mai marched over to the nearest patient. Smyth scanned the walls. "No cameras in here?"

Hibiki just laughed at him.

Mai touched one of the tubes gently. "This is a feeding tube. These people are kept in this state for days clearly."

"Mai." Hibiki's tone made her turn immediately. "They're kept like that for *months*."

"What?"

"I know this—these patients have been put into something deeper than the deepest sleep. It's some kind of neurological trance. They call it FX37. And all the doctors who work here? They're *neuro-psychiatrists*."

Mai shook her head. "What?"

Hibiki pointed out a bank of TV screens. "See those monitors? They measure brainwaves."

"Put a lid on the damn bullshit," Smyth grouched. "Speak English for God's sake."

"Have you heard the term 'hypnotic trance' before?"

"Oh yeah. Got it done to me in Vegas one time."

Mai raised an eyebrow. "I bet that was fun for everyone."

"Well this is more like a massively enhanced, technically brilliant version of that," Hibiki said. "And it is being put to a terrible use. These people. . .once they're wakened and rehabilitated. . .they will never find their old selves again. Only the thing they have been brainwashed to believe they are."

"You're saying captives are being brought to this island, brainwashed, and then sent back out into the world, mostly to America? For what?" Smyth nervously adjusted his grip on the gun he carried.

Hibiki spread his arms in an all-encompassing gesture. "For *anything*. You have only to listen to North Korea's news statements to know what they would like to do to America."

"This all started with you overhearing a comment regarding that senator," Mai mused. "I wonder what happened to him."

"We are working blind," Hibiki admitted.

"How's the comms room?"

"Last I heard, they had restored all communications. The fire did not destroy anything vital."

"We should go—"

At that moment there was the sound of many rushing feet. Mai and Smyth raised their weapons. Figures began to run past the lab windows, all jingling and jangling with guns and ammo, medals and camo fatigues.

The door burst open. The windows were covered from outside. Over thirty troops with steady weapons covered them. It had all happened very quickly. Mai glanced sidelong toward Hibiki as she lowered her weapon.

His expression took on an air of hurt.

A short man, stocky and puffed up with self-importance pushed his way into the room. A big smile turned a pudding-like face into Halloween tapioca.

"We have suspected Hibiki for some time." He sounded practically gleeful. "And allowed him to betray us further in hopes of attracting a bigger fish. But this. . ." His smile broadened even farther. "This will have to do. The legendary Mai Kitano. I have heard of you. Welcome to the end of your life."

CHAPTER THIRTY-SIX

Drake let the bikers close the doors to the hangar before dragging the three kidnappers they had abducted out of the back of the car. They had been physically thrown into the trunk, a tangle of arms and heads oozing blood, and now they were deposited onto the rough concrete the same way, without regard for their injuries.

"I want answers." Drake kicked his way among them. "And the first wanker to start talking gets his wounds tended to."

The suit with the thigh wound writhed. No doubt feeling precious life draining from him, he spoke up first. "We don't own this ring. We're just a part of it. Please—"

"Keep going." Alicia came up now, closely followed by Lomas and Dirty Sarah.

"It's big. We're a small part. Nothing more. The chain starts down the coast of Spain. All the cities down that way are targeted. The sleepers are sent to a halfway house in Barcelona before being brought here and then transported, by train, to Moscow."

"Interesting term." Alicia picked up on it instantly. "Sleepers."

"It's what the Russians call them. It's said the captives are put to sleep somewhere by the Koreans. For months. Years. But mostly—forever."

"Because they die en route? From wounds you give them?"

"No. It is the sleeping that kills the bulk of them. I don't know why."

"Experiments." Drake kicked a man in frustration. "You are providing human beings for experimentation. I've seen the other end of the chain. It's sickening."

"We are just a cog." The German clearly sensed his anger. "Nothing more."

Drake drew his gun and flicked the safety off. "Like fuck you are."

"Wait." Lomas stepped forward before the Englishman could pull the trigger. "If we kill the one who talks, we risk losing them all."

Alicia nodded. "Spoken like a true inquisitor."

Drake fought the darkness back. Thick black winds receded slowly from his vision and his soul. *Think of Mai,* he repeated the adage again and again. At last, he managed to lower the weapon.

Now Lomas signaled to Whipper. "Got some use for you, darlin'."

The leather-clad woman stalked forward, boot heels clipping across the floor. In her right hand, she held a thin black object. When she stopped she let it unfurl.

A bullwhip. A single-tailed length of braided leather with a twelve-inch, intricately formed leather handle. There was an even thinner piece of nylon cord at the whip's end, which allowed the weapon, if thrown properly, to exceed the speed of sound and send back a sonic boom.

"Now." Alicia grunted with malice in her voice. "Now you're in trouble."

One of the captives rose to his knees, shouting in defiance. Without warning, Whipper flicked out, arm muscles straining. The meat of the leather cracked the man across the face. The *cracker* snapped about a foot behind him. The clap of the sonic boom made everyone except Lomas jump.

The man, defiant no longer, thrust a palm against his cheeks as they parted in the middle. Blood poured between his fingers and dripped to the floor in a red torrent.

The suit stared, aghast. The words spilled from him faster than the other man's blood. "The orders come out of Korea. And. . .and from the States."

Drake's ears pricked up. "What about the States?"

"It's all I know. A powerful man is involved. An American. That's all. He has contacts in Europe. They direct us to where the expat Americans end up living."

"The Barcelona address," Alicia said. "Let's have it."

Whilst the man reeled off another European address, Drake fished out a cellphone and dialed Hayden. The new boss of SPEAR answered on the first ring.

"Drake. Thank God."

"Aye up. You guys still alive?"

"Barely. It's war over here, man."

Drake strode over to a quiet corner of the hangar, head down. "What's going on?"

"First off, we're all okay. But the HQ suffered major damage. The enemy attacked en masse. Dahl and the others are pulling up to a safe house as we speak. And Drake—Ben didn't take the fight well. He's totally freaked."

"Damn kid needs to go home," Drake said before he could stop himself. But he didn't apologize. He wouldn't apologize for Ben anymore.

"Keeps saying he's got blood on his hands."

Drake flashed back to the scene aboard the Destroyer after the Blood King vanished and started the blood vendetta. He saw Ben holding Kennedy's body, blood everywhere.

"He'll be right."

"Well, Mano and I are nearing the hotel." She paused, then rushed on. "For work. It's where this whole thing began. Looks as though a Korean general and an American got scared when a bunch of strangers accidentally saw them together."

"That's it?"

"Pretty much. As it happened, they had nothing to fear. But they didn't know that. Paranoia, my friend. Along with guilt, it's our best psychological weapon against the madmen who aspire to rule our world."

"We're starting to realize from this end that the kidnapping ring is directly connected to the island and even your American. And if the island is connected to your general, then he's been involved in this thing for years. Not weeks."

Hayden was silent for a moment. "Clearly, we're still missing a part of the puzzle. Somebody has to find out what really goes on at that island."

"Have you heard from Mai?"

"Not yet. But she's our best, Drake. She'll be okay."

Drake stared into space. "If you guys have been openly attacked at the HQ and even on the road, it sounds like our American and Korean friends have started their endgame. I'm getting on a plane today with Alicia. You need us."

The relief in Hayden's voice was palpable. "Don't be long, Matt."

Drake stalked back to the interrogation. "Everything's gone to shit," he said. "New plan. Alicia—you and I need to head back to Washington. Romero—you and some of the local troops need to organize a raid on that house in Barcelona. You up for that?"

The marine looked surprised but agreeable. "Sure, man."

Lomas met Drake's eyes with a keen stare. "And us?"

"Go home," Drake said, "with my eternal thanks. We couldn't have done this without you."

"We're going back?" Alicia was saying. "Right now?"

"Well, there's a Dinorock answer to that. 'Good Girls Go to Heaven, Bad Girls Go to Washington D.C.' Something like that."

"How about 'Born to be Wild?'" Alicia pursed her lips as Lomas questioned her with a look. "You heard of that one?"

"If you're still a part of this team, you should come with me." Drake saw now that his old friend had no agenda other than to follow her heart. She wasn't playing anyone. She didn't even know what she wanted from life herself.

For the first time, he found himself wondering what had happened to her. What made a young girl aspire to become an elite member of a world-class Special Forces group?

Maybe a story for another time.

He waved a hand. "If not, you should stay with them."

He walked away. Alicia threw a stone at his back and then grabbed Lomas by the hand, leading him toward his Ducatti Monster.

"Fuckin' hell, Drake. I just meant give me ten minutes."

CHAPTER THIRTY-SEVEN

Hayden pocketed her cell, buoyed by the news that Drake was on his way back. The team needed every one of its members if they were to put down this latest threat. She spared a moment for Mai, hoping the Japanese agent was okay. If anyone could come out of that ordeal alive and enriched, it was, without doubt, Mai Kitano.

The room around her buzzed with activity. They had been authorized to request the local PD's help. Within half an hour, they had a forensic expert and a fingerprint team scrutinizing the suite where Lauren Fox had spent the night on January 10th.

With the techs swarming and searching every nook and cranny, it left Hayden and Kinimaka with little to do except watch. The hotel management had so far been of little use. It seemed the place was often used by passing celebrities, and the management respected their right to privacy. With supervisors stalling and decision makers unable to be reached, Hayden had taken the decision to examine the room instead. They might find a whole bunch of fingerprints, but the prints they found would surely be more revealing than a guest name of Joey Tribbiani.

Even now, the manager was still grumbling about a warrant. Hayden had left Mano to deal with him, citing national security issues, which was awfully close to the truth.

Now Kinimaka watched the bustle passing them by. "These guys rock, don't they? Reminds me of my days in the Honolulu PD."

"Those days," Hayden said, referring to her own in the PD as well, "at the time they seemed so hard. So manic and rough around the edges. Now—" She clicked her tongue. "Feels like they were a cakewalk."

"Good days. Good friends." Kinimaka stole a glance at her. "Nothing's changed."

"Oh, I've changed, Mano. I used to do everything for my dad." She held a forefinger and thumb an inch apart. "Every. Little. Thing. Now, I do them for myself."

She took hold of his hand and led him into the bathroom. She closed the door and locked it. She stared hard into his eyes.

"You got something to say to me?"

Karin Blake stared at her brother as if he'd suddenly sprouted wings.

"You're *what?*"

"You heard me, sis. The call of the wild and all that."

Karin frowned in worry. "You're not making any sense."

"Says you." Ben threw back the standard brotherly reply. "Mum and dad are chuffed."

"Of course they are. You're talking about moving back home. Leaving a potentially dangerous job. You can't run away from real life, Ben."

"There's no *talking*. I'm doing it. The band wants me. Mum and dad want me. Here—" He stared around the safe-house's untidy kitchen. "Nobody needs me."

Karin held back a face slap, but only just. "You broke up with your girlfriend. Big deal. That can happen back in England too, you know."

Ben fiddled with a switch. "Kennedy died protecting me when she should've been helping herself. So did Colin Patterson. Do you even know who that is?"

"Of course. It's the soldier you tried to help back at the third tomb."

"There's too much blood on my hands," he said, checking his phone when it vibrated. "Taxi's here. I'm off to the airport."

"Now?"

"Right now."

"Are you even allowed to do that?"

Ben turned away. Karin watched his back, stiff and resolute, an answer in itself. She watched him walk past Torsten Dahl and Komodo without so much as a glance. She watched him walk out the front door.

She heard the car pull away. Sadness filled her. Ben was a pain, but he was her brother and still one of the few people alive with whom she had shared the terrors of her past. It was a rare day when Rebecca Westing's name or face didn't nudge its way into Karin's thoughts.

It did now. As Ben left for the airport, Karin found herself remembering that distant day when she had lost her faith in people, and life.

Kinimaka's eyes grew huge. He stared at Hayden as if she were the Devil. After a second, she raised herself up on tiptoes and brushed her soft lips across his cheek.

"Next time," she said, with a cheeky smile. "Be ready."

Next time?

Mano watched as she turned and walked out the door, unable to take his eyes off her body. How did the saying go? *Hate to see you go. . .love to watch you leave.* That about covered his thoughts for the next sixty seconds. He had no doubts that he wanted to take her out. That wasn't the issue. But Mano had been raised by his mother to respect authority, to adhere to the rules and the chain of command.

Was it ethical to ask his boss out? Hayden had been his boss for so long the dynamic was set in stone between them. How would that dynamic then transfer itself to a relationship?

It couldn't hurt to find out, the hot-blooded side of him whispered.

Oh, but it could, the more conservative side shot back. *It could ruin everything.* He loved his job. He loved his boss—as a boss. He loved the new team, even Alicia. The hours he'd spent with her and Belmonte in that bar in Vienna opened up a whole new side of her. Alicia was a woman with no agenda, but with a past that was, literally, explosive. Mano had only heard a brief part of it, but his heart had instantly melted.

After a while, he realized he was alone in the bathroom, staring through the open door. The techs were staring at him. With a grunt, he strode back into the main room. Hayden stood by the big window, framed in sunlight, her long, blond hair on fire.

She turned at once, happy. "Drake and Myles will be landing tonight. 8 p.m."

A tech guy stood up so fast he knocked a kitschy brass table over. The noise didn't even reach him or make him stop turning a tablet computer around and around in his hands.

Hayden put a hand on his shoulder. "You okay?"

The man stared at her and then thrust the tablet into her face. "Shaun Kingston," he said. "Owner of Kingston Firearms. One of the biggest legit arms dealers in the country. If he's in bed with the Koreans. . ."

Hayden stared at the picture. "Then we're up shitstorm creek."

CHAPTER THIRTY-EIGHT

Mai Kitano faced the facility's commander, disdain twisting her face.

"Those rags you wear," he said, sadistic glee making him look like an evil circus clown. "They're torn. Muddy. Maybe we should remove them for you."

She and Smyth had been tied by the wrists to upended bedsteads, their hands twisted through broken, rusty springs and then secured to the iron side rails.

"You can try."

The grinning base commander faltered and took a step back, reading the certainty in her eyes. A soldier stepped from behind, clearly not interpreting the situation, and strode forward. Mai instantly took the weight of her body on her wrists and kicked out with both feet. The first strike knocked the soldier to the left, straight into the hard, oncoming right.

The sound of his neck snapping silenced the room.

"No! No! Tie her feet." The commander's expression turned from uncertain to livid in a millisecond.

The other soldiers hesitated, not trusting their own skills. Mai smiled viciously.

"Fools!" The commander blustered, but didn't repeat the order.

One of the soldiers leaned into him. "Should we shoot her?"

"Probably." The commander let out a deep sigh that made his fat jowls wobble. "But not yet. Wait." He stalked from the room, shouting at a subordinate to go and fetch him the sat phone.

Smyth regarded her with the utmost respect. "Even tied up." He laughed. "Even tied up you're lethal. Maggie, I gotta say—you're my dream girl."

Mai shook her head, unable to hide the smile. It soon evaporated though when the sound of Dai Hibiki's groans filtered through the battle rage. The undercover Japanese agent had so far borne the brunt of the ill treatment. The Koreans had beaten him to the ground, then kicked and stomped on him until he stopped moving. Mai had heard more than one bone break in the onslaught. Her heart and mind wept, but her outward facade remained carved in stone.

"What is this place?" she asked, always digging. "What do you do here?"

The soldiers just stared at her. Then, from the corner of the room, came a clicking noise. A man, as thin, ugly and repugnant as a stick insect, rose, finely knobbed cane in hand. He didn't stop moving until he could reach out and touch Mai, well within lethal range.

"You still want to know?" His voice cracked, old with pain, old with terrible experience. "Even now before all these weapons. You still want to know? That is why I love you, Miss Kitano. The legend of Shiranu is *real! It is real!"* He cackled on like a man driven insane. "That is why, even locked away here in this purgatory, I have tried to follow your every move, your every victory even before Tokyo Coscon." He raised the tip of the cane and shoved it against what he could see of her flat stomach. "It would be a pleasure to die by your hands. Or feet. As you prefer."

Mai looked momentarily at a loss. A weapon rattled and clicked. "Come away from her, Doctor."

"Doctor? You run this place, bud?" Smyth rattled his bedstead. "C'mon. What can it hurt? You done life here, man, longer than any prison sentence. What gives?"

The doctor bowed his head. "At first, we outlined a proposal to propagate super assassins. Sleepers. It eventually became a leadership-run People's Republic program."

"Assassins?" Smyth almost laughed. "You kiddin' me, doc?"

Mai watched the end of the cane being pressed into the flesh just below her navel. She let her gaze run along its length and then up until they met the doctor's eyes. "Is this what you want?"

"Yes, Miss Kitano."

"Then speak."

It was one of the oddest situations imaginable. The captive promising death to the captor if they played nice and spilled the beans. Only Mai Kitano could conjure such extreme and fatal adoration. And the inept guards watched partly in fascination, and partly because they had no orders to the contrary.

"These assassins pass no blame on to Korea. It's what's known as a 'sparkling blow' against the West. Clean. Spotless. Death. It can be attributed to a chance act of ferocity, triggered by a single predetermined phrase."

"So why use them now?"

The doctor nodded ever so slightly at Mai and dug the end of his cane into her stomach. His next words caused a furor.

"Officially, they are not yet in use. General Kwang Yong has commandeered the program for his own personal means and gains."

Soldiers rushed forward, cackling. Mai raised both knees, swinging viciously under the doctor's chin. His head snapped back hard, breaking the connection with his spine. The body slithered lifelessly between her legs and down to the floor. Once again, the soldiers backed off.

"If I could choose a way to die"—Smyth tested his bonds—"it'd be between your legs, Maggie."

The lab door opened and the chubby-faced clown commander walked back in. "It's done. The general will return and take care of this. What happened here?"

"The doctor." One of the soldiers pointed at Mai in explanation.

"I have never known a prisoner like you before." He drifted closer. "You give grown, armed men nightmares. Which clan are you from?"

Mai whispered a word in a voice pitched too low for anyone else to hear, but the commander's frame visibly wavered. His entire body shook and he was an inch from having to pick himself up off the floor.

"Clear the room." He hissed. "The general will have to take care of this." Without ceremony, he forced a path through his men. "We wait. Now, we wait."

CHAPTER THIRTY-NINE

Shaun Kingston sat without moving, betraying no emotion as the calls came in thick and fast. General Kwang Yong thrust an encrypted phone back toward a subordinate and started smoothing out his cuffs.

"My people need me," he said quietly. "I must return to the island. Immediately."

"Anything I should know?" Kingston asked inoffensively.

"They have captured Mai Kitano."

"I assume that's a good thing." Kingston didn't pretend to recognize the name.

"It is an interrogation fit only for a General." Kwang Wong puffed his chest out self-importantly. "And as regards our own enterprise—I need to know what she knows. Only me."

"Understood. Germaine? What do you have?"

The bodyguard had been busy fielding half a dozen calls. "We're about to get fucked more times than a porn star. The bastards have exposed us, sir."

"Be more specific."

"They know you were at the Desert Palms. They've even figured out why we zombied-up to take out those drunk pricks who barged in on us. In hindsight, sir, that might have been a mistake."

Kingston didn't miss the gentle irony. "So it seems. How easily our best laid plans can fall apart, eh, Germaine? Years of toil and strategy flushed away in a second by four idiots and an expensive hooker."

Germaine nodded. "Since time began, sir."

General Kwong Yang interrupted them. "I too need to leave. I wish to use the same airport I arrived at."

Kingston nodded. "Goes without saying, General. My jet's kept in constant readiness there. And I have more properties and friends throughout the European and Asian continents than I do in the Americas. We'll head out together."

"Very well. I will prepare."

"General," Kingston said softly to the retreating man's back, "do we still have an arms deal?"

Three seconds of silence passed saturated with such thick tension it could have absorbed the thrust of a knife. Then the North Korean spoke without turning. "Of course we do, Kingston. If you wish I could always awaken our army. . ."

Kingston shuddered. He knew the effects an army of sleeper agents would have on American soil. The chaos and terror that could be triggered by random violence. He also knew how much the Korean relished making each and every call that turned a sleeper into a zombie-like assassin. The power in his voice could turn a respected, everyday American into a horrific extension of the North Korean army. Kwang Yong had invited Kingston to watch once, to bear witness to the wickedness. Kingston had felt obliged to acquiesce, just once. What he saw in Kwang Yong's face was something he'd never seen before.

Undiluted hatred. Gleeful malice—the kind a priest might associate with an avenging demon. Wanton and immoral rage.

Just six words: The Devil is in, Miss Jones.

If a man could have a sexual, corrupt and psychotic experience whilst delivering a message on the phone, then Kwang Yong had stolen the gold.

"You would do that just to cover our escape?"

"Wouldn't you? Mr. Kingston, you have made a deal to supply models of advanced weaponry and top secret blueprints to, quite probably, America's worst and most proficient enemy. Did you think there would be no collateral damage?"

"Not beyond a certain scale."

"Then on whom did you think we would use your DREAD system? Your XM-25's?"

Kingston hadn't actually taken his thoughts much beyond private island parties, a decadent, faceless lifestyle and megayacht ownership. Now, he pushed it all aside. "We have much to do."

"Then I should really go and prepare."

"You do that, General." Kingston exhaled noisily. "It's all unraveling. How long do we have?"

Germaine considered the question, whip-thin frame coiled with tension. "We have half a dozen material assets they will check first, but we need to be gone from this house by dawn, sir."

Kingston checked his bespoke Rolex. "It's five p.m. now." He turned to his assembled men. "Load up the trucks, boys, and prep the armored cars. We move out in twelve hours."

CHAPTER FORTY

Matt Drake felt the heavy burden that weighed heavy on his heart and shoulders ease a little when he walked into the safe house. Some of the world's most capable people stood ready for action, preparing to take the fight to the enemy and erase his entire operation.

Dahl walked straight up to him and clapped him on the back. "Good to see you back in one piece."

"Cheers."

Hayden met his eyes from across the room. "Hope you're taking that little desert-island jaunt off your vacation allowance, Drake."

Alicia sniggered beside him, then crossed over to a quiet corner, already checking her phone for missed voicemails or texts. Drake nodded to Karin, Komodo, Kinimaka and Gates, already noting Ben's absence. He fielded some questions about Mai and tried to put all speculation as to her fate out of his mind, lest it completely debilitate him. He described the dramatic overland trip and the exploits of Romero. When speaking about the Russians, he was far more forthcoming, describing the Moscow HQ and what little he'd seen of the operation, the ancient maps of Babylon and the tower of Babel, and the monstrosity that called itself *Zanko*.

Two new people sat staring at him from the farthest corner of the room: a grizzled, middle-aged man wearing a denim jacket and cowboy boots, and a dark-haired woman wearing tight hole-in-the-knee jeans and a ragged sweater.

"Ya know," Alicia drawled, "you'd think when a girl gets told she's going to a safe house, it'd be a *house*, rather than a bloody underground basement."

Lauren Fox nodded in agreement. Hayden smiled. "Welcome to the CIA, Myles."

Drake took in the room with new eyes. "This is a CIA building?"

"Sure is," Kinimaka told him happily. "And it may be cozy, but it comes with *all* the mod cons."

He directed them over to a central console, much like what an airplane pilot operates. Above the console sat a trio of TV screens, flickering with grey static for now. Kinimaka tapped a button and all three screens burst into life.

"It's a direct feed from the main CIA building at Langley. This is what they're doing now. The bit that relates to us anyhow."

"CIA?" Drake wondered. "Doesn't this thing come under FBI jurisdiction now?"

"We don't have time," Hayden said briefly. "You'll see."

Drake watched as three ultra-clear satellite images appeared. As the resolution increased and magnified, some major activity could be seen inside what appeared to be a walled compound. The center was a sprawling old mansion, abutted by many low-slung buildings that resembled car garages. The outside was a maze of gardens, warehouses and dirt roads, exiting the property at several points.

"What are we looking at?"

"An estate that belongs to Shaun Kingston, our arms dealer. It would appear the man's getting ready to move out big time. See all the damn vehicles? That's a shitload of metal, a shitload of manpower and a shitload of weapons. And that. . ." Kinimaka tapped a moving figure surrounded by other moving figures. "As far as we can tell is General Kwong Yang."

Drake's eyes widened. "They're both together right now? Still in the country? Oh, please don't tell me that's in Europe. I just came from there."

"It's not in Europe, Drake." Jonathan Gates came over to stand next to his shoulder. "Kingston's compound is a twenty minute drive from here." He shrugged. "Maybe thirty."

Drake felt an instant rush of adrenalin. "Tool up, people," he hissed. "We'll make his last journey a ride he'll never forget."

CHAPTER FORTY-ONE

Just as the dawn rose, a sprawling convoy of vehicles hit the highway hard. The rising red hues painted their dark colors crimson, marking them red, as though tinged with blood. Drake and his team were racing to intercept them in three separate Humvees. Hayden and Kinimaka shared the first, Dahl and Komodo the second, with Drake's partner being Alicia. When they closed in on their prey and the convoy spotted them, the race was well and truly on.

Drake shook his head at the excessive procession. It was being led by a black supercar, what looked to Drake like a new custom-specced Viper. Behind it ran a trio of SUVs, a Ford F150 with an open bed, a shiny chrome Mack truck and, somewhat bizarrely, a stretch limo.

"That's the Korean." Drake flicked the comms open so everyone could hear. "In the limo. Gotta be. And Kingston will be in the Viper. The rest is pure firepower."

Dahl raced up alongside him, eyeballing him as the two cars sped along inches apart. "Are you quite ready for this?"

Drake gunned the Humvee, inching ahead. "Stop poncing around, mate. Mai's still on the island and this is our last chance."

"I find sometimes in moments of extreme stress it helps to set a little wager. What do you think?"

"What do you have in mind?"

"Simple. Count bad guys. The one who takes out the most wins."

"I'm in," Alicia said instantly, grinning.

Drake chewed his lower lip. Hayden remained notably uncommunicative.

Dahl said, "Scared you'll lose, Drake?"

"Nope. I just don't want to see you sloping off to Sweden with your tail between your legs when you get pounded. I'm in. Winner takes all."

Dahl's Humvee roared ahead, rapidly closing the gap between himself and the last SUV in line. At the same time, Drake saw the heavily tinted SUV windows being rolled down and weapons come bristling out as if the vehicle had suddenly raised its heckles. The huge Mack truck swerved over two lanes as its rear doors were flung back.

Four men stood in the opening, sub-machine guns ready.

Men popped their heads up above the F150's high sides just as the sound of cop car sirens and the thud of approaching helicopters hammered the air.

Drake wasted no time slamming the accelerator through the floorboards. "Game on."

CHAPTER FORTY-TWO

For once, the roaring engines of powerful vehicles drowned out the crazy fusillade of lead that erupted across the three-lane interstate. Drake didn't flinch as bullets pinged off the Humvee's windshield and frame, trusting the upgrade kits to protect the armored vehicle. Hayden switched to the left, aiming to put one of the SUVs between her and the truck. Dahl was already past an SUV and fast approaching the eighteen-wheeler, sparks flashing off his vehicle like a Disney fireworks show.

The F150 loomed outside Alicia's part of the windshield.

"Can't get too much of a good thing." The Englishwoman cracked her window, aimed her gun, and fired. A man twisted and collapsed into the flatbed, his gun flying through the air and clattering down the highway. A bullet somehow managed to fizz in through Alicia's open window, thudding into her headrest.

Alicia whistled. "Nice shot. Wow, you know, Drakey, I miss this."

Drake swerved. A police chopper thundered overhead. His rearview filled with the flashing blue lights of the speeding cop cars Gates had requested, some of them clearly modified as they began to catch up. He gasped as he saw Dahl's Humvee dart to and fro behind the Mack truck. The bad guys were leaning out of the truck's rear hold, trying to bring a rocket launcher to bear on the Swede's transport.

A terrible hiss signaled that the weapon had discharged early. The missile impacted against the road near Dahl's passenger-side wheel and skipped away, exploding against a barrier that ran along the verge. From above Drake came the sound of rapid gunfire. Bullets rattled against the truck, taking out one of the men in the back. The police chopper dove in low, passing right over Drake's windshield, so close he could almost have stood up in his seat and grabbed one if its skids through his window. The helicopter veered slowly in mid-air as its occupants continued firing. Dahl's Humvee squealed out of the way, itself strafed by errant gunfire.

The truck started a crazy swerve, a slow motion snaking of machinery so heavy its rear seemed to take forever to catch up to its front end. The cab flew into the right-hand lane, the trailer sliced across the other two. The chopper cut sharply left, chasing the wide-open back doors.

A sizzling explosion and a smoke trail burst from the back of the truck. The chopper shuddered as the rocket blasted against its side, veering wildly and losing altitude fast. One of the cops inside fell through the open door, only to save himself by grabbing a skid on his way down.

Alicia held her breath.

The chopper came down fast, the pilot trying desperately to keep it under control as fire licked its tail boom and rotor. The main rotor struggled to carry the damaged chopper, its tail fins hitting the interstate first and crumbling under the impact.

The body of the chopper came down hard. Men leapt out any way they could. The cop who was hugging the landing skid hauled himself around and began a slow, lumbering run toward the median. As Alicia watched in the rearview mirror, the following convoy of cop cars had reached their brethren and was stopping to tend to them. Three big vehicles powered on through.

The eighteen-wheeler slewed back into the middle lane, its occupants flung to the sides, somehow managing to stay inside the rear container by grabbing at the many ropes and ratchet straps that whipped and thrashed around. Drake gave a tight smile when he saw the RPG launcher clatter onto the road and bounce away.

They all passed a civilian vehicle on the inside, the lone businessman staring in astonishment. Drake started to thank their lucky stars Kingston and his cronies had set out so early, keeping civilian road traffic to a minimum, then realized it would've been even better if he'd been planning to set off about thirty minutes later. They'd have caught up to him back at his house. He'd assaulted enough houses, ranches and compounds in the last few months to rate his chances pretty highly.

Hayden was shouting across the airwaves, something about civilians being their priority, a point so obvious even Alicia rolled her eyes.

Then men stood up in the bed of the F150 and began lobbing hand grenades down the highway.

CHAPTER FORTY-THREE

Mai turned to Smyth.

"Well, it's been fun, my friend, but I think it's time to leave."

The marine raised an eyebrow at her. He knew enough about the Japanese agent now to take her at her word. "What's the plan?"

Mai studied the way her hands were tied for a minute, then started to slowly lift her legs until her ankles touched her ears. Her wrists took the weight, her body contorted back on itself.

Smyth whispered, "Jesus Christ."

Mai selected a sharp blade that had been hidden inside her boot. "Shut it and watch them."

"They just noticed. Be quick."

"One of the advantages of being a bit of a legend in the lethal department," Mai said as she slit her bonds, "is that no one normally has the balls to pat you down."

"Hurry."

Mai dropped to the ground, massaging her wrists and palming the knife. One of the guards was opening the door, another half dozen poised to file in behind him. Mai spread-eagled herself across Smyth's body, nose to nose as she chopped his bonds away. "You ready for this?"

"Just lead the way. I'll follow."

Mai coiled her body and spun hard, flinging herself across the floor as the first of the guards piled in. She crashed into his legs and the legs of the men behind him, scattering them like skittles. Guns and radios flew randomly, creating chaos. Men hit the floor with their collarbones, their faces and the backs of their heads. Mai wrestled among them, lethal with both knife and fingers, and not a man moved in her wake. Smyth took a running jump and leaped over the top of her, slamming straight into more guards as they breached the doorway. The marine flew into the corridor, rolling, unable to stop himself from hitting the back wall but clever enough to hit it right. With a second's pause, he reached down and claimed the nearest rifle. A bullet smashed into the wall right next to his head. He swung the barrel around, firing indiscriminately. North Korean guards were flung back by the impact, through the open door into their cell, and against the heavy windows.

"Stop."

Mai's command made Smyth rip his finger off the trigger. Then she stood there, not a hair out of place, but with a slight smile playing across her lips.

"Now we take this island."

CHAPTER FORTY-FOUR

Dahl growled in anger as he slammed his foot to the floorboards once more. No one alive had ever fired an RPG at him and got away with it. He wasn't about to let that change now.

Komodo, the seasoned ex-Delta soldier, swallowed hard. "Um, Dahl…"

The Humvee powered up to the very back of the big Mack truck, inches from touching it. Without a word, the big Swede opened his window and angled his body so he could slip out of the opening. Then he let go of the wheel and drew his gun.

Komodo yelped and threw himself behind the wheel. With inches to spare, the two huge vehicles sped along the interstate. Those left standing in the back of the eighteen-wheeler fired at the Humvee, seeing their bullets bounce off the windshield. Dahl leaned out the window and pumped half a dozen shots into the opening. A man pirouetted, spraying blood, slammed into the side of the truck and then slipped off the back end. His body bounced along the concrete and across the median at speed, instant roadkill.

"That's one." Dahl spoke into his throat mike and used the distraction to gracefully rotate his body until he was sitting out the window, arms rested carefully on the roof, sighting his rifle. Only his legs remained in the car. Komodo used every ounce of concentration and skill to stay on the truck's rear end. Dahl squeezed his trigger, taking out another enemy. A return bullet grazed the roof near the Swede's head.

Dahl had had enough. Gyrating quickly, he squeezed fully out of the Humvee, balanced on the edge of the window for half a second and then slithered down the windshield, landing on the hard metal hood. Wind buffeted his face and plucked at his clothes with enthusiastic fingers. The man who had fired the RPG at him raised another weapon.

Bad move, arsehole.

Dahl ran and jumped, one arm aiming his rifle, the other reaching for a thick rope that flapped gently around the back of the truck. As his hand closed around the rope, he fired his gun, taking the RPG firer's head off at close range. The rope flexed as it took his weight, rolling him out of the truck and around the side.

Dahl bounced off the outside of the eighteen-wheeler, gun aimed high, hanging on with grim determination.

Komodo let out a harsh expletive as his mouth dropped open.

Drake shook his head. "Now he's showing off." Alicia whooped with excitement. *"C'mon, Drake!* Get us into the action! The mad Swede's having all the fun."

Dahl's momentum sent him swinging right back through the open doors. Instantly, he let go. Bullets flew past him, fired in haste by the two remaining occupants. Dahl rolled as he hit the metal deck and came up on one knee, firing two head shots.

Both adversaries fell dead.

"Four." Came over the comms system.

Dahl wasn't finished yet. Buckling into a pair of ratchet straps, he shot out the lock of a forward door and again stepped out into the blasting wind. For a moment, he hung from the vehicle as he hooked a strap over a rail that ran the length of the truck and then began to traverse sideways toward the cab, one step at a time.

Komodo brought the Humvee around, now seeing the F150 running in front of the truck—thankfully out of grenades but still with men balancing in the open bed of the vehicle. Beyond that, three SUVs, the limo and the Viper sped, snaking through the sparse traffic.

Komodo gunned the engine as he spied guns being leveled at Dahl from the back of the Ford. As the first man fired, Komodo's heart leapt into his throat, but the Humvee gave an instant response and surged forward straight into the bullet's path. As more men opened fire, Komodo kept the big armored vehicle steady, giving the F150 men no human target.

Dahl crab walked along the side of the fast-moving eighteen-wheeler. When he reached the cab, he fired through the window. Glass exploded, but the passenger was ready for him. The man flung the door wide, leaning out with a machine pistol cocked and ready. Dahl froze. But the driver of the truck hadn't reckoned for the sudden explosion of glass. The shock made him jerk the wheel, the Mack swerved violently, and the passenger lost his balance, tumbling right out of the door and crashing to the concrete road below.

Even Dahl winced as the truck bounced over him.

The Swede grabbed the swinging door, unhooked his strap and brought all his considerable strength to bear as he leaped into the cab. The truck driver just stared at him—this mad Swede with fiery eyes and a face set as hard as obsidian—and licked dry lips.

"I give up, man. Whatever you want. Just don't kill me."

Dahl nodded at the wheel. "Stop the bloody truck."

The driver practically stood up on the brakes and Dahl smashed into the windshield. The truck jackknifed, back end swinging around at high speed. Komodo hit the gas even harder, urging the Humvee to outrun the approaching mass of metal, at first losing the race but then, inch by inch, gaining enough ground to stay marginally ahead of certain death.

Dahl waited until the truck began to coast, slowing down. He saw Drake's and Hayden's armored cars and the three fast cop cars flash by.

"Bollocks."

The driver gawped at him. Dahl motioned him out of the truck as the standard black-and-whites caught up. "Half a dozen small container crates in the back," he told one of the cops as he climbed down, shaking the road dust and grit from his clothes. "Probably full of advanced weapons so, whatever you bloody do, don't look inside."

The cop stared.

"Ever hear the saying 'if I tell you, I'll have to kill you?' Same principal applies here." He shrugged in explanation.

Then his eyes lit on something magnificent. "Oh, would you look at that."

And he walked off, hearing the cop mutter something about *"English ass"* at his back, eyes full of the gorgeous light blue Shelby GT500 Mustang that stood idling near the median of the highway. It seemed luck and good fortune was on his side today.

The Shelby's driver stared at him with frightened eyes.

Dahl gave him a feral grin. "Step aside."

CHAPTER FORTY-FIVE

Lauren Fox slipped off her old sweater and settled into the plush armchair. She watched admiringly as Karin quickly manipulated a host of shaky images and transferred the best ones to the main screen. From there, Jonathan Gates, Karin and Lauren watched the road battle on live T.V.

Gates used the Blake girl's cleverness to assist with his decisions. It was Gates who had originally pulled the mass of cop cars back. Gates who had recalled the choppers, ordering them to follow at distance. Gates who now told Karin to scroll ahead using the American government's own version of Google maps to determine Kingston's destination.

"Got it," Karin said. "Palicki airfield. Ten miles ahead. I'll put them on alert."

"Now that's bad news." Gates breathed over her shoulder. "It means they're on their own. We can't get any backup there in time."

"Maybe you can't," Lauren said. "But you have time to scramble some of those F-35's to make sure the asshole doesn't get away."

Gates looked approvingly at her. "I knew you would become a valuable asset, Miss Fox."

Lauren narrowed her eyes. *What was the old guy spouting?* She hoped to high hell that he wasn't angling for some kind of secret *rendezvous* or a big discount. She'd seen it before. The more powerful and rich these guys got, the more they wanted everything for free.

Yeah, even that.

But Gates didn't come across as the sleazy type. In fact, the entire team, bar Alicia Myles, had treated her with respect and even a form of acceptance. Still, it seemed odd that the truck driver, Mike Stevens, had been sent home whilst she watched events related to national security unfold right before her eyes.

Gates wandered over to the far wall, speaking quietly into a cellphone. Lauren didn't dare wonder whom he might be speaking too. She stretched surreptitiously, searching the room for hidden cameras for the third time. When dealing with government figures, you just never knew who else might be watching.

Then Karin gasped and Lauren joined her as they watched the Swede, Dahl, take the big truck out of the race. Lauren then followed his progress as he commandeered some guy's sports car and returned to the fray.

"That guy's frickin' awesome." She breathed heavily, eyes wide.

Karin glanced at her. "It's just Dahl," she answered. "He does that."

Gates was suddenly at her side. "Where we at?"

"Drake just went for the F150."

CHAPTER FORTY-SIX

Mai scrambled over to check Hibiki's vitals. Despite a lot of groaning and coughing, the Japanese agent managed to smile through a mask of blood.

"I knew I could take the fight out of them using just my body."

Mai laid a hand on his head, her own skin dappled with her enemy's blood. "I have the most important job for you, Hibiki-san."

Smyth, over by the doorway, growled low in his throat "C'mon, Maggie, move   it."

Mai waited for Hibiki's eyes to clear and meet her own. "I need you to go to the comms room. I need you to make a distress call."

Hibiki struggled to sit up. "SOS? Of course."

Mai moved away. "We'll draw them away. I'm depending on you."

Smyth charged up the corridor, firing as more Korean guards entered the narrow space. His weapon discharged quickly, but he had a second and a third slung over each shoulder. Mai scooped up every gun she could find as she chased him. Behind her, she heard Hibiki struggling to follow. Smyth passed the door that led to the lab and outside to the partially burned comms room, slowing as he saw it standing open. Mai was about to warn him when he switched left and chose a darker room.

Shot out the windows at a dead run. . .

. . . and dove through. Smyth landed headfirst, rolled, and came up with a gun nestled against his shoulder. Then the Korean guards opened fire.

A round sent him toppling back among shards of shattered glass. Mai barely missed landing on him, registering the bloom of blood and seeing his eyes close before opening fire with a machine gun in each hand. A lead curtain of fury burst through the soldiers. Within seconds they were dead or twitching.

Mai turned to Smyth.

But at that moment, another group of Koreans came running around the side of the building—the ones who had been lying in wait outside the open door. *Good,* Mai thought. *That will give Hibiki his window to walk or crawl over to the comms room.*

And judging by their cautious gait and by the way they huddled around their overweight boss, this was the last of them.

Mai focused hard and all fell into place. She saw the sway of the trees behind them. The way the wind blew little tornadoes of leaves from the brush toward the shorter grass. How the sunlight dappled the killing grounds. She heard the rush of the surf, the deeper pounding of the waves out on the ocean.

Her mind relaxed whilst her body prepared.

The chubby island leader strode forward, unable to contain his curiosity. "And how do you plan to escape from this, Miss Kitano?" His expression betrayed his worst fears.

"I intend to cut the head off the snake." Mai widened her stance.

The island boss frowned in confusion. "Are you talking about me? My head? Even in death the People's Republic will be victorious. Even with a thousand—"

Mai sighed. "Do it, Smyth."

The marine answered even as he fell into motion. "Now I can die happy." He crawled between her open legs, and shot the boss through the neck. The ground shook and birds took flight as the lifeless body hit the ground. The remaining soldiers froze, then glanced sidelong at each other.

Smyth remained where he was, savoring the moment. Blood seeped from an open wound in his shoulder where the Korean's bullet had winged him. Mai didn't move a muscle but she examined every face, looking for their tells.

They were beaten.

"Cover me." She marched forward and put a foot on the dead Korean's back. "Drop your weapons, boys. This island belongs to us now."

And even as the guns started clattering to the ground, her thoughts turned to Drake, wondering where in the world he was, and how they would react to each other when they met once again back in civilization.

CHAPTER FORTY-SEVEN

Hayden watched Drake speed up to the F150. Its occupants looked ragged now, not the force they had been only a half hour ago when this nightmarish interstate chase had begun. But they still had guns and plenty of volition. And it was now all concentrated on Drake.

Hayden quickly maneuvered her own Humvee, screaming past a civilian-driven Pontiac that idled sensibly on the hard shoulder, its driver and passengers perched on the concrete K-rail, pointing their cellphones at the streaming mass of cars that sped by. Hayden approached the black SUVs. Even as she came up close, the blacked-out windows didn't crack. The big cars just kept on going, forming a barrier between themselves, the limo and the Viper in front.

"Take 'em out." Hayden backed off a little, giving Kinimaka space to work. But before he had sighted his Glock, one of the SUVs veered sharply and smashed into the Humvee's front end. Hayden laughed. The SUV would destroy itself long before it wrecked the Humvee.

A second SUV slowed rapidly, tires screeching and black smoke funneling from beneath its wheels until it drew level with the Humvee. The third SUV performed a similar maneuver and came up slightly behind them.

"Boxed in," Hayden muttered. "I don't think so."

The second SUV turned sharply, slamming against the Humvee's side. Hayden struggled to control the wheel, forced into the left hand lane. And now, all the windows slid open and weapons were poked out. Even the wide rear window of the SUV in front powered fully open.

"Oh fu—" Kinimaka began, and then the deadly fireworks started.

Drake twisted the wheel hard. Alicia draped herself out the window shouting something like *"Here, boys!"* at the top of her voice, but the wind took her words and shredded them. He counted only three men left alive in the back of the F150. A second ago, they had thrown one of their dead brethren over the vehicle's tailgate to give themselves more room.

There was no love lost between mercenaries and hired guns.

Alicia fired. Bullets pinged off the F150. One took out the small rear window. The car slewed dramatically.

"Driver's hit," Drake said. "You crazy bitch."

"One," Alicia shouted back. "That puts you last, Drake."

Drake took matters into his own hands. These Humvees didn't come equipped with cruise control, but they did sport something similar called throttle lock. Only difference was this thing didn't turn off by applying the brakes. He clambered up onto the seat, keeping the wheel straight with his knees, and arched his back out of the window. His first shot sent a man flying over the side of the Ford.

"Now we're even."

Then the F150, driverless, careened across the interstate at fifty miles an hour and smashed into Drake's vehicle.

Hayden reacted without thinking, turning the wheel and veering toward the hard shoulder. She heard Kinimaka's matter-of-fact comment "It's what they want," and peered through the hail of fire.

"We'll lose 'em in the trees."

Kinimaka stared at her, then back at the highway. "What?"

Hayden wrenched the wheel hard just as the third SUV swung toward her. The realignment sent their Humvee across the hard shoulder and onto the grass verge. The car began to bounce as if they'd joined a dirt track, but the three SUVs followed her.

"Look out!" Kinimaka at last saw the trees ahead.

Hayden looked grim. She ploughed toward them, pulling left at the last minute. Two SUVs followed her; the third went right. All four vehicles lost traction in the grass and dirt. The straight line of tall palm trees continued ahead for as far as the eye could see.

"Let's slalom the shit out of this thing." Hayden skidded right, churning up grass and mud. The enormous frond of a palm tree whacked the windshield as they scrambled by.

Kinimaka stared. "You get palm trees in Washington state?"

Hayden grimaced. "How the hell would I know? I'm from Toledo."

Kinimaka held on tight as they cut sharp left. "Doesn't look right is all."

Hayden aimed the big car at the sharp camber of an upcoming curve. "Mano, Hawaii doesn't have the monopoly on palm trees. Get over it."

She used the momentum the camber afforded them to swing down the slope and swerve around another big tree. The Humvee banked sharply, all the weight suddenly on the passenger side, lifting onto two wheels. . .

. . .and drenched suddenly in fire as the first SUV smashed headlong into the tree with a sound like the collapsing of the sky and exploded into a fierce fireball. Hayden's face was bathed in hot red as she took a fleeting look through the side window. Kinimaka met her eyes. They were both consummate professionals and would never say it aloud, but that look spoke volumes.

I guess that puts the boss in the lead.

The second SUV clipped their rear end and spun out of control. Hayden struggled with the wheel, and for ten crazy seconds, they skidded from left to right with the second SUV spinning out of control and keeping pace with them. .
.

. . .then Hayden swung right to avoid the next tree and the SUV crashed sidelong into it. A second crunch made even the SPEAR agents wince.

The third SUV hit them at speed. Hayden jerked, saved by her seat belt. Kinimaka hit his head against the inner frame and dropped his gun. The SUV plowed on, pushing them hard. Trees and leaves, patches of sunlight and flashes of the interstate all tumbled by as if they'd entered a frenzied kaleidoscope.

Both cars came to a juddering halt. The Humvee rolled precariously up on two wheels for the second time, showing its underside before crashing back to earth, scraping noisily down the hood of the SUV as it did.

Hayden jammed the accelerator down. Wheels spun uselessly. "Shit!" The SUV pulled back. Kinimaka swore. "They're gonna hit us again."

Hayden and Kinimaka needed only six seconds. The Vehicle Emergency Escape system allowed both agents to remove the windshield by pulling out the locking pins, rotating the latch handles and pushing their respective windows out.

Hayden rolled off the hood, landing feet-first and already opening fire before the SUV pounded into their Humvee.

Drake and Alicia clung hard to the doorframe and then forced their bodies back through the window of the vehicle as the F150 ploughed into its front end. Drake retained enough presence of mind to land on the steering wheel itself, trying to hold it in place with his whole body. Alicia tumbled across the car, limbs flailing. Drake, stuck as he was with his body around the wheel and his face pressed to the window, was witness to the spectacular sight of the F150 actually *somersaulting* through space. The vehicle, propelled by a powerful momentum, hit the sloped front of the Humvee and flipped end over end. Men fell from the open bed. The huge chunk of metal crashed into the median, scraping and shuddering and vibrating to a halt.

Then, his hands were too full to think about anything other than saving their own vehicle. Desperately, he tried to undo the impetus that the F150 had given the Humvee, forcing it away from the median with brute strength, but that swift motion sent the vehicle into a spin. Tires squealed. Rubber coated the road. Thick smoke trails raged in the tire tracks. Drake held tight to the wheel with one hand and to Alicia with the other as the armored car turned over onto its roof.

At last, the world went still.

Drake groaned as he took inventory. A few bruises, a skull that pounded like the seven dwarves in a gold mine, a sprained wrist where Alicia had landed hard. When his head stopped spinning, he used the same method as Hayden to escape the car, helping to drag a foggy Alicia out after him.

Drake stood up, seeking only one thing. It came in the form of the three powerful cop cars that had so far been trailing the battle at a distance. All three were Dodge Chargers.

Drake flagged them down. The cops had been ordered by the offices of the Secretary of Defense to let the SPEAR team take the lead. That's was why they had been staying close, but not engaging in the fray. Now, Drake slipped behind the wheel of one of the fast Chargers and fastened Alicia's belt for her.

"Hope you're wearing your big girl panties, Myles." He tightened the strap and hit the gas with venom. "Time to finish this thing."

Ahead, a great gantry hung over the interstate. The main off-ramp was signposted as *Palicki Airfield.*

The Charger—a super-modified police chase vehicle—spurted forward like a thing possessed, eating up the interstate as Kingston's Viper, closely followed by the limo, Dahl's Shelby Mustang and Komodo's comparatively well-driven Humvee all hit the off-ramp together.

Hayden leapt onto the hood of the SUV, firing without pause. Kinimaka shot out its tires. Doors opened on every side. Even the rear hatch came up. Men hurled their bodies clear, trying to twist and fire at the same time. But Hayden didn't stop. She loped straight up the windshield, shooting ahead and to her left, darted across the roof of the car and then jumped clear, landing on a mercenary she had already shot. His body made for a soft landing.

In seconds her adversaries lay scattered at her feet.

All except one.

A thin whip of a man uncoiled himself from the back seat. The machine pistol in his hand didn't waver as Hayden drew a bead on him.

"Germaine," she said, recognizing him from the photos they'd seen of Kingston's associates. "Aren't you supposed to be at your boss's side?"

"Bitch, I just follow orders. Same as you. He threw us to the wolves to make his escape." The tense shoulders shrugged. "Comes with the territory."

"How about I cut you a deal? I could make the next twenty years of your life feel like a sandy beach next to what they might be."

Germaine pursed his lips. "What kinda deal?"

Kinimaka stepped around the front of the car, his bulk not designed to be stealthy. Germaine pointed his other hand at the Hawaiian, in which a stubby handgun magically appeared.

"Stay put, bud. Mountain or not, this baby will take you down."

Germaine then smiled at Hayden. "I'm all ears, darlin'."

Hayden saw his plan then. The role of the SUVs and every man inside, including Germaine, had been to slow the authorities down. What they hadn't planned on was coming up against someone like her. All three cars had taken only two agents out of the race.

Hayden cocked her head. *Maybe not.*

A chopper landed on the nearby hard shoulder. Cops armed with rifles and wearing Kevlar vests stormed out, closing in on Hayden's position. Germaine saw his fate and lowered his weapons. "Worth a try."

Hayden's gaze zeroed in on the idling chopper. Moving fast, she grabbed Kinimaka by the shoulder and manhandled him toward it.

"Mano," she said, "Kingston's still running. We ain't out of this thing yet."

CHAPTER FORTY-EIGHT

Dahl blipped the Shelby Mustang's potent throttle, feeling all five hundred and forty horses respond to his touch. The Korean's limo weaved in front of him. He could take it any time, but held off until he perceived Kingston's end game.

It wasn't exactly subtle. But then, what had they expected from an arms dealer?

Five vehicles blasted onto Palicki airfield, soon to be joined by two more. The Viper streaked ahead, racing around the entrance to the parking lot and aiming for the mowed-grass borders that separated the airfield's civilian frontage from its runway system. Dahl knew that with this being strictly a low-key private airfield meant that the fences inside were easily breached, but then he saw that even that didn't matter. Kingston must have called ahead. Gates were open and a Gulfstream IV was taxiing out of a small hangar. The G-IV was a twin-jet engine aircraft. It would take a two-man cockpit crew and up to nineteen passengers. Kingston was running, no doubt about that, and he wasn't planning on coming back.

Was he even planning on taking the Korean General with him?

Dahl closed right up to the limo. Behind him, Komodo sat at the wheel of the surviving Humvee, his face a mask of concentration. Now, fanning out to the left, the Swede could see Drake and Alicia, making a police-decaled Dodge Charger scream in fury. Then, crazy to see, a helicopter blasted from out of nowhere, swooping low over the tops of the cars as it joined the race.

Hayden.

Dahl tweaked some more speed out of the Mustang. The Viper raced toward the jet aircraft as the plane began to accelerate down the airfield's longest runway. The limo roared as it struggled to keep pace. Drake's Charger edged past them on the outside. Komodo's Humvee tucked in behind. The Helicopter swept at an angle, arrowing hard toward the Gulfstream.

Without warning the plane's forward hatch slid open. Two armed men leaned out with what looked to Dahl like multi-grenade launcher weapons in their hands.

He looked across, reading Alicia's lips: *Fuck me!*

Dahl gave Drake half a smile as he goosed the Mustang to its limit and wrenched the wheel sideways, passing *under* the tail of the speeding Gulfstream and in front of the limo. The limo driver gave up the ghost, slamming hard on and sending the vehicle into a multi spin. The Viper roared as it raced alongside the jet aircraft, closing in. Drake's Charger gained new swiftness as it pealed out to the Viper's offside. The helicopter dove in, drifting sideways as it flew, enabling Hayden and Kinimaka to draw beads on the two guys and take them out of the picture.

Their guns bounced off the runway; their bodies bounced back inside the plane.

Dahl swore loudly. The shock, elation and danger of the chase urged him to keep going. But he could see Komodo stopping beside the damaged limo and knew the ex-Delta man needed back up. The Mustang responded without complaint as he blipped the brakes and jammed on the handbrake, performed a swift one-eighty, and took off again fast enough to leave smoke obscuring his wake.

Komodo stepped out of his vehicle and approached the limo's driver side. "Hands up!" he cried. "Come quiet, now. My little friend here would love to make a meal of you."

Dahl stepped on the brakes, leaping out as the Mustang still drifted forward. He approached the limo's passenger side, slipping out a Glock. The doors opened slowly. Both Dahl and Komodo stopped walking, taking aim.

A Korean stepped out of each door, hands held high. The first, a driver, fell to his knees, clearly more than petrified. Motion sickness was making the man was throw up all over himself, his body weaving even as he tried to remain frozen.

"On the ground," Komodo said. "Arms behind your backs."

Dahl glanced wistfully back at the ongoing race. *If only he. . .*

Then a fifth Korean emerged. He wore the tunic of North Korea, the flag stitched to the lapel. He glared unflinchingly and fearlessly at Torsten Dahl and he held a cell phone to his right ear.

"Engage final protocol." Dahl heard him say in English, clearly for the Swede's benefit as a last *fuck you*. "I repeat—engage final protocol. Blow up the island."

CHAPTER FORTY-NINE

Mai was standing right next to the communications console when the call came in. She was tending to Hibiki's wounds whilst Smyth secured the Korean soldiers with twine and rope and anything else he could find. The marine had even started to eye the soldiers' feet in consideration of using their socks as gags if they didn't shut up jabbering about freedom and victory and the Goddamn People's Republic.

Then, the console started flashing in front of her. Balancing on her knees beside Hibiki, she looked up. The console was made up of various toggles, big colored buttons and what looked like a sat-nav system. Around it were arrayed various sized monitors. A vivid blue light began to flash, a claxon-like ring tone sounded, and then some kind of automation program answered the call.

A hasty voice filled the room, "Engage final protocol. I repeat—engage final protocol. Blow up the island."

Mai turned swiftly. The Korean army at last went silent. Smyth met her eyes. "Are you fuckin' kidding me?"

With that, another ominous noise came over the brash loudspeakers, a noise that filled the room. The alarm—the intermittent clang of a horn of doom, and then a robotic voice. *"Warning. Warning. Final protocol engaged. Final protocol will occur in four minutes."*

And repeat.

Mai leapt into life. "Which one's the most senior?"

Hibiki pointed someone out. "Him."

"Final protocol?" Mai bounded over to him. "Does it really blow up the whole island?"

The man swallowed nervously. Mai had no time to waste so she threatened him where it would make the most impact but still give him focus. "Your balls." She said and twisted hard. "You can have them back for an answer." Alicia would have been proud of her.

"Ye." He gasped in Korean. "Haeng un eul bile o yo."

"What did he say?" Mai shouted.

Hibiki translated. "He said 'good luck.'"

More Korean rhetoric spewed forth.

"What did he say?"

"Umm. My hovercraft is full of eels. As near as I can tell."

Mai took it to the next level. A wrench and a three-quarter twist sent the man to his knees, squealing like a terrified warthog. The clang of the alarm deepened. The disembodied voice announced "*Three and a half minutes to destruction.*"

"Why's it speaking in American?" Smyth wondered.

"It's speaking in English because the call transmitted in English." One of the Koreans stepped forward. "It's adaptive. Like North Korea itself, it bends to better understand its enemies and then bends again into the shape of the hammer that destroys them."

Smyth stared.

"You think we are all ignorant fools? Conscripts. Brainwashed by a tyrannical leader. Well—not all of us. Not even half of us. Have a good death, *Americans.*"

Mai sent Hibiki a hopeless look. "You know nothing about this protocol?"

The Japanese undercover agent shook his head.

Mai felt her death approaching. It was do or die time. She raised her gun and started shooting. The English speaker was the first to go, shot through the forehead and sent tumbling back into an array of instruments.

The mechanical announcement droned on, "*. . .three minutes. . .*"

"I'll kill you all!" Mai promised. "One by one." She pulled her trigger each time she spoke a word. Korean soldiers jerked and spasmed. Blood spattered each man's neighbor and the walls behind.

"Tell me!"

"*It's not unstoppable!*" One man screamed in Korean, instantly translated by Hibiki just as loud. The man held his hand up as if to ward off Mai's bullet, putting his head down. He was not a soldier. This man was one of the island doctors.

"Your life for information." Mai shot another Korean as she spoke.

"There is a missile in a silo beneath the island. It is programmed to launch, return, and explode on impact with the compound. But it's not a one-man protocol. Not even a madman would allow that. The failsafe is that *two* men have the authority to launch and abort."

Hibiki suddenly stopped short and stared at the doctor. "No," he said in English. "That's so unfair."

Mai chewed her lip. "What?"

"General Kwang Yong and the base commander both have the authority to abort the launch," Hibiki said. "By the fingerprint scanner on that console."

". . .final protocol will occur in two minutes. . ."

Mai ran like never before. She hurdled a body, hit the door at a dead run, shouldered it aside so that it almost crashed off its hinges. She jumped down the steps, felt her feet touch the grass and accelerated to full sprint. She vaulted a drainage ditch, leaned her body down without losing pace and scooped up the first discarded rifle she passed.

All the time counting the seconds off in her head.

"Ninety. . .eighty-nine. . .eighty-eight. . ."

She found the clearing where the overweight island boss lay. His dead eyes and chubby face stared up at her with the mocking appearance of a smile—a last laugh. Mai stepped in and didn't give her next action any more thought. She set the rifle to auto and pulled the trigger.

Bullets slammed through the boss' arm at the elbow, churning up dirt, blasting apart bone and flesh until the appendage separated from the rest of the body.

Mai scooped it up, dropped the weapon with a crunch, and hurled her body back the way it had just come. *Forty-three. . .forty-two. . .forty-one. . .*

Pounding across the uneven grass, springing from one rise to the next, a full-flight hurdle across a fallen tree, now seeing the distant comms building, seeing the door standing wide open.

. . .nineteen. . .eighteen. . .

She wasn't going to make it.

CHAPTER FIFTY

Her life was measured in seconds. The distance between her and the fast approaching comms building seemed to elongate like some special effect, making it seem farther away. Smyth was at the door, screaming. She felt an ill-omened rumble begin under her feet. The ground shook.

The arm she held slapped a tree on the way past. Mai barely kept hold of it. If she dropped it there was no doubt—*game over.*

But it already was. *Nine. . .eight. . .*

Mai flung her entire body at the top step, skidded across the threshold and into the room, twisted in mid-slide and dug her boots against the concrete for purchase. Then like a hundred-meter sprinter, on her knees with her hands against the floor, she was out of the traps like a gold medal winning Olympian.

Smyth had cleared the path to the console. He was even pointing at the fingerprint pad.

. . .three. . .two. . .

Mai lunged.

"One."

"Final protocol engaged."

Mai jammed the boss's fingers to the pad. She heard a click. But then the threatening rumble beneath her feet grew to a shaky groan. Smyth ran to the door and Mai followed him.

Above the distant trees, a trail of light and fire shot high into the sky. Mai spared a despairing glance for Hibiki and then stepped close to Smyth.

"At first I thought you were an insolent prick, my friend. It is strange that I grew to like you so much. It has been. . .a life experience."

"That it has, Maggie." Smyth's eyes tracked the boiling stream of light as it painted the skies. "That it has."

The rocket attained the end of its vertical flight and began to turn. Mai was surprised to feel Dai Hibiki's hands suddenly resting on her shoulder. "You must go." He coughed. "Run. You might make it."

Even Smyth laughed. "I doubt even the great Mai Kitano could outrun a rocket, bud."

"Well, not with a marine in tow." Mai's thoughts turned to Drake. Here she was, staring into the scorching face of her fate, unsure if the man she already knew she loved was even alive. She remembered their first meeting so well she could recite every line, recall every event, simply because she ran it through her head at least once a week. Chechnya had been a hellhole, a veritable outpost of purgatory and a den for all the Devil's demons, but Mai knew it as the place where she'd met the love of her life.

Amidst battle. Amidst war. A fitting occurrence that defined all her days since the clan had bought her from her destitute parents. To be a human child, and then for that child to be remade into steel, into the hard edge of the night, and then to be turned human again by a single chance meeting with a great man.

"What the—?"

Lost in her thoughts, in her unfulfilled dreams, Mai hadn't even been aware of the rocket anymore. Smyth's outburst brought her back just in time to see the burning fire trail flutter out. In the same instant, the terrible weapon stuttered and fell, like a bird killed in mid-flight, straight down toward the ocean.

The doctor, the last Korean standing, sounded very matter of fact as he spoke up. "I did say the base commander could *abort* the missile. *Abort.*"

Mai resisted the urge to turn around and shoot him.

CHAPTER FIFTY-ONE

Drake drove the Charger faster than any car he'd ever driven in his life. Even then, the Viper stayed ahead, its whole façade—its color, its shape, its name, its occupant—radiating an unrestrained predatory instinct. The Gulfstream jet hustled along beside it, separated by mere meters.

Kingston was running level with the open forward hatch.

"What the hell is he doing?" Alicia shouted. "He can't get *in.*"

That's what worries me, Drake thought. Kingston had called ahead. The arms dealer knew what he was doing.

"He has something," Drake said. "He designs advanced weapons systems. Devising something that gets you out of a car and onto a plane would be child's play for him."

"Shag it." Alicia sighed. "Guess I'm shooting out the tires again."

Just as the Englishwoman started to writhe into shape, Hayden's helicopter blasted overhead. Drake grinned. He'd forgotten about their hardy boss and her new toy. So, it seemed, had Kingston. Maybe the fleeing arms dealer had been plucking up courage, but when he caught sight of the chopper, he set off an explosion that blew the driver's door off its frame and sent it tumbling down the runway. Simultaneously, a huge robotic arm shaped like a car door and carrying a harness shot out of the planes forward hatch, probably gun-bolted to the plane's floor inside. The arm slowed dramatically as it reached the car, air brakes popping like pistol fire, fitting around the Viper's doorframe.

Kingston must have engaged the cruise control. The runway at this point was as smooth as it was ever going to get. The arms dealer must have been waiting for just this moment to implement his carefully rehearsed plan.

But he still hadn't reckoned on the chopper.

As the arm reversed its movement, bringing Shaun Kingston aboard the Gulfstream, Hayden swung the helicopter across its front end. Drake wrenched the wheel to avoid the driverless Viper as it veered off the runway.

"Look out! Shit!"

Kinimaka hung out of the chopper's cabin, rifle nestled from chin to shoulder, taking aim at the jet's cockpit. The Gulfstream's engines began to scream as the plane accelerated to takeoff speed. Drake mashed the accelerator pedal against the Charger's floor. The plane's tail passed over the car as the forward hatch slammed shut.

Kinimaka opened fire. A storm of bullets hammered into the airplane's body and tore through the cockpit window. Red flashed across the ruined glass. The

Gulfstream lost its impetus in a second, powering down and changing direction, now heading straight for the grass verge.

Drake tailed it closely. Hayden brought the helicopter to rest a few yards from the tip of its starboard wing. Drake, Alicia and Hayden jumped out of their vehicles, drawing guns and staying low. Kinimaka kept his rifle trained on the cockpit lest Kingston be inclined to use the jet as a getaway vehicle.

The hatch remained closed. Hayden nodded to both Drake and Alicia and then used her cell. "Do we know how many were on board?"

Drake heard the reply easily enough. "Only two pilots. It seems Kingston prefers to travel alone."

Now Dahl and Komodo pulled up in the Shelby Mustang, the Swede giving the throttle an extra blip before stepping out, grinning from ear to ear.

"We passed the general on to the cops. Hey, is there any way we could keep this thing?"

"Question is. . ." Hayden nodded at the plane. "Who gets to go in and drag Kingston's pathetic ass outta there? He's alone."

Drake studied the windows, the door. "Who will interrogate him? Make him squeal?"

Hayden shrugged. "The FBI, I guess. Gates will pull us away from the aftermath of all this. SPEAR doesn't do mop up, but will still be privy to the intel."

"Aye, well. There's your answer." Drake touched Hayden's shoulder firmly. "Our priority now is to get Mai and Smyth off that island."

"General Kwang Yong should be able to help with the tactical side of that," Hayden said.

Dahl looked down at his boots, an unusual trait for the Swede. Drake discerned it immediately. "What's wrong?"

"Ah, the general." Dahl flicked his head in the direction of Kwang Yong, still lying with his belly to the concrete. "He called in a last order before we got to him. To destroy the island."

Drake wavered. *Not after all this,* he thought. Not after dragging his arse all the way from Asia, through China and Russia and Germany and then taking down the operations ringleaders. Not now.

A blackness stole in at the edge of his vision. He hadn't asked Mai to trust him with her life, but he had fully expected her to survive all this. He barely heard Dahl's next optimistic comment or Hayden as she took a call. He didn't register the Gulfstream anymore and the fact that its forward hatch had just cracked open.

Even though he was staring right at it.

Then, Hayden thrust her cell in his face. "Matt!" She sounded as if she'd been shouting his name for a while. He focused on her.

She smiled. "It's Mai. She's calling for you."

Drake said a soft *hi*. He listened as Mai told him the rocket had been aborted, as she explained how she'd been able to send a distress call from the island's comms room to the nearest American special forces Recon team—one recently stationed on nearby Guam by none other than the U.S. Secretary of Defense— and how she missed him every second of every single day.

"You're famous, Drake." Mai laughed. "I asked if they knew of a Matt Drake and they replied 'Yep, hasn't everyone? He's fine.' The team's inbound now. We'll get out of here before the Koreans arrive. We made one of their men call up and garble something about an accidental release." The Japanese woman laughed, the sound like soft, summer rain to Drake's ears. "It'll keep them guessing for an hour or two."

Drake still stared at the forward hatch, which was now closed again. "Did you figure out what the lab was for?"

"That's why we hung around so long. It's a sleeper operation. They kidnap down-and-outs, transform them, and bury some kind of 'wake' command deep inside their subconscious. A doctor here says it can be triggered by some guy— General Kwang Yong—verbally, or by a machine at this end. And don't worry. The machine's about to get some Mai-time."

Drake grinned. Fucking Wells' legacy would never die. "And the down-and-outs who are there now?"

"We'll take them with us."

A good outcome, Drake thought. Romero and he had destroyed the body. Mai had chopped off the head. And SPEAR had caught both ringleaders.

"And that general?" Mai went on. "Kwang Yong. The doc says he was always scared, always paranoid. He was acting without permission. He needed to cover his tracks somehow and used the sleepers. That's all I know."

Drake couldn't stop thinking about her face. "It's enough. Be safe, Mai. It'll be good to see you again."

Drake ended the call and gave the cell back to Hayden. When he looked around, Dahl was grinning at him. So was Komodo. Even Alicia had stopped texting her biker boyfriend for a minute to stick her finger down her throat.

"C'mon, Drakey. It's not like you haven't been there before."

Then, the Gulfstream's forward hatch burst open and out stepped a nightmare—Shaun Kingston, outfitted in all his advanced weaponry: his prototype "killproof" full-body armor, his bulletproof weapons-synced, computerized helmet and goggles, and toting two of the craziest, meanest, most radical guns Drake had ever seen.

"Crap!" Hayden dove for the concrete.

With no cover, they were all exposed. And they weren't wearing their Kevlar anymore. Not even Torsten Dahl could cover enough ground to prevent Kingston from opening fire and they all knew it.

Kingston screamed as he jumped out and managed a textbook landing. "This is what I can do!" he yelled. "I am the future."

Drake ran straight at the guns. So did Dahl. Komodo followed a second later. Kinimaka stepped in front of Hayden.

Kingston's fingers tightened on his triggers, the sound of manic laughter fitting for this futuristic figure so decked out in all his advanced weaponry, his cutting-edge hardware with its electric-blue and blood-red lights flickering all over the killproof vest.

He waited an extra second. "Time to shred me some Goddamn pork!" he bellowed and opened fire.

The knife, the primitive shaft of sharpened steel, thunked loudly as it slammed through the lower half of his face—the only exposed part of him—just below the nose and around the mouth. In the millisecond it took for his brain to register death, the force of the blow sent him reeling backward, his weapons shooting at nothing but sky.

The last words he ever spoke were in shock. "A knife?"

Drake slowed and turned. Dahl followed suit. Alicia knelt on one knee, still poised in a throwing stance, eyes narrowed.

"A knife," Drake echoed. "All that bloody technology. All the money they spent. And he gets taken down by a biker chick with a blade."

Alicia shrugged. "I want that back. Lomas gave it to me as a keepsake."

"Whatever you say, Myles." Hayden used Kinimaka's proffered hand to pull herself upright. With a quick scan, she inventoried the assorted machinery scattered around the airfield.

"Now, who's driving *what* back?"

CHAPTER FIFTY-TWO

Days later, Jonathan Gates prowled around his office as night pressed implacably against his uncovered windows. He preferred exposed, unadorned casements and skylights—it helped him see clearly in more ways than one.

The new agency had pulled off a great accomplishment but there still remained a few man-eating sharks on the Hill, their cold eyes examining and their bloody teeth bared, ready to swoop in for the kill. Gates knew it didn't matter how many times you were successful; it just took that one bad day or unlucky decision to wipe it all out. The sharks would always circle. It was their nature.

His plans were afoot. SPEAR was about to get a new HQ courtesy of Hayden Jaye's old agency, the CIA, one better equipped and more clandestine this time. That damn reporter, Sarah Moxley, continued to bug them, and with more clout behind her now. Gates felt that both he and the agency owed her some kind of an explanation.

But that problem would save for another day. Now, Gates walked around to the front of his desk and picked up the photograph he kept there. It showed his wife, Sarah, and he in better times. He held on to the frame as he clicked a button.

"Show Miss Fox in."

The door opened almost immediately. Gates replaced the picture and turned around. Lauren Fox closed the door and stood with her hands folded across her breasts. "I really don't know why I've been brought here, sir. Or *summoned*, I guess you could say."

Gates gave her a wry smile, sensing her discomfort. "Don't worry. I don't wish to engage your services." He gestured to a chair. "Sit."

"I'm fine."

"Please?"

Gates settled himself as she finally perched on a chair opposite him. "I grant you, it's unusual for a Secretary of Defense to *summon* an expensive hooker to his office. We could have met in secret, or in public, but for what I have to propose"—he met her eyes—"this seemed more appropriate. *Official.*"

"Won't people wonder?" Lauren was clearly thinking of the staff.

"They're my people. They know me. Now, Miss Fox, I liked the way you handled yourself."

"Excuse me?"

"First—you saved lives during the attack on our HQ. You showed amazing bravery. Second—the assassin. You beat him, and that was no mean feat. The man was well-trained as we're starting to understand from General Kwang Yong."

"Are there more of them?"

Gates gripped the bridge of his nose. "Undoubtedly. We don't yet know how many. We'll most likely never know who they are. But the head has been cut off that particular snake. Now we wait for the next one to rise. And, Miss Fox, we need all the. . ." He paused. *"Specialist* help we can get."

"Call me Lauren. Now what the hell are you saying? Sir."

"You'll fit right in," Gates said to her and then proceeded to outline his proposal. When he'd clarified the dangers and then secured her acceptance, he watched her walk out of the room.

Damn.

Quickly he occupied his mind with picking up the phone and dialing Hayden's cell. It was around eight o'clock in the evening, but his second in command needed to know about his newest recruit and the parameters he'd set for her.

Hayden took the call as she and Kinimaka sat down to dinner. The restaurant was crowded and noisy, but her Hawaiian partner gawked in happiness. Hayden had brought him to Washington DC's one and only Hard Rock Cafe.

"I'll get us cocktails." Kinimaka's huge fist almost fully concealed the drinks menu. Hayden heard her boss out, at first shocked but then seeing the usefulness of an expensive asset like Lauren Fox. At least now she knew why Gates had been asking all the odd questions. Time would tell if she was up to the job.

Hayden thanked Gates and then told Kinimaka. "Good move," he said. "She sure can get into places we can't."

"We'll see." Hayden was more worried about how many times they'd have to go in and save Fox's ass. But for now, she focused on Kinimaka.

"I kinda brought you here for a reason," she said a little nervously. "Other than to buy you a shot glass."

"To get me drunk?"

"Maybe. So Mano—" She touched the top of his hand where it rested lightly on the table. "You got something to say to me?"

The misgivings rose like a castle wall before his mind's eye. "You're my boss. I respect you for being my boss. And if it doesn't work out—how could we work together?"

"Geez, Mano, nothing's ever gonna be that predictable. And wouldn't life just get damn boring if it was?"

"We've known each other a long time. . ."

"I can't promise we'll always be friends." Hayden thought about real life and how it always took away those you loved. "Whether we hook up or not."

Big cocktail glasses full of mixed spirits, gaudy umbrellas and slices of pineapple were placed on the table. Hayden had known her oldest friend would try the Hawaiian-based drink, just to compare it to the island offerings. She also knew he'd go with the island. He always did.

Friendship. Trust. An almost psychic intuition for what each other would do next. That's what they had. Why risk it?

"There's always another level," she told Mano, though she'd never found it with Ben or any other of her past boyfriends. "There has to be."

"Hayden Jaye." Kinimaka took her hand and squeezed gently. "Will you be my date tonight?"

The atmosphere at the table suddenly changed. The dynamics shifted sideways and a thrill shot through Hayden's body. "Sure will," she said with a grin. "But first things first—I have to pass on the information Gates just gave me. Actually, I'll tell Dahl to do it. He's reliable."

Kinimaka waited patiently. He'd waited for Hayden so long he couldn't even remember when he fell for her. Another five minutes wouldn't hurt.

Dahl took the call without feeling an iota of surprise. He trusted Jonathan Gates now. The man had a plan, and a bloody good one at that. Dahl's only continuing concern was the distance this job put between his family and himself. Johanna would not pack up and move to the United States, nor would he ever ask her too. And it wasn't fair on the kids. Their early youth was an impressionable, grounding experience. He wanted familiarity and stability for them.

But how grounded would they be with a father figure who only flitted in and out of their lives?

Dahl checked his watch. It would be mid-afternoon in Sweden. The kids would be at school but at least he could talk to Johanna. But first, he'd make a call to his newest comrade, Komodo. The Delta boy had taken it all the way in that final battle. A quality Dahl appreciated. He trusted the man to pass along Hayden's information.

After that, Johanna would be eager to hear his voice. And he hers. Already, a wide grin was spreading across his entire face and making his dark eyes shine. He set up the video link on his laptop and crossed to the window. The dome of the White House glowed in the distance. Johanna would love to see it.

Komodo seemed agitated to Karin by the time he'd finished talking to Dahl. The soldier was standing completely naked at the window, seemingly oblivious, and no doubt making some passerby's day. The street was only three floors below. The lights were on. Karin studied the width of his shoulders and the play of the muscles down his back.

"Is Torsten okay?"

"Yeah. He just called to tell us the hooker has been made part of the team."

Karin let it run through her quick mind. "The idea is a good one, T-vor." It was her private name for him.

"He wants me to pass it on to the team."

Karin raised a wicked eyebrow. "Well, you probably needed the break anyway. Felt like you were about to peak early."

Komodo looked a bit self-conscious. "It's been a long week."

"Just ring Drake. He's reliable. I need to try Ben anyway. Haven't spoken to him since he left."

Karin wrapped her body in the soft bed sheets right up to her neck. "You can stay naked, soldier boy. That's your punishment." The connection whirred and clicked and then the ringtone began. Ben's phone was one of those annoying ones that played a preset tune in the caller's ear.

She heard Komodo talking to Drake.

Ben didn't answer.

Without further ado she jumped up on the bed, letting the sheets fall away. Komodo fell at her feet so that she landed perfectly on top of him. His hands grabbed her hips.

"And since you've done nothin' but sit on *this* for the last week, let's give it some exercise."

Drake listened to Komodo. The appointment of Lauren Fox would raise some issues, not to mention some eyebrows, but now was not the time to address them. Although Mai had been back for days, this was the first time they had been alone, totally alone, since they had hit the island.

Neither of them was the kind to make small talk. Neither were they the kind to emphasize how much they'd missed or thought about each other. Drake knew all he had to do was sit next to her. "I'm supposed to contact Alicia."

Mai studied her hands in her lap, almost coming across as shy. Almost.

Drake yawned, stretched and put an arm across her shoulders. It was intended as a joke, but went straight over the Japanese woman's head. She snuggled in.

"Glad to see you didn't fall for Smyth, then."

"He takes some getting used to but he's a good man."

"Romero too. He helped finish off the Spanish side of the trafficking ring. Almost single-handedly I hear."

"Special Forces people," Mai said. "No matter the nationality, they share a bond. They respond to each other."

Drake kissed the top of her head. "A theory I'd like to test."

But then his phone rang. It was Alicia herself, ringing *him.*

"Bollocks."

But he should've guessed she would ring. Alicia Myles was *always* the exception to the rule.

"Drake? Didn't catch you two shagging, did I?"

"Nice to hear your voice, Alicia. What's up?" A hesitation made Drake narrow his eyes. Almost instantly, he sensed a bombshell. "Alicia?"

"I have something to tell you, Drake. And you're not gonna like it."

"Do you know something? About Coyote? Don't tell me you've been keeping something else from me. Is it Cayman? The Shadow Elite? This new Russian thing."

"What new Russian thing?"

"I told you. The seven swords and the saber dance. The Pit of Babylon. The Devil's tower that led straight to the doorway of the gods and all that."

"Sorry, mate. Must have been kipping."

Drake closed his eyes. "Yeah or texting your new boyfriend." Another hesitation. This time Drake let her think.

"I'm leaving, Drake. I'm quitting the team."

His heart fell so far he was sure it hit the floor. "But. . .what? . . .*Why?*"

"I miss Lomas," Alicia said easily. "I miss the others too. With them, it's all about the ride. The journey. Not the destination. I kinda like that idea. Bloody hell, Drake, you know me by now."

"I do."

"No agenda. I just want to live whilst I'm alive and have fun."

"That's what I love about you."

Alicia's voice softened to almost nothing. "Me too, Drake. Me too."

"So..." Drake blinked away more than shock. "Will we see you again?"

"If it comes to the apocalypse. . . call me."

CHAPTER FIFTY-THREE

Nikolai Razin was not a well man. At one time he'd been a bare knuckle boxer, and had broken every bone in his hands. Now, he could barely move his fingers, but the frequent doses of morphine helped. Now, he had men to fight for him. Now, he liked to watch them break other people's fingers.

But the longing remained. His youth had been a hard, brutal, fleeting thing and now he wanted it back. That impossibility bred anger and hate in him, the kind that festers and sours. The highlight of his days was recognizing fear in another man's eyes, the tremble in their shoulders. He had honed a stare, the unblinking, unnerving gaze of a madman that could agitate even the bravest of men.

And he had honed the team he surrounded himself with like a knife edge is honed on a whetstone. He had grinded them. Sharpened them. Molded them with violence and longing and more—with reward. With sadism. With a cruel love.

Zanko was his meanest, his most potent. Maxim, his stealthiest and most intelligent. Viktoriya, his most beautiful and resourceful.

The four of them sat around Razin's big table with the wall-size picture window at his back, the Russian night falling and the deep-red sunset washing their faces with blood. Out there, madmen and killers might walk. In here sat the men and women who controlled them.

Razin spoke first as was protocol. "Tell me, Zanko, what have you found in Iraq?"

"Ancient Babylon." Zanko spread his arms expansively, ever the showman. "The city of sin. Debauchery. Murder. Greed. All the good things in life. The place where every bad thing began and criminals were invented, no? Ha, ha! They say Saddam Hussein built a palace overlooking the ancient ruins of Babylon. But he didn't have the cunning to search for what we have found. If he did…" Zanko shrugged his muscle-bound shoulders. "Perhaps he would still be in power."

Maxim spoke little, but when he did, it was usually fast and to the point, like the strike of a snake. "Did you find the swords?"

Zanko picked up several rolls of paper from the floor. He placed them on the deeply polished surface, sorting through until he found the right one. "We think the swords are there, and next week we should know more. But. . ." He jabbed the paper and the table urgently. "We found the *original* pit . The one from which Babylon was forged. *That* is what we found, my happy friend."

"And inside the pit?"

Zanko gave them a grin like a cartoon shark. "You are all invited to come and look, of course."

Razin tapped the table, reigning in Zanko's zeal. "And the other site?"

The huge Russian held out both hands, palms up. "Insanity."

"Zanko?" Razin's tone held a note of warning.

"Seriously, my old friend, I mean what I say. It is impossible to describe. Imagine the size and breadth of a foundation that once held a tower reaching all the way to the clouds. But no swords at that site. Yet."

"The Devil's Tower." Viktoriya breathed in her super-smooth, silky voice. "The tower of stone. Who'd have thought it once actually existed?"

"*They* existed," Zanko corrected her. "That's the wonder of it. The legends state that these towers were erected by almost every ancient civilization. Could they all be wrong, *moyo sladkaya*? And collectively, what do they mean? What do they form? We. . ." He patted his mighty chest. "*I, Zanko*, will find out."

Viktoriya curled a lip in distaste. "*Moyo sladkaya?* Be careful, Zanko. The last man who called me his 'sweetheart' ended up wearing his guts as a noose."

"The doorway to the Gods?" Razin speculated. "The seven swords that were part of the saber dance on Alexander the Great's deathbed? I remain skeptical. We will see. And the writings you have found, are they a positive match to what the westerners found in the three tombs?"

"It's being checked," Zanko admitted. "With all the secrecy—it is not an easy match to make."

Razin accepted with a nod. "And so now. . .now on to more mundane things. The man who raided our yard. Killed our men. He must pay for the devastation he brought to us. What has been done about him and his associate?"

"Matt Drake is part of a covert American agency with maybe a dozen operatives. Officially, they handle special response and recon around the world." Maxim was reading from a prepared sheet. "If we strike at one we strike at them all. They are regarded as a 'first strike' team. Highly skilled."

Zanko guffawed. "I promised to smother the little man with my armpits. I promise it again. I will not wash them until the job is done."

Razin didn't take his eyes off Maxim. "Do we have him yet?"

The man's eyes glittered with intelligence and malice. "Within seventy two hours."

THE END

Keep reading for more information on the development of the Matt Drake series:

Well, it's that time again. Another Drake adventure draws to a close with the promise of an even more exciting one to come. The next two books, Drake 6 and 7, tentatively due October 2013 and January 2014 will form the Sinners Cycle in which we will unravel more ancient mysteries and, hopefully, explore more about the myths of the gods, but then. . .

Matt Drake #8 changes everything. There's a developing back-story. Take Coyote out of the equation and then imagine Drake's worst nightmare come true. Big things will happen and big changes will occur.

Next up, it's the start of the new series – The Disavowed. Those readers who have visited my website will know a little of this series already and I will soon be posting much more information. Hope you like it!

Printed in Great Britain
by Amazon

25057259R00106